THE VEILED LADY: A Miao Juzheng and George Silver Elizabethan Adventure

I

THE VEILED LADY: A Miao Juzheng and George Silver Elizabethan Adventure

Written by
M.E. Eadie

Edited by
Karin Vogel-Eadie

Adam
Books

ISBN: 978-1-927586-05-1

Book design: M. E. Eadie
Cover design: M. E. Eadie

Published by *Adam Books*
Web site
adambookhouse.blogspot.com

Dedication

To my family, past, present and future, and one little daughter with albinism.

Chapter One: Murder most Horrible

Mid spring, London: it was the choice between rain and fog. The night was moderate in temperature which invited the rain instead of the fog. It came down in a constant, pluvial damp that covered the cobblestones in a glossy slick, not enough to wash any of the thick street filth away. Then the rain came. It was a deluge of water that pounded onto the roofs and poured down onto the street. At first the water piled up, gaining weight with each passing moment, exerting its primal strength. Eventually the dam of sewage and garbage broke, and the wall of filth gave way to small rivulets which grew to a raging torrent that ripped through the barrier and ran the grade, carrying the night soil and refuse down to the river. A piece of crumpled cloth was gently pulled from one eroding pile and began its journey twisting and turning on its way. It was a gentle trip, but soon the cloth gained companionship, a rotten apple core, the entrails of some animal and someone's ear. Together they collected speed and plummeted into the river beside the three men chained to the bank. Their crimes many, their punishment very gentle: to be washed for the duration of three tidal periods. The symbolic conceit was lost on the punished, the hope that they may be cleansed from their sins through the washing. More likely, if they survived, they would return to crime and end up losing an ear, or a nose, or a hand, or be drawn and quartered.

One of the chained men tilted his head up to the rain and opened his parched mouth. His lips were cracked. He hoped to take some drink. If anything could cleanse them it would be the rain, nothing else was fit to drink, except ale and no one was about to give them that. He watched, balefully, as a piece of cloth rode the gushing water out onto the river. The current caught it, and, it sank. Most things in London did. Sometimes it seemed everyone who came to the city in hopes of a better life eventually sank into the filth of despair that was the city. Without a benefactor or family that was the way of things.

The downpour soon ended returning the night to its encompassing mist. The streets seemed abandoned, but that was not true. Life never ceased to thrum in London, night, day, wet, cold, it didn't matter. There was always life, and death. Only tonight the life hid in the dark and watched. A door opened and a rectangle of light shone into the darkness. For a moment the cold gloom was dispelled and the shadows were chased away. Out onto the golden rectangle stepped a cloaked form. Even swathed in the bulky fabric it was obvious that the form was of a slight woman. She looked about, wary of the eyes in the dark that must surely be watching. There were always eyes. A lock of red hair fell to hang against her cheek, just outside her hood. A calloused hand reached up and tamed it, tucking it away from the wet. She held the candle lantern out to ward her way and stepped charily into the street. Tonight she would brave the eyes in the dark, because there was a commission and money to be made, good money. Her footfalls, quick and rapid, soon gained confidence and they took her to the river, to the wharf, where the men were chained.

The chained men heard gentle feet on the wood of the wharf, heard their lightness and for a moment entertained the hope that some compassionate soul had come with drink or food. Their hope sank when the heavy footfall of studded boots followed the light. They knew that sound.

He was one of the Lord Marshall's men ordered to keep the Queen's peace, and his domain was a twelve-mile radius of the Palace. He was fortunate to have employment, unfortunate to have drawn the night's watch. So he had thought until he had been approached and offered a bag of coin. He looked past his big, bulbous nose at the slight girl on the wharf and counted his luck and the new coins.

But the fact was that this was noble business, and that was a little disconcerting. Nothing good came from associating with the Palace Hoppers. He stepped up behind the poor girl and startled her. She turned about, lamp up as if to ward him away, but the light only revealed his nose and the white scars on his face.

"You're late," he growled.

"I'm sorry," she apologized. She needed this money. Her family needed this money. They were always short and the need always great.

Out in the darkness of the Thames came the clunking sound of wood on wood and a running gurgle as something moved through the water. It was coming towards them. Out of the darkness she could just make out the long oars sweeping over the water and then ducking beneath the water to pull the wherry along. The oars moving in their locks made a plaintive, almost human moaning sound. A sudden light illuminated the bow end of the wherry. The Marshal's man caught the rope as it snaked out of the darkness like a fly catching the web from some unseen spider. The man deftly wrapped the rope around a cleat.

He was starting to feel sorry for the slight girl; he had a daughter of his own about the same age. He had to harden himself to the emotion, because when the Palace Hoppers played, it was nobody's business but theirs. Their laws, their rules and damn them to Hell for it, because the price was always paid by the poor. Still, she was so slight and fragile, as though a slight wind might blow her away. He hoped she was street tough.

"Best get in, luv. It doesn't pay to keep them waiting. Leave your lamp here. You can get it when they row you back." He hoped the words would comfort her, but he wasn't at all sure she would be coming back. Sometimes they did, sometimes they didn't.

The young woman took some relief from the turn in the man's voice; he sounded as though he almost cared. She found herself near the edge of the wharf staring down at the man in the bow who was holding out an expectant hand edged with lace. She could still run. She could turn around and run and they would never catch her. She could lose them in the narrow streets and then return home. That was the problem; they knew where her home was. When she had accepted the proposal, she had invariably committed herself. There was no backing out now. She took a deep breath and reached out for the strong hand that closed on her and guided her down into the wherry. She looked up as the Lord Marshal's man tossed the rope back down. In the flash of faint candlelight she thought she saw an inexplicable expression on the man's face, the expression of pity. She suddenly bridled at this. He could keep his pity, life didn't offer such sentiments; life was hard and you needed to get what you could where you could.

The dark man had strong hands and an overwhelming presence smelled of soap as though he had freshly bathed. She knew that smell because once, when she was tiny, she had labored at soap works mixing the lye with the fat to make soap. It was hot, dirty work. The smell made her wary and cautious, only the very wealthy bathed. It was even said that the Queen bathed once a month. Therefore, his soapy smell placed this man close to the Queen. One of her baths was like a giant, open clamshell where faucets magically poured out hot water, or so the stories said. But that was a tale for children. The dark, the damp, the stink of the river was her reality.

She examined the two oarsmen who set a rhythmic pace. Even though it was too dark to see clearly she could feel them avoiding her. To them she was invisible and this caused a cold feeling to root in the small of her back. She didn't want to look at the man she sat beside because he terrified her. She focused on the movement of the boat, surging forward and the sounds of the water and they soothed her, a bit. It was amazing how they were able to navigate the many moored boats that populated the river. In an eternal, weaving dance they continued to make their progress until the density of boats began to thin. It was a good thing they were on the upstream side of the bridge, because downstream, the boats made a virtual forest of masts for over a mile. There were people onboard those boats, guarding their cargo, she could tell; only a fool would leave cargo unguarded. What began to concern her was why they weren't taking any interest in them. They must have been near the middle of the river because the smell wasn't nearly so bad when they began to slow.

Then the dark man beside her stood up and held out his blacked out lantern. He told the men to stop and they stopped, but the wherry continued to glide forward. He took away the shield on his lantern and the dim light of the revealed candle became painfully bright. It was the way of light in the dark, to seem startlingly bright. He opened and closed the shield several times and then waited. Off in the inky dark of the water a light blazed, repeating the same pattern.

"Over there," said the man and she noticed he had an accent. It wasn't Spanish but it was close. It definitely wasn't French. There was a French Huguenot bakery just down the street from where she lived.

The wherry's oarsmen steered the boat in the direction of the light, a beacon for them. The rain had stopped, which she took as a good omen. It only took a few moments of strong pulling before they came alongside the barge. Even in the faint light of the candle lanterns, she could make out the gold and crimson paint and the ornate woodwork along the rail. She had seen barges before, but only at a distant. It was a vessel for the divine, not for her type, not for the profane. She found her hands shaking involuntarily. She was going to tread where only the gods tread, or those close to the gods.

The candle lantern was handed to one of the oarsmen as the other steadied the rope ladder that hung down the side of the barge. The laced hand flicked towards the ladder. Obviously he wanted her to climb it, so she reached out and began the task of pulling herself up one rung at a time. It wasn't a difficult thing to do because the ladder's rungs were made of wide strips of wood. Other strong hands and arms reached out of the dark and pulled her aboard. The clean man followed. She heard the clink of a money purse being tossed to the oarsmen and the water swirling as the wherry pulled away. For a moment panic gripped her; how was she going to get back to shore? More lanterns were lit revealing the curtained cabin at the front of the barge. She stared at the sumptuous crimson and gold cloth used to drape the cabin: cloth fit for a queen but used for a covering. It was awe evoking. She felt the overwhelming power of the man beside her and couldn't help notice his sword jutting out from beneath his cloak. He was calm, relaxed like a cat. There were other oarsmen in the belly of the barge, but she couldn't see their faces from how they were sitting, heads covered by deep hoods. Why did they need to hide?

The dark, soapy man smiled down at her and held out his free hand to guide her to the cabin. When she hesitated, he moved forward, parting the curtain to show her that there was nothing to fear. Again he invited her to enter. She noticed that the warmth in his smile did not reach his eyes. Gathering her courage she entered.

Inside the cabin there was a lot more light, enough to make her feel more awed. The room was bracketed with benches and in the center was a stool. It beckoned to her, but that was not what gripped her attention. What held her enthralled was the curtain of sheer cloth and the silhouette behind it. Sensitive to the intuition of her kind, she felt the woman's eyes on her, assessing her. The figure shifted behind the sheer.

Berto Della Massa, the dark man who smelled of soap, pulled back the curtains and tied them so that they draped. The obscured figure was now more visible. The woman in a dark gown, stood before them. A dark veil hid the woman's face, but her hands were free and they were entrancing. Those hands, those pure white hands that fluttered like the wings of doves when they moved, they were what the girl stared at. She gave a rough, awkward curtsey as she remembered her place. One of those unblemished hands waved instructively to the dark man who nodded.

"Please," he said, "if you would be so kind to sit. The lady wishes to sketch your likeness."

Still at a loss for words she arranged her simple, stained skirts and sat on the stool. She felt the dark man's hands on her face, tilting her chin, angling her head, then, when he was done they retreated, careful not to disturb the pose.

"There, please do not move, until finished." The dark man moved smoothly over to the bench where with a flick of a cloak he sat down sideways to provide room for his sword. His legs lounged lazily forward stretching out to their full length. His own pose was one of contrived boredom, but there was a feline lethalness there, waiting, watching.

At first she was able to hold the pose easily, but after a while it became difficult. The cramps started to build in her shoulders and spread through her back. Her eyes were transfixed by the deft movements of the pale hands of the veiled lady, as they moved across the paper, or parchment, she was too far away to tell. She wondered wistfully what it would be like to have the unblemished hands of privilege, and then chased the thoughts away. Her hands were thick and cracked and raw from labor. Suddenly, a feeling of apprehension took her breast, a feeling of dread. It was somehow tied to the movement of those perfect hands that when the hands stopped her life would change. Maybe it was because of the money she would be paid, but she suspected something else, something as elusive as the lines the lady was drawing. For some reason a scene from a play rose up in her mind. She had seen a play once, hadn't understood half of it, but that wasn't the point. The point was that there were all sorts of people there, lords and ladies and the small folk and wealthy men and everyone between. Some of the actors, she knew, had been lifted up by wealth, and if them, then why not her? Had she been a man, she would have been able to perform, but this was much like acting...

Then the white hands that had been manipulating the lines stopped.

"I am done," said the long, drawn voice from the dark veiled silence. It was a voice that glittered with triumph.

Della Massa rose to his feet and approached the place where the lady sat. She handed him the paper and he considered it. Several times he looked up at the girl to compare the rendering; after a long moment he nodded.

"Truly, my Lady, one of your best pieces."

The girl shifted restlessly, not sure whether it was now all right to move or not. She swallowed and meant to quietly clear her throat, but a tiny squeak came out.

Della Massa gave her a cold look as though any noise made from her presumed too much. "Oh," he said moving to her side in one stride. He held out the rendering. "Would you like to see," he said. His deep voice was friendly, but his eyes were still cold, terribly cold.

She nodded and he handed the rendering to her. She had never held paper before, only parchment. She wondered at how something could be made so smooth, maybe that was why it was so expensive. She looked at herself. The coal black lines formed the face of a young girl. She stared gap mouthed at the drawing as if it was alive. It was more than an image in a mirror, so much more. It was as though the woman had stolen something from her life and imbued the paper with it.

"Witchcraft," she said, suddenly horrified.

Della Massa laughed. "No, not witchcraft, talent. Would you like it? My Lady doesn't have any use for it anymore."

"No, no, I couldn't. You've made me look like a queen. I could never take this." She went to hand it back but the dark man's hands closed on hers.

"No, it is yours. My Lady insists, and now for your reward."

She had hoped for this, been promised this, but had been too afraid to ask. She felt the dark man shift around behind her. Out of her peripheral vision she saw him pulling something out from beneath his cloak. It looked like a long necklace; maybe it was made of gems. It looked like a rosary but there was something different about it. It caught the dim light and glimmered. A necklace. He held it so that she could see them.

"Do you know what this is?" he asked.

"They're beads..." her throat suddenly became thick. What was he doing showing her some beads? Glass beads were to be her reward?

"The rosary, you've seen them before. But these have ninety-nine beads not fifty-four. Each one represents a name," he said instructively.

"A name," she said not understanding.

He leaned down to show her the beads more closely. He held the simple glass beads close to her eyes so that she could see. She felt his hot breath on her face.

"Yes, it is a misbaha and each one of the beads represents one of the names of Allah."

His fingers were rolling one of the beads.

"This bead has a name on it. Do you see it?"

She looked closely at the bead and as she leaned in he slipped the beads around her neck, and pulled. Della Massa twisted the beads and pulled so hard that he lifted the girl from her stool. It was so easy and she was so light. She clawed at the beads and flapped her arms about trying to release herself, but she had no hope. She had no hope once the Lady had seen her that day in the street and desired to sketch her. From that point she had been dead. This was a favor he extended to her. It was better for her to go out like this then end up in some plague pit. All men and women died, he had seen it countless times. She slumped as she passed out. He knew she was not dead, so he hefted her in his arms and carried her out of the cabin, to the edge of the barge and let her almost tenderly roll away from him and over the side. A splash broke the calm of the night and he noticed that it had begun to rain again. He wound the prayer beads back up and stuffed them into his pocket. Instead of enlightenment and hope, these beads gave death. He had feigned conversion once to escape death and as a result of his piety he was given the beads. He had killed the giver.

Chapter Two: Lotus House

It was hard to tell whether it was a dream or not. Miao Juzheng could only describe it as an awareness, a sense of being that was part memory and therefore part reality, but one thing was real and that was the pain.

In her dream she was sitting in front of Old Lao, her teacher and mentor, dipping a wolf hair brush into a pot of ink and practicing her characters. Old Lao was smiling, directing her hand and correcting her downward stroke that was too narrow.

"Press, but do not press too hard or the stroke becomes too wide. Too little pressure and you do not have the strength to make it straight. The pressure must be just right."

There was warmth in that voice, warmth that reminded her of hearth and home and pain.

Then the first scream came. It was a mortal scream full of unbelievable terror and death. Then the sounds of male voices and things breaking came, shouts that threatened to shiver her spirit from her body.

Old Lao had always known what needed to be done, known what others had needed. So he spoke to her in quiet, calm tones and guided her away from the table. It had the desired effect, and the need to bolt, to flee, subsided within her. She looked to Old Lao for desperate instruction.

He took the brush from her hand and placed it gently down and rose calmly to his feet. The violent noises and rough male voices were getting closer. He held out a gentle hand and she took it, putting her shaking hand in his. She felt it then. She felt his calm power enter into her and she felt strengthened by it. It helped her lock the panic away, to put it in a place where the muted screaming could not get out.

"I think it is time for us to leave." They walked calmly out of the room and into the night. Behind them the men burst into the room where they had just been. The men kicked the scrolls and upturned tables in frustration. The men were carrying torches and their distorted and misshapen shadows danced across the grass.

The dream shifted. She was on a wharf now. The violence of the night was behind her, but she also sensed the danger in front as well. It was a different type of violence. The violence of betrayal; now, she understands, it was not betrayal, but a desperate act to save her life. There was sadness, a resignation about Old Lao that made her sad as well. Her mother, her father were gone because she could no longer *feel* them. They had always been that way, able to sense each other; now that line was cut. She looked up into Old Lao's eyes and saw change there, but there was also courage. He squeezed her hand. She heard the footfall, wooden and empty, as the Portuguese slaver walked down the gangplank from his ship.

She did not know he was a slaver then, but she thought it odd that Old Lao was handing him a bag of coin and in return she was being escorted up the gangplank. The captain, who looked so different, smelled like a sweaty pig and his porcine eyes bored into her with a feverish intensity. Maybe he was sick. There was something on the other side of that bearded face that made her ill at ease. She turned around to plead with Old Lao not to do this, but he was gone. No sooner was she on the ship then she was thrust down into the ship's belly. There, darkness and the press of others greeted her. She placed her face desperately to the planking on the ship's hull and gripped one of its massive ribs. She was truly in the belly of a great beast. Even as she dreamed she was able to take some comfort in the knowledge that although the beast had consumed her, it would also birth her in a new world.

She did not understand then that Old Lao's betrayal was his last effort to save her life. Upon returning to the palace he would be questioned and then executed.

The dream changed again. She was beneath the waves. There was no need for her to breathe because she was part of the very water itself. It was hard to see through the murky depth as she kicked and pulled herself through it. She seemed to be looking for something, or someone. She swam on through the murk. Then, off to the right, there was a blur, a shadow. The closer she got, the more detail the shadow took on: dark wisps elongated to form arms, and legs. The shadowy form was human. She swam up to it from below. Around the corpse's head an aura of hair fanned out like a luxuriant growth of sea weed. The figure was that of a woman. Miao reached out and touched the hair. Suddenly, the corpse flipped over, and she was staring into the open eyes of the dead girl, barely a woman. Not of this world, was the gaze of the dead girl, but of the world where she had gone. There was something in her hand, something crumpled, something pale as the skin of the girl.

It came to her suddenly: the desperate need to breathe. She clawed urgently, her fingers and arms cycling through the water in an attempt to get to the surface. She knew she wouldn't make it, that she was about to drown. All she had to do was open up her mouth and breathe in the water and it would be all over, she would find out what the girl was staring at.

Then strong hands gripped her shoulders and she was being pulled out of the water. Bursting up out of her dreaming state, she gasped for breath.

"Lady Juzheng, M'lady, wake up."

The voice was deep and rough as though it had been scraped with sand paper, but it was familiar and she was grateful for it. She clung to George Silver's arms until she was sure she really could breathe; then she composed herself.

"It was another dream, wasn't it?" George's voice was full of worry, but also cornered with fear.

"Yes, George, I'm afraid so. I have to dress. We have to go out."

"It's the middle of the night?" He knew when she set her face the way it was set now, she would go no matter what he said. He grumbled. "Fine, M'lady. I'll wait outside."

"George," she said as he was leaving the room, his big form made bigger by the flickering of the candle. "Don't call me M'lady. Call me Miao or I'll cast a spell on you."

There it was again, the flicker of a fear, but he then smiled. "As you say M'... Miao, but you're as much a witch as I am."

From what she knew of these people, they were pathologically superstitious, and they often used that superstition as a weapon. It was fear; maybe it was the Emperor's fear that had destroyed her family. She had an amusing thought as she robed; maybe she should get a black cat. There were plenty enough of the poor things wandering about in the city. She could hear George outside the door shifting uneasily.

The man was always in motion, born to combat rather than home, which made her wonder how Sir Water had gotten him to take on such a domestic assignment. George, on first meeting, had impressed her as an adventurer, but as time went on his domestic aptitude began to show. He was as good as any servant she had seen, even better, because not only could he cook, and bake, there was none better at fighting. At times, much to her chagrin, he was worse then a mother hen, a mother hen with a sword. He would have been a gem in any noble's entourage. To be associated with the best swordsman in the land was indeed a gem. But when she asked him about this he just replied, he always had a hidden desire to bake, cook and keep house. Then he would wink past his broken nose, and say no more. He must have owed Sir Water a hefty debt, but she was very grateful to have the big man close to her. She slipped the cloak over her homespun dress.

"Almost ready, George," she called out.

"You know," came George's deep rasping voice on the other side of the door. "My mother had a touch of the sight."

She adjusted the cloak over her shoulders and tied it off. She liked how George's voice sounded, deep, but rounded with a thick smoothness on the ends. It was comforting. She began looking for the purse she carried. "The sight?"

"Just a touch of it. She could see things. She knew when one of my cousins was run over by a cart and killed, even though she was miles away."

Miao couldn't find her purse. "Damn," she tried out one of the swear words George had taught her.

"No, it's all right. He was a cripple anyway and this world is none too gentle with cripples."

"No, I'm sorry, George. I can't find my purse. Do you know where I put it?"

"On the stand," said George. "You probably knocked it off again. Check beneath it."

Miao went down on her knees and reached beneath it, exploring with her fingers. There it was, exactly as George said. The man had an amazing memory. He also never forgot a face or what people said. Perhaps she could remember faces, if she could see them clearly. She opened the door and joined him. The top of her head didn't even come close to being level with his shoulder. He was holding a candle lantern.

"Thanks."

"There's no way I can talk you out of this?" he asked cautiously.

"No."

"Right, let me get my sword and cudgel then and we'll be on our way."

Even though his language was disapproving, there was a note of hope in his voice, the hope that he would have an opportunity to use one of his tools.

A fine mist met them on the streets, a fine mist that made the night darker than it already was. The only light came from some of the second story windows of the buildings that overhung the street. It made them feel like they were moving through tunnels. She could feel George's discomfort. Miao didn't mind the dark. In a way she saw things better in the dark than in the day. Her nose she tried not to use. On first arriving in London she thought nothing could smell so foul, but she had been wrong, because it was all perspective. Once she had become one of the hundred thousand souls living in the city she had acclimatized to the stench, which bothered her, because it probably meant she smelled as bad as the city. She reached out and found George's hand.

"Just don't let me stumble into the mew."

"No mew for Miao," chuckled George. "Where to?"

"The wharf; the dream had water in it."

George grumbled. "Probably a lot more than just water, am I right?"

Miao's answer was a gentle push to get him moving.

George led her down the slick cobblestone street. There was one section where the paving stones changed from being small and rectangular to being wide, flat and uneven. Miao almost fell when her foot caught an edge, but George held her up.

"Easy, M'l...Miao."

Just then a shadow moved off to the left, Miao saw something shifting out of the corner of her eye. She found it easier to see things by looking at them obliquely, much like a bird, but she tried to do this covertly because it bothered people. Her constantly moving eyes also disturbed people and so, when she went out into public she wore a deep hood to hide her eyes.

"We're being followed," whispered Miao.

"Hopefully," rumbled George.

The water was closer now; it's damp rising up around them along with the burbling sound as the streets struggled to drain into the river. It was the sound of movement and of death. The image of the dead girl floated before her eyes called to her. She slipped her hand free of George's and ran for the wharf and the water. Inadvertently she had hit George's candle lantern and it fell, clanked on the stone and went out.

She didn't know why she ran. The girl was dead, she felt it. There was no way she could save her, but she ran nevertheless and was not satisfied until she felt the wood of the wharf beneath her feet. In her swiftness a space was created between them and the great black gulf of night flooded in. Suddenly, the two shadows that had been following them rose up behind her, large and foul. A large, rough hand latched itself onto Miao's shoulder while an arm slipped around her waist and lifted her into the air. Putrid breath filled her nose and she kicked. The man's face rubbed painfully against her skin. He squeezed her causing her to cry out in pain.

"Stop kickin' or I'll cut you in half."

"I'll take the bottoms," cackled the second voice. "You can haves the tops. I likes the bottoms, I does."

"Let's have a look."

The clumsy hands tried to rip the cloak off her, but the broach which held her cloak about her shoulders caught painfully against her throat. Then there was a whistle of wind as the cudgel pounded into the flesh with dense, meaty sounds. There was a snapping sound and a howl filled the night and big hands dropped her. The two scrambled away into the night like rats. George was around her protectively, lifting her up gently, sustaining her.

"Sorry about that," he said, "you took me by surprise. Shouldn't have run off."

"I'm sorry, but I thought they were behind us."

"They still are," whispered George, "We just stumbled on a different type of rubbish. The others are still out there, watching."

"If they can see anything in this," said Miao feeling about the dark, "then they are welcome to watch. You didn't kill them, did you?"

"No, I didn't kill them," he said plaintively. "I used the cudgel, although I should have used the sword."

"Thank you George, for not killing." Miao eschewed killing because of the effect it had on the person who killed. It often left them worse off than the person they killed. The dead are dead, but the living can die over and over again.

George struggled to get the candle relit, and after a number of strikes managed to. He held the lantern out over the water. He squinted his eyes trying to search the darkness for her.

"So, why are we here?"

Miao scanned the water more with her mind than her eyes and eventually found what she was looking for: a white wisp floated along the surface of the water. It looked like an ethereal flame. Recognizing it was being observed it began to draw close. Miao moved to the end of the wharf, closest to the shore and stepped down into the mud of the river. She sank up to her knees. The current was driving the wisp towards her.

"Miao, what do you think you're doing? There's nothing..."

As the white wisp came by she made a grab for it. Her fingers passed through it and it dissipated. The body of the dead girl, white face staring up, bumped gently against her, exactly where the wisp had vanished.

"George, come here. I've found her."

There was a splash as George entered the water.

"You've found her..." and then he saw the corpse. "Oh, I see. You dreamed this didn't you? I'm glad I don't have your dreams."

The girl floated gracefully as Miao gathered her in. Her red hair fanned out waving like seaweed. She touched her eyes and shut them.

"Those who are killed do not go gently. There is a ripping of their spirit from their body. It was on the water, telling me where she was. Her hand, George, what's in her hand?"

George noticed it and reached down and carefully took the sodden paper from the dead girl's fingers.

"Is it like the others?"

George wanted to groan but he only nodded as he thrust the paper into his pocket. It was like the others. This was the fourth in the collection that were pinned to the wall back at Lotus House. They were all pictures of dead girls, all with red hair.

Chapter Three: The Queen's Request.

The Queen's Glories were rosy cheeked and puffing as they tried to keep up. Their skirts, much lighter than the fare of court, and much less adorned with ribbon, lace and gems, whisked in agitated effort. When the Queen walked, she was intense. It was nothing more than the physical manifestation of her agile and overactive mind. It was her way of working out the demons, and the demons Queen Elizabeth walked from, were particularly dark. When she was a young woman, under custody, walking was the only freedom allowed to her. It kept her from going mad.

Not two months ago she had signed the warrant which had culminated in the removal of another

Queen's head: Mary Queen of Scots, the granddaughter of her father's sister. She had stalled, and equivocated, but the evidence had been irrefutable, both contrived and real. The killing of a Queen was no small matter. Kill one of God's anointed and you obscure the lines of those chosen to rule, but her father had done that, in spades. He had killed both Mary's mother and her own, one by breaking her heart and the other with the sword of an executioner. She, like her father, had blood on her hands and no matter how much she washed she could not get it off. Walk, walk hard and what chases shall never catch, but she knew that to be false. Eventually her health would fail and her demons would catch her, but not today.

Today she felt good, optimistic. Today she knew she would find a replacement for Doctor Dee. She had a special place in her heart for the Doctor of Mort Lake, her astrologer and physician psychic. She understood the weakness of men and often played to them, but the doctor was not weak, not in the attitude of telling the truth, at least.

If anyone were tempted to lie it would have been a court astrologist. A bad telling often had the cost of being shortened, or lengthened a foot. But there was one thing the Queen prided herself on, was to know when someone was lying to her. Most knew the difference between truth and deception and she could use those, but the ones who believed in the lie so much that they believed it true, well, that's where her crows, Walsingham and Lord Burghley, came in. Without them she would have been dead years ago.

Doctor Dee had read her stars and in them he had seen much. So fascinating was the man that she had studied his works and when his wife died she had descended from Richmond to attend him, in person to assuage his grief. He had told it true and she had been a true friend. So, when the prudish in her privy council conspired to have him arrested for heresy, she had Walsingham assign him a commission to gather information on Laske, the visiting Polish Prince. In this way, he would take his skryer, the unstable Edward Kelly, and their wives and children and leave the country. That seemed like years ago. Indeed Cecil had heard that Kelly had uncovered the mystery of the philosopher's stone, the elixir that could transmute base metals into gold. She smiled at that, her Captain of the Guard, Sir Water, had shown her how to turn smoke into gold.

The rogue had bragged about being able to weigh smoke. She took the bet. So, he weighed his tobacco, smoked it and weighed the ashes. Much to her delight the Queen had paid up. No doubt one of his wits from his society had advised him on this. She missed Dee terribly. They were in Prague now, at the court of The Holy Roman Emperor, Rudolph II. She had even heard that Dee had told him to repent. Well, we all need to repent, she thought and the dark, headless spectre of her cousin threatened to rise from her spilled blood. She felt the primal scream build within, but she would never release it. She knew Dee would come back to her, but until then, she needed guidance, a path finder so that she could find her way amongst the stars. True, she could retain any number of astrologers, but they would all lie, she needed someone of character, someone of Doctor Dee's innocent honesty.

Water had whispered in her ear, while wreathing her in smoke, of the possibility of a man who could find this rudder. The man was a brilliant playwright who was also part of his society. And so Sir Water had summoned him, and now she would commission him. She caught glimpses of her guard slipping through the greenery parallel to their course, flashes of silver armour through the trees. She demanded private walks with her Glories. They made their way through the woods down to the pond she had stocked with fish and swans. She tried to teach her Glories the virtues of the swan. It was easy to teach the graceful attributes, but the feral attack instinct was harder to teach. The swan was beautiful, but those wings, once extended could be lethal. That's why she loved Sir. Water, he had the grace of a literary man with the instinct and reflexes of an adventurer.

She just hoped his instincts about this rudder were good, because she felt, even while walking, the black humour caused by her headless cousin rising in her.

She stopped and her Glories, at the point of exhaustion, nearly collapsed. There were a number of stone benches about the pond and she told them to sort themselves out accordingly.

"Rest," she said, "while I investigate something of interest – alone."

They were too busy gasping for air while she slipped off into the woods. She was safe enough with the slashes of silver armour still following. She soon found what she was looking for, just as Sir Water said she would.

At first he was a shadow attached to the large bole of an ancient oak, much like a dryad, she thought. He had sat down against the tree and fallen asleep. She looked down at the young man's feet and was disappointed. From the way some talked she had hoped to see the hoofs of some satyr.

"Disappointing," she mumbled.

Christopher Marlowe scrambled up in a confused haze. Then realizing who was standing before him, he bowed and then dropped to his knees. "I am sorry if I offend your Highness."

She *tusshed* him and pulled him up. "None of that sycophantic nonsense; I get enough of it at Court. It is business I am about. Let us not stand on class division, shall we?"

Kit felt like shaking his head. This was not the Queen that the myths had constructed. This Queen, his Queen, seemed almost human. Of course she was human, idiot. When Sir Water had summoned him and told him of this surreptitious meeting, he had not known what to expect.

"You don't look like a cat, more like a goat with that little tuft of hair on your chin. Come, little cat, do not be what you are not."

"I dare not aspire to more than what I seem."

"Aspire not and rise not," she said with disappointment. She was about to turn and leave but then Kit said something to catch her attention.

"I will rise through my words, even though my thoughts pale in your presence and shake as though they have palsy."

Elizabeth took the fan she held and rapped him on the right shoulder and smiled. "Better. Keep that up and I'll raise you to Sir."

"I have no ambition to be Sir."

"No ambition?"

"Only to have my words heard. In that there is release for my mind."

She paused on that. She was familiar with suppression; she had suffered under her sister Mary too long, until God, and her sister's death released her. She was familiar with the budding playwright's work, the stunning darkness and horror of Tamburlaine the Great, of how a Scythian Sheppard could rise to rule the world.

"Oh, they will hear your words. I am sure of that, but beware new ideas dressed in old clothes; they tend to trip one up. Tell me something true."

Kit had been told how the Queen sounded people out with banter. If the mind was proved wanting, she would have no use for them. Even her fools, especially her fools, had to be sharp. Richard Tarlton was one of the sharpest, even when he was drunk, which was most of the time.

He cleared his throat in order to meet the test. "Will Somers said this to your father:

'The difference between counterfeit and
real wit is the difference between a
fart and a tempest, unfortunately you
are surrounded by too many foetid farts.'"

At first he had thought he had gone too far because the fan leapt to her face to cover her mouth. He had heard that the Queen's teeth were bad and that she had developed the habit of hiding her mouth when she laughed or smiled. It gave the false assumption that the Queen was coy.

She was anything but that, thought Kit. What he didn't expect was the neighing laugh, more of a horse than a human. It reached its crescendo then descended into a dying rasp. He controlled his reflect response. It would not do to laugh at the Queen's laugh.

When she was done, she rapped him on the other shoulder with her fan. "There, done. Now, you have heard me laugh. This means you are now sworn to secrecy, or, of course I will have you killed."

Kit shifted uneasily not sure this was some jape or real, or both. "You're secret – your laugh is safe with me."

"See that it remains so. Now, I shall name you Sir Cat. Does this please you?"

Kit dropped to his knee and bowed his head again. When he looked up she was glowering down at him. "It does not please the sun that a shadow should kneel before its luminance?" he asked.

She wagged her fan at him again. "Get up," she said tersely. "If you insist on falling down again I shall be tempted to leave you there. Come, walk with me."

They followed a small, beaten path through the woods. The silver armour followed, obscured by the trees, except for the flicker of the sun against metal. She wanted her Cat to see them, so that he knew that he had not yet passed.

"I will tell you something, my Cat, that I only tell a few."

Kit stiffened inside, but forced himself not to show his apprehension. This was a test. She would confide in him and if he betrayed that confidence it would be a knife in the dark, or poison, or his head, or worse.

"I will keep your confidence."

"Good, good. Do you think I am divine? No, truth now; I am not looking for any sycophantic platitude. I can get that at court."

"No," he responded cautiously, "I think your divinity is an act."

She stopped and regarded him with piercing eyes that seemed to ruthlessly enter into his very being. It was a gaze that quickly rummaged through his mind, separating at will, his lying shadows from truth. "Good. Indeed, it is an act, and for any act to be effective, the audience must believe it, even though I do not."

"You do not believe you are anointed of God?" asked Kit. He felt himself swimming in such dangerous waters that he might as well swim bravely. If something dragged him down, it dragged him down and he drowned, but maybe, just maybe, he might make it to shore.

He had his Masters in Divinity and had felt that any Christian authority had died with Christ and his apostles. That the anointing of Kings and Queens was purely imitation of the anointing of Saul and David, a tinkling sound without substance. After that, things had become more of a mummer's farce than anything else.

"Have you seen God, Cat?"

"No."

"Listen closely, Cat. God counts, but it's what the people think that matters. Win the people and you win everything. Lose the people and..."

"That's the act?"

"No. That much is true. I fill the empty heads of my Lords and Ladies with contrived love and fashion. Listen, what do men want most?"

"Power, to win a woman."

"To bed a woman you mean, and power is a means to that. If I am unattainable, then what do men seek?"

"Power."

"And it is power through the courtly words of love, of worship, that I demand. Then I reward. Now, ladies, what do they desire?"

"To be desired, and thereby, power."

"Oh, you are good. And through the use of cloth and the wearing thereof, I have achieved that. And through this I control my royal family. That is the act, none of it real, all of it pretence."

Elizabeth stopped walking, a pensive look on her face. "It has been many years since my father's fool died and yet I hear his voice in yours. I must advise Tarlton there is a new wit on the rise."

Kit bowed his head and thanked her. He was sensing a feeling of emotional turmoil within the Queen, an unrest that not even the intellectual acuity of her mind could tame. The Queen was not well. She seemed to be making up her mind moment by moment.

"Perhaps you will do. Do you love me? Do you worship me?"

Kit bowed his head cautiously. "I live to serve and serve to worship."

"Does it not bother you that you worship a heretic queen, one who has been marked an enemy of God?"

"No, this would not bother me, even if it was true."

"My father was a good Catholic and would have remained so had the Pope granted him his divorcement. But his hand was forced as all our hands are. We are forced to do things – we do not want to do.

What work have my Raven's been giving you?"

"Letters mostly, I deliver them and they pay me. It allows me time to write."

"Never fear, if you will do this thing for me, you shall have money."

"How can I be of service?"

"I am in need of a physic spiritualis, someone who can heal my broken soul."

Kit's heart leapt into his mouth. The Queen was confessing things of such intimacy to him that he knew he was both blessed and condemned. He hadn't a clue where to find a person of the quality of Doctor Dee. Such brilliance came along only but seldom.

"May I ask a question?"

"Ask."

"You are surrounded by brilliant and profound counsellors, could they not be better for such a task?"

"More patience give me," she said in an exasperated tone and placed a gloved hand against Kit's face. "This must be done in secrecy and my Captain says you are the man for the job."

"I doubt myself."

"Are you being pertinent with me?" There was a dangerous tone to her voice.

"No."

"Get someone to replace Doctor Dee, until he returns. You have until after the Maundy Ceremony at Windsor. Please," her voice softened, "do not look so distressed. I am seldom wrong about the men I choose. Those I choose find themselves very resourceful to me as well as themselves."

Kit almost fell to his knees again, but instead gave a slight, jerky bow. A cooling presence, he felt her hand on the crown of his head, and her face close to his ear.

"Very good, my Cat, stay like that until I am gone, and remember that the sun has chosen to shine on you. And Cat, this meeting never happened."

When Kit lifted his head, the Queen was gone, as were the armoured slashes of silver that had lurked close by during the interview. He took a great gasp of air realizing that he had been breathing in suppressed gasps while he had spoken with the Queen. His cold forehead was covered in sheen of sweat. There was terror here, but also triumphant exhilaration. He had just spoken to his Queen, his emotionally unstable Queen, and been sworn to service and secrecy. The next time he saw Sir Water, he would have to thank him.

Chapter Four: Sword Play

Lotus House was tucked away in the Vintry, a district that included the Three Cranes, three very large cranes that were designed for loading and unloading cargo, especially wine from France. It was where Sir Water held his favour from his Queen, the tax on sweet wines. The entrance to Lotus House was unassuming. In fact, a busy person would trudge by it without notice. Its front was as normal as any other building, but inside was the difference. The house had an inner courtyard, greened with grass and shrubbery and open to the sky above. There had been a bench and a pond in the centre, but George had the pond filled in, now all that was there was grass, well beaten, almost to the point of being dead. The stone benches had been moved to the periphery.

George preferred to practice in a full suit of doublet and hose including a cloak. His point was you should train in the clothes you are going to fight in. Invariably, with everyone in London carrying a rapier (those who could afford it), a fight was bound to happen in the course of a day. He trained his students to fight to win, because losing meant death, or with the new laws, maiming.

The Queen had become upset with the deaths of her young nobles, young cocks strutting around waggling their rapiers. Dying in defence of your country was one thing; dying because someone made an obscene jest about the size of your ruff, was quite another. So, with the support of her Privy Council, a law was issued. It did not outlaw fighting, but if you killed, you hung. So, the young dandies started to maim. There was no law against maiming.

Before Sir Water retained George to be the companion of Miao Juzheng he had made a good living teaching the techniques of fighting, now he made a better living being a companion. When he trained, he preferred to work with the commons. Those lads didn't care about wrist flicks or fancy Italian twirls, or tricks, more designed to entertain than anything. No, those lads he taught with sword and buckler or long sword and pike. He taught them to stay alive, which was rather ambitious of him, because if the enemy didn't kill them, sickness did. The Queen was rather parsimonious in her pay, and most of it was tithed on its way to the men, so they often starved. The court dandies and the gentry were a different matter. They paid quite well to be trained in the use of rapier and dagger. Before Sir Water approached him, his business was taking quite a hit from the Italian imports. They were great showmen and to the dandies, show was what mattered, still those who really wanted to learn how to win still came to see him on occasion, but most of his time was taken up with educating Miao Juzheng.

George undid his cloak from its clasp and tossed it down onto the stone bench. He looked up. Overcast with a chance of rain, more like a slim chance of sun he thought wryly. In his opinion, women had no business learning sword play, but Sir Water had strange ideas and he had issued his commands. He commands and I obey, as long as the command was lined with silver, and indeed it was. He had already given her the rudiments; now it was time to take things to the next level. On the whole, she was satisfactory, not bad for someone who was sight impaired, which in itself amazed him.

"Just throw your cloak down onto the bench, beside the buckler, although I don't think we'll get to that today. Now, let's see what you remember from the last time..." George turned about to find himself looking down at the blunted end of a rapier.

Miao was clothed in similar doublet and hose, and looked more like a boy than a young woman. George put his finger on the tip of her rapier and pushed it away.

"What was my last lesson?"

"The element of surprise."

"Ah, yes. It seems that you've remembered, and I have forgotten."

"George?"

"Yes?"

"Why do I have to fight in doublet and hose?"

"Ah," he was about to say that that's what she would be wearing if she got in a fight, but she had just pointed out the flaw in such reasoning. "Right, being a lady, you would be in a dress, but right now I'm a little short on Farthingales. So, we'll just have to make do. Besides, girls don't fight."

Her blade flashed at him and he parried. Miao began to circle to the left. That was good. She was an apt student. He taught his swordsmen to move in a circle to utilize the area, to never get caught in the forward and back movement of the thrust and parry. Movement kept the enemy guessing.

He darted in and she parried.

30

"Make sure your feet are turned out. It gives better balance with lateral movement."

She attacked low again and he used a low parry.

"Good, would you like to learn how to maim your opponent today?"

Miao shrugged. The truth of the matter is she didn't really like to sword fight at all, well, not the killing part, but she did delight in the exercise. It felt good to move, to work up a sweat. "I suppose," she said as she tried a right mid torso attack, spun about to hack at the left.

George blocked both with a little half-smile on his face. "Careful with that move; if you were to use it again in a fight, you'd end up with a sword in the back."

He went in with a three count, high, low and mid, all of which Miao was able to block, however the third left her rattled. George had put about half his strength into it, just enough to send painful vibrations up her arm.

"Stop," he said. "Sword at standby position. Warm are we?"

Miao nodded.

"Now, one of the best maiming moves is to use the edge of the sword on a pass, to strike the Achilles tendon. I have yet to see a man fight on with a severed tendon. Cut the tendon and he is done."

Miao watched his movements carefully, which feet went where. She found seeing detail impossible, but the general movement, the flow she could grasp. Faint, move in, one, two, block, pass, turn and as you pass strike low severing the tendon.

"Right?" now you do it, "nice and slow."

Miao replicated the sword master's moves to perfection. George felt the slap of the dulled steel against the lower part of his calf. Had the swords been sharp his flesh and tendons would have been nicely sliced open. He saluted her. She had an excellent memory for movement.

"Well done. I don't often complement my students..."

Miao laughed. "You never complement your students; you insult them. The greater their ability, the greater your insults."

"Am I really that bad?"

"Worse."

George went to the bench and picked up a towel to wipe off the sweat. He tossed it to her. Miao caught it gingerly and held it far from her body as though it was infected with plague. She let it drop to the stone bench. She had a sensitive nose and the towel reeking was in desperate need of a cleaning.

"The thing I still can't figure out about you is how you actually see," said George. "With your eyes doing that fluttering thing, back and forth, it's hard to believe you can see anything."

Miao had been over this with George before. It was why she liked to wear deep hoods, to hide her eyes. Most people thought she was possessed and that could mean accusations of witchcraft. Sir Water had warned her.

"I can see quite well," she said defiantly and untruthfully. It took effort for her to focus. The truth of the matter was that she had learned to trust her other senses more, her smell (which was useless in London since everything stank), her taste, her touch, but most importantly, her intuition. She could feel movement before it actually happened. Impossible to explain, she had always been that way.

"So, we have someone who draws the victim before killing them," she said trying to change the subject from her eyes. It was a sensitive topic to her, something she preferred not to discuss.

George smiled. He knew exactly what she was doing. He lifted his sword up. "As the froggies say 'en garde.'

He lunged, his sword point darting for her head. She dodged and struck at his arm, which he parried.

"Keep your sword up. Always expect an immediate counter."

His sword slid effortlessly past her guard and tapped her on the shoulder.

"Oww, that hurt," said Miao.

"It hurts a lot more when it slides in between your ribs. The worst is a lung puncture. They linger until their lungs fill with blood and they drown."

Miao tried the same move on him and this time she recovered sufficiently enough to fend off his counter.

"Are you trying to scare me?" she said nervously.

He laughed with an insufferable, half mocking smile on his face. "Not at all. You know what I think. I think," he said as their swords crossed again. "I think you see better than most because you have the gift of anticipation. You know which way a person will move by the way they stand. I can teach that, but I rarely find people born with it."

"It's rare?"

"And dangerous." He stood back, sword in the standby position. He pursed his lips and his brow creased. "It is very dangerous, because of dissimilitude."

"Dissimilitude? Lying?"

George nodded his sword suddenly at the ready. She noticed his weight was shifting to his right, which meant his strike would come on her left. She prepared to counter, but then everything changed. The right changed to left and the sword's point was hovering only inches from her eye. She blinked, her mouth going dry.

"I see what you mean."

"Never let anyone know what you have now revealed to me, that you depend mostly on motion instead of sight. If you do, you'll be dead in a blink of an eye."

Then the sword's point was gone and she swallowed.

"Not that I'll ever be in a position of fighting for my life, right? After all, like you said, I'm a woman."

"Right," he said, but not with a lot of confidence.

George was wiping the sweat from his face again. He sweated a lot when he trained, which was odd. She had never seen him fight a duel, but it was said that when he did he was as cool as a fall wind, and cool winds did not sweat. She smelt the ale scent in his perspiration.

"With swords, maybe not, but you've been fighting for your life ever since you got here." He shrugged his broad shoulders, "now you are fighting for justice. I can respect that. Can I be perfectly honest with you?"

"Please, do." Miao, sensing that her instruction was over, had put her sword away. She was now pulling the cloak over her shoulder. She found dressing in men's clothing rather liberating; skirts, with the weight of the layers, rather encumbering.

"When Sir Water asked me to watch you, I did it because of the money, but now, I do it because I'm afraid of what people would do to you if they found out about you."

Miao approached George and placed a hand to the side of his face. "You have a good soul, George..."

George looked hurt but then covered the awkward silence with a laugh. "I never said I was falling in love with you. I'm just protective that's all, besides, I like my women with more meat on their bones. You're so skinny you could pass for one of Leicester's boy actors."

She punched George in the arm, relaxing. Distance was important to maintain, because as soon as men got close to her, bad things happened to them. The thought of something bad happening to George made her feel sick to her stomach. Besides he was old enough to be her father.

George grunted: "We have to find these killers, but I don't think we have much chance at justice with them."

"Why not?"

"Because I get the feeling that the killers are not on our level. The gentry have their own rules, their own justice." He took a look at his rapier before sliding it into its sheath.

Miao shrugged. "Let's catch them first and then we will let Sir Water sort them out. We have to get in front of them, George. Instead of finding the bodies, we have to find the living. We need information."

"I know where to go for that," said George bracingly, "but first breakfast. Ready for a bite?"

"A bite. Where are we going?""

"You eat like a bird. Eat a nice, big, English breakfast and I'll tell you."

Miao knew what a nice, big English breakfast was and the mere thought of it made her full: Eggs, sausage, bacon, beans, and toast, all fried. George may have been a sword master, but his first love was eating. She knew he wouldn't budge unless she promised.

"All right, George. I will eat your English breakfast, as long as you don't force feed me for the rest of the day."

George laughed. "Deal."

"Now, the information? Where do we find it?"

"St. Paul's Walk," he said examining her, "but you can't go like that."

"I know that."

"And you can't go in that black, hooded robe you like to hide in. I'll not be seen in public with a little monk on my arm. No, you'll have to go as a lady, a shockingly beautiful lady in all her glory. And fortunately you are nobility, so you can get away with it."

"And you?"

"I fake it. Sir Water has a few of his outfits upstairs, just in case."

Miao was tired of finding dead bodies, but she was hesitant in showing herself in public. Her white hair, constantly moving eyes and pale, almost translucent skin tended to disturb people, and she was cautious about this. "You know I don't like people to see me..."

"How badly do you want to catch these killers?"

"Badly, very badly, George."

"Then, you're going to have to show yourself, because nothing gets noble tongues wagging like gossip, exotic gossip, and I hope you forgive me for saying so, you're as exotic as it gets."

"But Sir Water..."

"It's better to ask for forgiveness than for permission, besides, leave Sir Water to me, one Devon man to another."

Chapter Five: The Theatre is the Thing

"I think you need to be more aggressive," barked Ned Allyen trying to direct.

"Sure 'nough, Ned. Don't get mad," said George Bryan pleased to see the rubicund response of the actor, the stiffening, the puffing up of Ned's big chest.

Richard Burbage gave him an admonishing look.

"I am not mad. I just think it would be more believable if there was more intensity."

"So," said Will Kemp who was lounging on the stage, "you want them to get mad."

"No, not mad, just intense!" responded Ned irritably.

"Sure enough," said George. "Intense, like you?"

"Yes, yes, like me!"

It wasn't that they didn't like the big, dramatic actor. He was the best at the major roles. No one could compare to his Hieronimo in Kyd's 'A Spanish Tragedie' and it seemed that Marlowe's Taburlaine the Great was written just for him to bombast and blow across the stage. What bothered the other players was that not only did he have the major roles, but he had also taken it upon himself to direct. The problem with Ned was that he lacked subtlety. His direction tended to digress into shouting and bellowing matches. It was one of the reasons Ned refused to direct Will, because Will loved a good yelling match. So, to manage Ned, they used subtlety, something Ned had a hard time understanding. Telling him he was mad had the strange effect of not only confusing him but it also took the bluster out of his direction.

Thomas Pope, who was standing beside Ned watching the fight scene, stroked his whiskers pensively. "Really, I don't know about that, Ned. This is the new bit you know. Usually if there is any killing or fighting it's a simple matter of an exit, tumultuous noise, pig's blood and then staggering back on stage pretending you have a dagger between your ribs. Do this wrong and..."

"Tom's right," said Augustine Phillipe, who was lounging beside Will on the stage. Everyone knew him as Augsy. He was tightening the strings on one of his many instruments. "One slip and our company is one short." To emphasise this he plucked one of his strings that gave a dissonant TWANG.

"Remember that pyrotechnic display?" said Will. "Killed a young, pregnant woman and a child. Bad luck that. A dead woman would be enough, but pregnant, and a child.... It's a wonder the entire company wasn't hauled off to Tower Hill to have their sausages displayed for all."

"Fine," spat Ned, "fine, but something is missing. I just don't believe you two are fighting to the death."

James Burbage rubbed his head in bewilderment. "If you want me to try to kill George, I think you're nuts."

Ned stomped his feet on the boards and yelled: "I am not mad!"

"He didn't say you were mad," said Tom, "he just said you were nuts."

Ned threw his hands dramatically into the air, gave a great groan, spun about and stalked off the stage.

"Exit, Allyen," said Will chewing on another grape and spitting out a seed. He held one up and examined it. "When I was with Leicester in the Lowlands we had grapes from Burgundy. He popped another into his mouth and spit the seeds out. "I'd prefer wine."

"Why don't you just hold it in you mouth until it ferments," offered Tom.

"Just might do that, Tom, might just do that."

"That being said," said Richard. "I think Ned was right. There is something missing, but where? At the beginning, in the middle, near the end?"

Augsy tapped his chin. "It's not bad. The swordplay is good: the sound of metal on metal rather rhythmic. It's just when you go to kill each other that it falls apart."

Will had dispensed with the grapes and was now eating an apple. "Augsy is right. There is a certain rhythm happening here. Maybe I could teach you some..."

"No," shouted Richard, "there is no way I'm going to do one of your stupid jigs, in the middle of a fight scene. I'll be a laughing stock."

"That's the idea," said Will with a mouth full of apple. "Better to leave them laughing than heckling. Let's see it again, from the little swirly bit."

George and Richard worked the scene back and forth, swords clashing. Will leapt to his feet.

"Stop, right there. Didn't Silver, when he set the fight, have you do a jab thing with a dagger, right there?"

Richard stared at him with exasperation: "I think I would know if I was using a dagger, wouldn't I?"

"A pity; could use a dagger there, don't you think, Augsy?"

"Absolutely, a nice dagger with a gem in the hilt."

"A gold hilt," confirmed Tom. "I like gold."

"Don't we all," said Will, "don't we all."

"Stop!" shouted Richard. They were just continuing the game they had just finished playing on poor Ned, except now they were working him over. He turned his attention to George. If they were going to solve this, they would have to do it sans nut gallery. "Just, shut up. George and I will work through this."

They started to mark the choreography set down by Silver. He had been particularly meticulous so that nobody would get hurt.

George waved his sword. "Here I do my little Italian trick."

"Right," confirmed Richard, "then I do my trick."

George took the required steps until he was on the other side of Richard and turned. "Then we both do the French thing."

Raucous laughter burst from Will, Tom and Augsy.

Richard felt like telling them to shut up again, but that would be like throwing fuel on the fire, so he did the next best thing. He ignored them.

Richard and George were standing facing each other. "This is the English bit where you try to kick me in the nackers and I trip you."

George did a controlled fall onto the stage.

"Good," said Richard, "now, roll away."

"All right, all right," bellowed Will. "Now you stick each other, do a little dance and give us a laugh."

Richard looked at Will drolly. "I know you may find this hard to understand, but that's what we're trying to avoid here."

Augsy clapped his hands together. "I know what you're missing. You're missing a song."

Richard dropped his sword onto the stage where it clattered. His head was giving him a great pain, and other than killing his friends, he had no idea how to get rid of it.

***

Shakes, on coming to London, had pieced together a reasonable existence. He worked with his friend, Henry Field, in his publishing business, did some spear holding for the Burbages and occasionally wrote for Lord Strange who had his own troupe of actors. It was from there that he met Christopher Marlowe. They were the same age and made an immediate connection. Looking for work, Kit introduced him to Richard, who had offered him some work dressing the actors and holding spears, swords or anything that was required. Eventually, when the time was right, he would slip him some lines on a play he was working on. Right now, Shakes couldn't understand why Ed wasn't fitting into the dress. True, the boy was getting a bit too hairy to remain a boy actor for long, but nothing that a good shave and some makeup couldn't handle, but that was a two-edged sword. Start shaving and the hair would come in faster. Unfortunately, Ed's days as a female were coming to a close. He placed the sole of his foot on Ed's backside for leverage and gave the cords on the corset a tug.

"Easy, Shakes," complained Ed. "Pull any harder and you'll cut me in half."

"Sorry, Ed, but I've got to get you down to a size where you'll fit the dress."

"I fit yesterday," yelped Ed as Shakes gave another tug as he worked his way up the back of the corset. "This is the rack, it is, just gone vertical and backwards."

Shakes had a strange vision of the Queen's pensioners prancing about in their precipitous hats lining up to have the rack lengthen them because it became fashionable.

"One more tug, then we will see if the dress fits; one, more, deep breath."

Ed took a breath.

"There, done."

"How am I supposed to do my lines when I can't talk?" asked Ed, his voice squeaky and breathless.

Strange, thought Shakes, admiring Ed's wasp like waist. He took the verdingal from off the armature. "Look at it this way, Ed. You got your high voice back."

"I did, didn't I? Well let's try it on again."

Shakes lowered the cone shaped hoop skirt over Ed's head and arms, but again the skirt caught on his chest. No matter how hard he tugged, the dress wouldn't go down any further. If they couldn't get the verdingal on they wouldn't be able to get the kirtle or the forepart or the gown and the sleeves on. Everything hung on the verdingal fitting.

"Sorry, Ed, you must have grown overnight. The verdingal just doesn't fit. We're going to have to get James to pay for a new one."

"Are you serious? He'll have my head and someone else will have my job."

"We show tomorrow night."

"It's all fine for you," lamented Ed, "you get to hold a spear. No pressure there."

"Not much money, either," reminded Shakes. He had a family back home to feed.

Shakes had removed the verdingal when he noticed something funny with stiffened ropes that were supposed to define the A-line structure to the skirt. "Hold on," he mumbled to himself.

41

Ed tugged desperately at the corset binding, trying to open it up when the laces broke. The corset sprung open, popping off Ed. He groaned in despair. James Burbage, the principal owner of the company, wasn't going to be happy. The dress had not come cheap, even though the mild Cuthbert Burbage would probably pay for it, he would still have to suffer James' wrath. A dress for a leading lady, one designed to meet the exacting standard of the nobles, was not cheap. The Bel Imperia dress had cost a large chunk of change, more than he could make in a year. Ed's girth left him no recourse; he was going to have to diet.

"Strange," mumbled Shakes.

"What's strange?" asked Ed in despair.

Shakes held up the ribbing of the verdingal. The stiffened cords had been sewn together so that they bunched up. He ran his fingers over the thick, clumsy stitches. Someone had altered the width of the skirt's waist.

"I'll kill him," said Ed, the blood flooding back into his face.

"Everything all right?" asked Richard who had escaped the futility of the sword practice on stage. He was at the point of throwing the entire bit out and giving Will his jig in its place.

"Look at this, Richard," said Shakes. He showed him the stitches. "Who do you think?"

"Bloody Will," groaned Richard, "sorry, Ed; I'll have a talk with Will."

They did this every show. The closer they got to the opening of a new play, the more pranks they pulled. It was Will's way of dealing with the stress. The more stress, the more pranks. But Richard had had enough.

"Will," he yelled, "bloody Will Kemp!" Richard grabbed the hoop skirt and dragged it out onto the stage. He had left them arguing, but when he found

Ned yelling at George Silver, his fury left him. Silver was someone you didn't want to yell at.

"We paid good money for this scene, and it doesn't work! Never in my life have I seen such shoddy choreography."

Richard tossed the dress at Kemp who caught it. "Will, tear your godless stitching out and help Shakes fit Ed will you."

Will sighed at Richard in disappointment. "I was waiting to see Silver run Ned through." Then he caught the murder in Ed's eyes. "Sorry, Ed, just a little humour that's all."

Shakes went off with Will and Ed to set the dress right.

Richard noticed the slight, almost wraith like form of Miao Juzheng standing off to the side of the stage. She was dressed in her usual black robe, her hood pulled up over her face to hide her features. Normally, the players, being a curious lot would have wanted to investigate, but with Silver as her companion they had learned to respect their distance. He nodded greeting to Miao who nodded in return.

Ned was continuing to complain in his best declaiming oratory, when Richard stepped in. Silver was well connected with Sir Water and it wouldn't do to insult him, although he suspected it would take some insulting to bother Silver. For a moment he thought about letting Ned go on. He could do with one less leading man.

"Thank you, Ned, but I'll take it from here."

Ned opened his mouth like a fish in need of oxygen and then shut it after seeing Richard's demeanour.

"I understand," said Silver gravely, "that there is some problem with the fight choreography?"

"No, not at all," clarified Richard. "The problem is we can't make it realistic enough."

Silver nodded. "Show me."

George and Richard took their places on the stage and quickly came to the point where they were having difficulty.

"See, no matter where we turn they'll see that we're not really skewering each other," said Richard with a pleading voice.

Silver rubbed his chin.

"Cloaks," said Miao. "Give them cloaks."

Silver gave an assenting nod. "Absolutely my Lady; that would solve the problem no matter which way they turned."

"Cloaks," shouted Richard, "fetch some cloaks."

Once they had the cloaks, Silver was able to arrange the actors so that when the fatal thrust came, the cloaks were able to effectively mask the swords, making it truly look like the rapiers were passing through their bodies.

"Marvellous," clapped Ned his surliness suddenly gone.

The others were nodding their approval.

Augsy stooped over the two bodies on stage, took a third cloak and threw it over them. "Just for dramatic effect. Now nobody can see them breathing."

Tom continued to stroke his beard. "The only question is, should we drag the bodies off the stage or have them stand up and take a bow."

Beneath the cloak Richard muffled something.

"What's that?" said Tom pulling the cloak off.

Richard sat up. "If it was part of the play, I'd say drag them off, but since this is only an interlude between acts we should stand up."

"I concur," proclaimed Ned. He turned and grasped Silver's hand and began pumping it. "You arrived just in the nick of time. What do we owe you for such propitious timing?"

Richard cleared his voice. "Ned, we've already paid Silver, and handsomely."

Silver gave a big grin. "That's why I'm here..."

Richard's mouth went dry. He already had to convince James and Cuthbert to increase the play's expenditure to pay Silver. "I'm sorry, Silver, but until we start the run we just don't have any disposable...

Silver shrugged. "How about a favour?"

Richard relaxed, but just a bit. "Yes, a favour will do. Name it, as long as it won't get us closed down."

"Do you remember the Bel Imperia dress?"

Richard knew the dress well. It had cost a small fortune, but a cheap one would not do at court. The Queen would not be entertained by fakes, even though acting was nothing but fakery. He gave a slow but cautious nod. "Yes."

My Lady needs a dress, just to borrow, mind you."

"She needs a dress?" asked Richard his mouth going dry again. The Bel Imperia dress was a marvel. It was made of gold and black and crimson silk. It had slashed sleeves and was festooned with pearls, but that wasn't what made Richard start to sweat. The problem was that only a member of the royal family could wear those colours. He looked again at the hooded form of Miao. He knew Silver to be rash, but not insane.

"May I ask why you need that particular dress?"

"None other would suit My Lady's rank. Don't worry, Richard, we just intend to go for a walk."

"That's exactly what I was worried about," responded Richard feeling as though a great void had opened up and he was about to be pulled in.

Chapter Six: To St. Paul's Walk

The wait was excruciating. Richard knew his brother and father wouldn't be back until the end of the week. They were away securing funds for some repairs on The Theatre's thatch, until they started Marlowe's Tamburlaine, the purse was very tight. They had a little bit of time to pull this off. However, how to exactly do it remained to be seen. Richard rubbed the toe of his boot into the slick cobblestone as he waited. He didn't know how it happened, but not only had Silver secured the Bel Imperia dress for Miao to wear at St. Pauls, but he also convinced him the loan of the sedan chair to carry her hence.

It was all really quite mad, and Ned and Will loved it. Silver wanted to stir the pot so that the Walkers at St. Paul would spread the word about a new mysterious lady. This would get tongues wagging and where tongues wagged answers to questions could be had. More likely, it would land them in gaol. Miao Juzheng may indeed be royalty from the Middle Kingdom, but that was a long way away and this was London where things could get ugly very fast. Just the other day a number of apprentices were hung, drawn and quartered at Tyburn. It had something to do with an extracurricular outing involving smashed eggs and breaking into a place and stealing something. One of Richard's greatest fears was to have his intestines paraded before his eyes.

"How long is it going to take her to dress?" complained Augsy who was also becoming nervous.

"It took Ed at least half an hour to get it on," said George.

"Not to worry, not to worry," declaimed Ned. "She will be out anon."

Ned Alleyn was a strange man, thought Richard. He was generally a vacillating pain in the arse, but when he made up his mind, and threw his weight behind something, he was an unstoppable force of nature.

Richard began to review what had happened to land him in this mess. Perhaps that would help him to never let this happen again. Will had appeared after fixing Ed's dress. He flippantly suggested they accompany Silver and Miao to St. Paul's. Ned and the rest, for some bizarre reason, had agreed. Ned even suggested the sedan chair. After that point everyone piled onto the adventure cart and Richard had become so loaded down he had to agree or risk revolt. It was either this or they would make the nearest tavern and get blind drunk. Drunken actors and a new show weren't a good recipe.

The door opened and Silver, dressed in one of Sir Water's courtier outfits, stepped out into the street. Miao's graceful fingers, much like the wing of a dove, floated down to rest on his forearm. Although the dress was mostly hid beneath her black cloak, the resplendent Bel Imperia dress still glittered when light caught pieces of it. Flashes of gold and crimson silk winked at them coquettishly. Will, in a flourish, took off his cape, and threw it on the pile of filth in front of her. He bowed himself to the ground. Will, when he wasn't cutting a caper could be quite fashionable.

"The trash is embarrassed before such beauty."

Miao laughed. Even though it had been a few years since fleeing the Middle Kingdom, she had not entirely eradicated the tonal accent from her language. It still came out, when she laughed, with sing-song sounds that filled the air.

"Will, you've ruined your cloak," she said stepping on it.

Augsy and Tom fell over each other to help her up into the chair. Will and Richard would lift the front while Tom and Augsy would handle the back. George would be rotated in when someone got tired. Silver along with Ned would lead the procession. Ed, still unhappy with the decision, had to stay behind.

"It's most likely," said Will, straining to lift the chair and setting it on his shoulder, "that this won't be the last time we step in it today."

Richard gave a discontented groan. "I just hope it doesn't cost."

"Not to worry, James can just take it out of your wages," said Will with a straight face.

The weight of the sedan chair was manageable, because Miao was not very heavy. Sometimes her slightness gave the impression that she was a changeling from Faerie. A stiff wind could have toppled her, but the players knew she was made of stiffer stuff than that. She had to be for Silver to take an interest in her. To outward appearances Silver seemed to be made of steel, but Miao, when she let people see her, was made of diamonds.

Progress through the crowded streets was made quickly with some notice, but people tended to mind their own business and the daunting forms of Silver and Ned in the front made quite a procession. Once a black cat appeared from one of the side streets and Ned yelped giving commands to double the pace. Richard didn't have to be encouraged. The sedan chair had sped ahead and the startled cat dodged away. The people they nearly ran down, cursed them. Afterwards the chair slowed down.

"That was a close one," said Richard breathing a sigh of relief. "We need all the luck we can get today."

As they approached Bishopsgate, the street became more crowded. People tended to set up their vegetable stalls just outside the gate. It was a perfect selling strategy. As they got close Ned began to bellow, "Make Way, Make Way." The people parted not necessarily out of respect, but because they were curious, and because most people knew Ned and his acting style. They loved his bellowing manner.

"It's Ned, Ned Allyen," went the mumble through the crowd and some even decided to delay their business to follow along behind.

"You know," said Will, "there's irony in this."

Richard was feeling a bit nasty towards Ned, but he had to admire the man's pluck. He played the part of the self-confident courtier so well that everyone believed him. They should see him before going on stage. Ned would have a pail between his legs as he filled it with vomit.

"How?" snapped Richard.

"Can't play inside the walls, but that's what we're going to do isn't it?"

Richard got a sick feeling inside his stomach. He hadn't thought of this. "Oh, Lord."

"I didn't know you were a religious man," quipped Will. "I just hope Silver and M'Lady don't lose their heads over this. I heard it often takes seven whacks with a dull blade, but that's if the person doesn't start running around."

Richard's complexion became tinged with green. "Would you do me a favour, Will, and just shut up."

Bishopsgate was crowded as usual. The guards were being obnoxious as usual, stopping people and questioning them as to their purpose of entering Bishopsgate's ward and the district of London proper. Within the gates the Mayor's Law was oppressive, while outside there were some liberties. The Mayor hated theatres and brothels equating them as the same. It was why Richard's father, James, was forced to lease land in Shoreditch to build The Theatre.

"What if the guards stop us?" whispered Richard into the back of Ned's head.

Ned gave his big shoulders a shrug. "They won't."

"They're irritating," said Silver, "but they won't cause any trouble."

Richard still had a sense of foreboding as they made their way to the gate. Just as he thought they would, the guards stopped them. There was a pair on duty while several lounged about looking vigilantly bored.

When they saw the sedan chair their interest piqued and they became guards with purpose. "Swords," said one oily looking fellow. "May we see your swords?" Although his voice rang with authority there was a tone of apprehension about it as though he didn't know what to make of the troop.

"You want to see my sword?" asked Silver his voice lethally flat.

The guard hesitated and then nodded.

"My good man," began Ned, "do you know to whom..."

Silver stopped Ned and pulled out his sword. The rapier, as far as he was concerned was a strange domestic weapon. They were often too long to draw normally, so, in essence you had to grip them by the hilt and flick them forward to get them out of the scabbard. Silver handed the man his sword. The second guard held a stick against it. Silver's sword was a few inches shorter than the stick. The guard handed the sword back and apologized.

"To what purpose is this?" demanded Ned.

"Your pardon, Sirs, but the Queen has ordered all swords entering London to be measured. If they be found to be over a yard and half-a-quarter they are to be cut down to size. Your dagger, Sir."

Silver handed him his dagger and the guard used a shorter stick about a foot in length to measure that also. Satisfied, he handed it back to Silver. Ned was looking a little pale.

"Your turn, Sir."

The other gate guards had taken an interest in the sedan chair and had approached it. They weren't so interested as to be brave enough to enquire who rode in it. Miao had her cloak pulled up over her head to hide her features.

Ned handed the guard his rapier. Feeling he had to match Silver, he had grabbed one from the theatre's armoury. It was the newest and shiniest one he could find.

Richard recognized the blade immediately. His father had bought it as a joke. Rapiers were getting longer and longer, in order to give the shorter man a longer reach. This one was so long that the guard had to help Ned get it out of the sheath.

"Oh, ho," said the guard, his eyes lighting up. "We've got one here boys." He didn't even bother to measure it. The guard turned his grinning face back to Ned. "I'm sorry, Sir, but we will have to cut it down to size." He handed the blade to a guard, as big as an ox, who took the blade wedged it in between two stones, and promptly snapped it in half.

Richard gave a little whimper.

The guard handed the sword back to Ned.

"Dagger?"

"No dagger," said Ned weakly.

"Any spiked bucklers?"

"No," said Ned. The natural bombast seemed to have drained from him.

"Pass."

On the other side of the gate Richard was glad he had the sedan chair riding on his shoulder because he would have cuffed Ned on the head. "You know how much James paid for that?"

Ned gave a weak sorry.

The rest of the journey to St. Paul's was uneventful. The yard around the front of the old cathedral was congested with stalls full of produce from the country, but the principle thing being sold, outside as well as inside were books, and pamphlets. Only the wealthy could afford books, but for the price of a chicken anyone could afford a pamphlet. A good business had risen up around the sale of pamphlets. A preacher who was pounding away on his pulpit no doubt had a few stacks of pamphlets to sell. Richard recognized the selling technique right away. A moderate crowd had gathered around the preacher who was continuing to pound away on his pulpit. The man, most likely a puritan Brownist, was working himself into lather. He was reaching for the sky, hands outstretched in supplication, as though he was about to summon down divine fire to destroy the wicked.

"That's a neat pose," whispered Will to Ned. "You have to remember that. Call it the appeal to the gods."

Ned who was still embarrassed over the sword refused to answer.

St. Paul's was old and it showed its age. It was said that its central tower had been blasted away by lightening years ago, but everyone knew the cross had been pulled down during Edward's reign, not a very long reign, before the delights of bloody Mary. Time had ravaged St. Paul's, but its size and big rose window stared on defiantly. The ornate window dominated the church yard. In a direct line down to the river, the window spoke of the mysteries of a bygone age. There was even a story that the Knights Templar had used their philosopher's stone to effect the reds of the stained glass. Even in her dilapidated state she was still beautiful.

The preacher yelped again and began pointing his accusing finger directly at them.

"Hubris! Pretentious hubris! Those who are anointed to their glorious destiny to rule are blessed, but there are those who pretend beyond their station..."

Tom turned to Will. "Do you think he knows us?"

"How convenient," sniped Will. "I suppose yon preacher is also partial to his guts."

Almost on cue, the preacher hefted his large stomach and took a gasping breath "...but on those who presume beyond their station..."

"It's all about station, isn't it," said Kemp his face taking on a wicked expression.

Richard gave him an apprehensive glance. "Will..."

"Has always been, will always be. Ned, Silver, let's put M'Lady down. I am in the mood for some black bird pie."

"I'm not going to put her down," said Richard stubbornly, but when he felt the weight increase with the angle of the sedan chair he was forced to do so. "Will, so help me..."

Both Ned and Silver turned around to see what was happening. The expression on Kemp's face made them stop. Like Dick Tarlton, much of Will's humour was in his face: it was rough and malleable, able to portray any emotion he chose, as a result, it was often hard to tell what Will Kemp was really feeling. Will, at the moment wasn't hiding anything, and it made both Ned and Richard start.

However, Silver had seen it before, in the face of men who were about to kill.

"Not a good idea, Will. Let's just get Silver and M'Lady inside..."

Then she was there, standing beside Will. There was something about Miao's presence that calmed men. She reached out and took Will's hand. Some of her warmth flowed down into the fool's hand. His face became less harsh, less brutal.

"Will, are you all right?" Her voice was like a whispering breeze.

Will gave a brisk nod unable to remove his eyes from the preacher. "I will be. Not to worry, M'Lady, I won't be long."

The preacher pointed at them in a rude, accusatory fashion. His focus was on Miao. "You, you, who wear the attire of the devil, know you not that you keep the company of dogs."

Will growled.

Richard put his hand on Will's shoulder but Silver caught his instructing eye and he let him go. The preacher had just insulted his charge and he or Will was going to answer. Richard gave a despairing groan and let his friend go, because, when everything was said and done, and no matter how much trouble Will got them into, he was still his friend.

"Don't do anything stupid."

"Always." Using his stage voice, Will turned his full attention to the preacher. "Dregs and dogs it is!" There was some laughter. The crowd was his. "It appears that yon crow knows us. I think I saw him with one of the working girls when we were in the labours of birthing Kyd's Spanish Tragedy."

There was more laughter. People had stopped their business to inquire.

"I thought I recognized them," shouted a man, "those are Liecester's Men, and that's Will Kemp."

"And I, am Ned Allyen," said Ned stepping up to join Will. He couldn't stand being left out.

"It is, it is," said a woman in a swooning voice.

Another man shouted. "Will, Will, give us a jig."

Soon the entire crowd was chanting rhythmically: "Jig, Jig, Jig..."

"Sedition...evil...fornicators...." screamed the Preacher at the top of his lungs hoping that his tirade would overwhelm the crowd with it fervid brilliance.

Will turned to Silver who was standing with Miao. He gave them a roguish grin.

"I think everyone is distracted enough. Why don't you and M'Lady slip into the Walk while I and the lads deal with yon lard mouth."

Silver gave a terse nod and threw the preacher a nasty look. "Don't be gentle on him, Will; he insulted M'Lady."

"Non gentle, it is," he said cracking his knuckles and doing a little, springy two-step.

Will was born to dance. His mom and dad, when he was little, would bring him out, like a trained monkey, and make for him to dance and spring about for their amazed friends. Dancing for groats they called it. He had never stopped dancing, because dancing meant wealth and wealth meant power. He gave a bounding leap and the crowd cheered. He doffed his hat, gave a bow and did a little twirl.

"I'll give you a little jig," he declared. "And a song."

"Will, you're going to get us arrested," said Richard from between his teeth.

Will smiled. "Probably."

"Augsy, you bring your pipes? Tom, your tambour?" asked Will.

They waved their instruments in the air and the crowd cheered. The preacher still blustered but he could make no headway against the humour filled wind that the crowd was giving Will.

Richard threw up his hands and gave in. He might as well make the best of the moment. One thing he had learned was that when you had the crowds' attention you had to make good use of it. "This is just a taste," he shouted over the crowd and the preacher who was still blustering away, "of what you will get when Ned does Tamburlaine at The Theatre."

Ned wrapped an arm around Richard. "You are shameless."

Richard nodded and smiled waving to the cheering crowd, but below his breath he said, "You know we're most likely going to end up in the gaol today."

Ned waved and grinned. "True, true, but we are Leicester's men!"

"And that means?" said Richard.

"And that means we can even make Newgate jump with joy," comforted Ned. "We will always land on our feet."

"That's cats, Ned," said Tom. "People tend to land on their heads."

Will, as the pipe and the tambour sounded, began to dance. The crowd backed away to give him space and began to clap along, breaking out in cheers when he did a leap or twirl. Then he began to sing. Will had a rough voice that was ill suited for carrying a tune, but it warmed the heart with its deep, earthy tones. It was everyman's voice. He widened his circle moving closer to the preacher who was now beet red because he had been forced into silence by the crowd.

"A man of words and not of deeds is like a garden full of weeds," sang Will.

"I've got weeds in my garden, Will," said a large woman with arms as big as any wrestler's.

The crowd laughed.

Will blew the woman a kiss, and jumped up on the little dais that held the pulpit. She caught the kiss and stuffed it down her bodice. He dodged behind the preacher and when the man went to turn, Will tipped the man's hat down over his eyes.

"And when the weeds begins to grows it's like a garden full of snow."

The preacher went to open his mouth, but nothing came out. He knew his cause was lost because the crowd was fully behind Will, cheering and egging him on.

"And when the snow begins to fall it's like a bird upon the wall. And when the bird does fly it's like an eagle in the sky. And when the sky begins to roar it's like a lion at the door."

The audience knew the well tried tune so that when Will said the word 'roar,' many in the audience did just that.

"And when the door begins to crack it's like a stick across your back."

Suddenly Will snatched a stick from someone in the crowd and thwacked the preacher across the ample backside with it. The man promptly screeched. Will threw the stick back into the crowd.

Richard groaned.

Will leaped down from the platform and spun about to face the preacher. Before Ned could do anything he had relieved Richard of his dagger. He pointed it at the preacher.

"And when your back begins to smart it's like a penknife in your heart."

The preacher sensing a change to Will's temperament from playful to lethal raised his hands in defence and began to back away.

Will advanced.

"And when your heart begins to bleed, you're dead, and dead, and dead, and dead indeed."

A few flourishes from the dagger were enough to cause the preacher to screech again, turn and run. Will bowed and tossed the dagger back to Richard who caught it and quickly sheathed it.

"Well, that's that," said George.

Richard shook his head glumly. "No, it isn't."

The preacher had not run far. He was now in an argument with a constable that had the dower, unyielding look of the law about him. He was gesturing violently at them, and they had fallen under the stern eye of the Mayor's law.

"We best be off," said Tom, "before we're arrested for an illicit production."

"We could fight," said Augsy flourishing his pipe like a tiny sword.

"We could run," said Tom.

"Ned, what should we do?" asked George.

"Don't ask me," said Ned, "Richard's in charge. It's his sedan chair."

Richard gave Ned a baleful glare.

Will gave a big whooping laugh. "We shall do what we have been trained for. Whenever faced with the cold steel of reality, we run."

Lord Leicester's men artfully put the crowd between them and the law and ran.

Chapter Seven: The Spider enquires

The only thing that greeted Kit was the absence of light. It would surely have been a walk of light, beneath the high stained glass windows, but it was night. Darkness was the cloak of secrecy, so it made sense that he should be summoned at night.

He was still rattled after his encounter with the Queen: shaken and stirred. Envoys from all over Europe had sought Elizabeth's audience and been refused or simply ignored, and Kit, a mere son of a Shoemaker from Canterbury, had talked with the Queen about issues so private that they marked him as a dead man, if others learned of the interview. The operative word was 'if,' but he knew that that meant when. Just thinking about it made his stomach churn. Death held no fear for him, just the nasty manner in which it was dealt out. He had no desire for his head to adorn a pole on Southwark Gatehouse.

On the sides of the hall, hung the heraldic pasteboards, false shields upon which were painted, in the heraldic glory, all the great families of England. A strange, bizarre thought entered into Kit's head. What would his board look like? Probably a hanging man with his tongue torn out: 'here lies a presumptuous man. Truth was foreign to his tongue.'

The muse turned to terror as a white hand shot out of a dark alcove and grabbed him around the neck. Kit was thrown up against the wall, the full weight of his assailant pinning him. The man's breath was hot and foul against his face. He knew that smell and the sickly pallor of the man's skin. It was always greasy looking, no matter how clean the man might be, as though he was tainted with an illness of the spirit and it was trying to work its way out from the inside. He knew the man and wished he didn't: Richard Baines.

"Hello, Kit. It has been a while," Baines said in a slobbering snarl, his voice full of threat and promise.

"Listen, I'll get you the money…"

"It isn't the money, or the lack thereof, I have problems with." He shoved him further into the wall. "It's you, just you, Kit. I have problems with, just you."

"Me?"

"Yes, you."

"That's nice," said Kit trying to summon up some bravery. If Baines had wanted him dead a dagger would have found him by now. No, this tormenting was just the game of a mad man. Kit shoved back to get some room. "What's your problem?"

Baines spat out in the dark: "You spread lies about me, filthy lies."

"I don't know what you're talking about." If Kit reached for his dagger, he would have little chance in the hallway. Baines was a lethal killer and would not hesitate, while Kit was governed by morals. This was the irony; Baines was as close to being a trained papist priest as you got. Killing for the cause, one way or another, was something Kit had a hard time wrapping his mind around. Instead of the dagger, Kit shoved back against Baines again creating more room between himself and the oppressive man. "The Lord has summoned me."

Baines hesitated, and then gave a rough, whispering laugh. "The Lord calls us all."

The man was insane. Fortunately, at the end of the dark corridor a door had opened and a rescuing light cracked the darkness. Kit couldn't remember feeling so grateful for light. It's why he had chosen to study Divinity – light. The gospel was supposed to grant light, but all he had found was darkness and men both secular and ecclesiastical intent on twisting words to gain power. Baines made a hissing sound at the light as though he was being burned and slipped away.

A lantern lit the man who stepped into the corridor. The dark, slightly protuberant eyes belonged to Arthur Gregory, Lord Walsingham's forger.

"Master Marlowe, is that you? You best not keep the Lord waiting."

Kit approached the forger.

Gregory was a drawn, sallow faced man. It seemed as though all the colour of his face and hair had drained away, most likely from spending so much time inside. He had a long nose that gave the impression it was permanently dripping. He pointed his nose down the hall and sniffed. "Who was that with you?"

"Baines."

Gregory rolled his eyes. "Baines again: that man leaves a stench wherever he goes. Come this way, the Lord is waiting. It is best not to keep him in that state."

Kit noticed Gregory was stooped as though he had been permanently frozen in the attitude of working on some cypher or parchment. He moved with a halting gait as though he had a clubbed foot. He followed Gregory through an empty room that revealed, dark empty chairs. A waiting room, most likely. It was said that Walsingham was liberal with his wealth and as a result found no lack of suitors.

Gregory reached to open the second door. "What was that about, you know, Baines?"

"A theological discussion gone bad," offered Kit.

"Yes, yes," said Gregory dismissively. "You both went to Cambridge, Corpus Christi, two peas in a pod."

Kit felt offended. "I wouldn't say that." He found being compared to Baines rather distasteful. But why not, weren't they both the same creatures, sired in the dark. Baines had just lost himself on the road.

"Take my advice, young Sir, stay away from that one. His humours are black, black indeed."

"Then why does Sir Francis employ him."

Gregory opened the door.

"It is exactly for that reason that he continues to employ him."

Kit felt the icy hands of foresight creeping up his spine and he shivered. When he looked into Baine's eyes was he looking into his future self?

Kit followed Gregory into another dark room, but this one was dimly lit around a desk at the opposite end. Washed in candle light, bent over a pile of paper, was the somber form of Sir Francis Walsingham, the head of the Queen's own spy network. He was dressed in a black gown, with a black muffin cap on his head. The effect, as he worked, was that of an aging white face with white beard floating above white hands. They stood in front of the desk waiting to be noticed.

Walsingham lifted an envelope and held it close to the meager candle light to examine it. He took particular notice of the red wax seal on the back. Then he lifted his dark, lively eyes and regarded them. He held the letter out to Gregory. There was a look of frustrated bewilderment on his face.

"Arthur, this letter is sealed."

"Would appear so, Sir," said Gregory.

"Well, take the infernal thing and unseal it. I cannot read an unopened letter."

Gregory took the letter and held it up to his nose and sniffed it, and examined the seal. He gave a humph. He tasted the wax with his tongue. "It's papist by taste."

"You can tell that by taste?" asked Kit amazed.

Gregory nodded. The bee's wax they use has more honey in it, you know, Italian bees, definitely papist. They are the only bees that can access red clover."

"Arthur," cautioned Walsingham.

The forger gave a petulant look, turned and left the room.

"He's a good man, Arthur Gregory. I have never met one who could forge a letter and replicate a seal after simply looking at it. He truly is amazing, and truly invaluable." Sir Francis Walsingham motioned to a chair waiting before the desk. "Please, sit, Master Marlowe. Arthur will be awhile, so in the interim I thought we might address a point of business."

"I'd rather stand," said Kit. He had a feeling that if he sat, he would be trapped.

Walsingham shrugged. "Only so right. Then I shall stand also." He groaned as he slowly stood, straightening. "I've spent too much time at this desk as it is. You are wondering why you are here?"

Kit shifted uncomfortably. He knew when he was in the presence of a superior mind, one that could work at many levels at once. The Queen knew exactly what she was doing when she placed herself between Lord Burghley and Sir Francis Walsingham. She was the white, linen brilliance surrounded by the black book boards of her councillors. Her courtiers she toyed with, but these two were the workhorses. Without them the Queen, like a book without binding, would simply fall apart.

"I thought you wanted a message delivered."

Walsingham gave a sly smile. "Your play, Tambulaine the Great, is disconcerting. The Master of the Revels has brought it to my attention. A Sheppard that rises to displace an anointed King..."

"I don't think..."

Walsingham stopped Kit's defence with a dismissive wave of his graceful white hand. "I, nor the Queen, are alarmed. Your use of blank verse is quite inspirational."

"Thank you," said Kit who was beginning to suspect that Walsingham was putting him off balance for a deeper purpose.

The room filled with tension as the spy master watched him with cat like patience. Kit felt as though he was being weighed, assessed and decided upon. It made him very uncomfortable.

Having found what he was looking for, Walsingham took a deep breath. "The Queen's mind is troubled. She feels that the taking of Mary Stuart's head was murder."

"She signed the warrant," said Kit trying to understand where the spymaster was going.

"I know, I urged her to do so. It was treason which brought the execution order, yet, she feels as though she swung the axe herself."

Then suddenly Kit knew. "You know of the Queen's request."

Walsingham gave a tired, almost painful smile. "There's very little I do not know of Master Marlowe. Do you know why I do the things I do? Why I have men put to the question, why I have some men do horrible things?"

For a good show, thought Kit, but from the look on Walsingham's face this was not a time for humour. Instead he said, "No, I don't."

It was as though Walsingham had read his unvoiced thought. He laughed. "Thank you, for your tact. It has been a long time since I've laughed. I can see why Thomas has taken with you."

Thomas Walsingham was a good friend of Kit's and a close cousin of Sir Francis. Thomas hoped to replace Francis as the spymaster, but Kit doubted he had the mental acuity that Walsingham had, or his ruthlessness.

"And I with him."

"I wonder," pondered Walsingham, "I wonder if theatre has a proven affectation on the yielding mind."

"You like theatre?" asked Kit, feeling that finally they had something in common.

"No, not at all; I prefer the truth and all theatre lies, but lies are effective in appeasing your friends and deceiving your enemies."

Walsingham gripped his chest and started to cough. The fit became so bad that he doubled over in pain. Kit moved to help.

"No, please, I will be all right in a moment." He straightened. "There, better. By my sweet Saviour, London's perfume is of corruption. I would be free of this place, but the Queen lately chooses to spend much of her time here, so here I remain."

He moved back behind his desk where he sank back down into the chair and was absorbed by the dark. The desk, the papers, the quills all seemed to be a part of his person, an extension of his being. A strange expression came over his face as though he was looking miles away. His pale fingers toyed with a ring on his left hand, turning it about.

"I was there, you know: St. Bartholomew's Day. The embassy was not far from it all. Babes in arms, mothers, boys, killed and piled up like cord wood; thrown into the water like so much night soil. It is strange, how quickly something so terrible can happen. It was like I wasn't there, but I was, and there wasn't a blessed thing I could do."

His eyes seemed to spark with a keen light. "I know you hate religion."

Kit was more than a little startled. The man shifted quicker than tempestuous winds. Madness could have explained it, but it was the madness of a cold, keen, discerning mind. Kit cleared his voice and tried to make it sound solid. He had to meet strength with strength. "I don't hate religion. I hate hypocrites. I think many religions have a certain portion of truth."

"What of the papists?"

"In my studies at Corpus Christi, I came to the conclusion that no church today bares any resemblance to the one the Saviour instituted."

"Not even the Church of England?"

It was a question that carried much importance and Kit knew it. If he said yes, then he walked the thin edge of treason. Deny the Church and you deny its head, who just happened to be the Queen herself. Kit was beginning to wonder why he had suddenly attracted such attention, but then he realized that things in Walsingham's world never happened suddenly, they only appeared so. The saliva in Kit's mouth had abandoned him and he tried to swallow. His tongue cleaved to the roof of his mouth.

"No, not even the Church of England."

"Some ears would hear that as heresy. I remember the smell of burning flesh under Mary's reign. It was a terrible smell." He sighed. "Forgive me. It is the problem of age. To most, age brings the dotage of senility and the abyss of an idiot, alas; it is my fate that with age my mind becomes sharper in remembrance. I am cursed. You desire to be a courtier?"

"No, my Lord, I will hold court with my words and abide the perfume of the streets."

"Hah! Well said, Master Marlowe, well said, but beware the streets, for they are full of the stench of humanity."

"As smells the court, but masked with perfume."

"Indeed. You know, I can still see those flames burning. There's a storm coming, and we best be ready for it or our flesh will light the pyres of the inquisition."

Walshingham opened up a drawer and pulled out a fresh empty sheet of paper. He took a quill out of the apple on his desk, dipped it into the pot of ink and began to write. The pen scratched away, filling the room with its ominous sound.

"Master Marlowe," said Walsingham, continuing to write.

"Yes."

"You have some friends in the theatre, some friends that you and Sir Raleigh share? Two of those friends are trying to find a murderer. Watch over them and let me know where their trail leads them."

Walsingham stopped writing, stuck the quill back into the apple. He reached into another compartment in his desk and pulled out a pouch of coins. He threw the money and Kit caught it.

"To help you find the Queen a new physic spiritualis. You will also find enough there to pay Baines the money you owe him. He was never the same after Rheims."

Kit regarded the black pouch and felt the welcome weight of the coin. "Thank you. I will pay Baines. As to why he blames me...I have no idea. It is as though he blames me for what happened there. We were never there, not at the same time."

"You know, he thinks you were, and in his troubled mind he thinks you are responsible for all his ills."

"How can he think that?"

"He thinks you're an atheist."

"He thinks the Pope is both the angel Gabriel and the Anti-Christ."

"Ah, such is the fate of all double agents."

"He is a traitor?"

"No, not a traitor, a double agent; it is of my own design, may heaven have mercy on my soul. Just don't underestimate what Baines is capable of doing."

Walsingham dripped some red sealing wax onto the fold of the letter he had just written. Into the pool of wax he pressed his seal. He held it out to Kit. "Oh, you know, when I said I had no messages for you, well, that was theatre. I have something I want you to do for me in Plymouth." With that he reached into a secret drawer, pulled his hand out and handed him a second letter.

Chapter Eight: Walking St. Paul's

Up the steps and below the big circular rose window, walked Miao Juzheng and George Silver. George had taken her black, monk like robe and tossed it to a young lad to watch. The boy's eyes had dilated wide when he had seen the silk and the colours of Miao's dress. One of the greatest teachers seemed to be the legality of things. Had everyone been permitted to wear silk, black, gold and crimson, the boy would not have paid much attention, but because it was illegal, he was all eyes.

"And the lady will be wanting her robe back," growled George.

The lad nodded fervently. "Sure, Mr. Silver."

George gave a satisfactory nod. "Good, make sure it is so and there's another half-angel in it for you."

The lad shook his head. "Don't need another half," he said staring at Miao. "Not when I've seen one."

George gave a laugh and tussled the lad's head.

Inside the entrance, Miao leaned into George; people were already starting to notice her. She whispered: "Do you think he'll be there when we come out?"

"No. I'll buy you another cloak."

"I'm not worried about the cloak." Miao had always felt that the act of theft, or violence left its mark on both the doer and the victim. People could avoid such misery if they were only nice to each other.

St. Paul's Walk took the humanity, the mix of class, of colour, of sex, that existed in the narrow, crowded streets of London and amplified it. The ebb and flow of people outside was that of people about their business, on the Walk the senses were heightened by the accents of fashion and the sound of people speaking that hung in the air. A great concourse of people, dressed in finery walked, moving back and forth in the nave, while amongst the great pillars people sold and preached whatever seemed necessary to them. It was all here, at St. Paul's Walk, books, ideas, flesh, all the things that made humanity good and bad. Into this flow stepped Miao Juzheng and George Silver.

"So, we just walk?" asked Miao, glad she had George's arm to guide her through the swirl of people.

George gave a nod setting the green peacock feather on the top of his tall hat bobbing. "That's the idea. You are an oddity. With you in that dress the gentry will be drawn like moths to a flame."

A dirty little girl in rags kicked a boy in the crotch and escaped to the other side of one of the great pillars. While Miao had difficulty seeing detail, she could still tell what was going on. "Why is that girl running?"

"They're thieves. Their parents get them to steal because the law is not as severe on children. They only hang children."

"Oh," was all she said and she realized George had been protecting her from this, but the murdered women, out of necessity, had dragged her in. She braced herself with a deep breath.

"We could always back out of this," said George.

"No, we need information and if you believe this is where we will find information, then this is where we should be."

George was giving a salutary nod to some of the gentry they were passing, his feather bobbing. He had given lessons to some of them and his reputation carried respect with the others. The men were looking, but not as much as the women. The women feigned cold indifference, but he could see the envious, even offended glances thrown at Miao. It was just a matter of time. A few more circuits should do it.

Miao was beginning to have difficulty, not with the press of people, or the swirling motion, but with the sound. All the busy sounds of people moving and chattering lifted into the air and bounced back down on them from the fan vaulted ceiling. It was a jumble of confusion, and that was part of the problem, because Miao's mind was desperately trying to straighten things out. A sense of panic was beginning to grow in her and she wondered at how long she could remain at the Walk without screaming. Her fingers dug into George's arm.

"Are you all right?" he asked her.

Miao gave a terse nod. "Yes – no, it's the sounds. The sounds of all the people, I can't keep them straight."

"Straight?"

"I don't know how long I'll be able to handle the sounds, George. So many voices...I'm hearing everything...at once."

George didn't understand the distress, but he guided her over to a book seller's stall and out of the flow of people. He took her by the shoulders.

"Look at me. Focus on me. I promise, if we don't get what we need in the next few minutes, we'll leave, all right?"

Miao gave a tremulous nod. "I'll try. I'm sorry."

"Good, don't worry about it," said George picking up a book and pretending to thumb through it, "because we've already gained some good notice."

On the other side of the nave a group of gentry had stopped to discuss something. They were casting glances over at them, and were embroiled in a heated debate. There was another group that had also noticed them. Dressed primarily in black with modest white ruffs and hats with broad rims, they stared at them in a more sinister manner.

Miao smiled. "Good. That's good, isn't it?" most of the crowd to her was just a blur of movement and colour.

"I've got to get you out more," lamented George handing the book back to the stall owner. "The fellows in black aren't good news; the other group may have potential, let's see."

Both groups had chosen to act and were now slowly moving towards them through the flow of walkers.

"Here they come. Let's go over things before they get here."

Miao straightened herself in her dress. "Right."

"Now, you're absolutely sure you come from a royal family in the Middle Kingdom? Because they're like hounds, their snobby noses will smell out a fraud. You can change your accent but not your blood."

"My father was the Emperor's first aide, until my family was put to death. We were cousins. If Old Lao hadn't sold me into slavery I also would have been killed."

"The former is good, very good, but the latter, I wouldn't mention that. Remember, talk little and look down your nose. That will make them gossip more. They won't be able to stand not knowing who you are. And try not to let your eyes flutter back and forth."

"I can't help that, but I'll try."

"Good, we don't want anyone accusing you of being possessed, because some of these people are wicked enough to do so."

"These men, do they know who you are?" asked Miao.

"Me? Yes, most likely, but they don't care about me. There are plenty of clowns showing up dressed in someone else's hand-me-downs. It's you they're interested in and your white hair."

"So, we wait?"

"We wait." George idly picked up a pamphlet, opened it up and mumbled into it. "I'm more concerned with the ravens than the clowns."

George suddenly became interested in the pamphlet he had opened. Across the pages were printed images of swordsmen. He became more and more agitated as he read, his broad finger poking at one of the illustrations.

"What's this tripe about?" he asked the stall owner.

The stall owner, Richard Field, who had publishing interests at both Blackfriars and Bishopsgate gave a hapless shrug. It wasn't too long ago that he had been a mere apprentice, but the death of his Huguenot master, Vautrollier, and marriage to his widow, Jacqueline, had elevated him substantially. He knew what sold and this little pamphlet written by an Italian fencing master was selling like hot cakes.

"It's an instructional guide by Giovanni Travoni, a foremost master of the Italian school," explained Field.

"Yes, yes, I know the man," said George. "His tricks are artful, but they're more likely to get you killed than not."

"Well," Field had become skilled in dealing with the hubris of the gentry, but he sensed there was more to this man than just that. A latent, organized violence was just lurking beneath the surface. "Why don't you write something? You know, counter his 'artful tricks?'"

"It's all paradoxes you know, paradoxes of defence, because everything begins with a good defence. If you don't have one, you're dead before the fight even begins."

"I don't mean to be disrespectful, but who are you?" asked Field.

George didn't hear the question. He had dived back into the pamphlet and was engrossed in some other offensive point.

"George," reminded Miao. "The man asked your name." Another person had just entered the stall carrying a stack of books. He placed them down and began to move them about. Miao reached out and touched his sleeve. He looked up, his eyes, wide and startled. "You look familiar," she said.

Shakes smiled. "Of course I do, M'Lady; sometimes I work for the Burbages at The Theatre. I carry spears, dress actors, that sort of thing. I also do a bit of writing for Lord Strange, and sometimes I help out my friend."

Field turned to Shakes and said something so heavy in an accent that Miao couldn't understand them. He was apparently asking him something and Shakes didn't know.

"What did you say?" asked Miao. She had taken a keen interest in accents. Ever since she had learned English she had made it a habit of tying to match the accent with its place.

George looked up. He was aware of her habit. He had heard a Warwickshire accent a number of times when he had been hired to train troops. It was an accent so thick that he had had to hire an interpreter. "Warwickshire, they're from Warwickshire, some place there. I trained some lads from there once." He then said something equally incomprehensible.

Field's face which had been a rather glum looking brightened perceptibly. His hand shot out to shake George's.

"Stratford, from Bridge Street," he said in understandable English, "and Shakes is from Henley Street."

Miao nodded. There was something about the man that smelled of leather. If she were to close her eyes she could almost 'see' a man taking the hides from animals and working them into leather. "Your father is a tanner?"

Field nodded his grin fading from his face replaced with amazement. He went to cross himself, but Shakes reached out and grabbed his hand to stop him.

"And mine? Can you tell my father's profession?"

Miao could sense George stiffen. He had warned her about doing this. He had warned her against looking at people and reading them. She really didn't know how she did it, but she could. Even at a very young age she could tell things about people, see things about them.

"Miao," cautioned George.

72

"It's all right. I sense they are not dangerous, just deeply religious." She turned to Shakes. "Your father..." she could see fingers, fingers forming into what seemed like gloves – gloves with long, flaring cuffs. The cuffs consisted of white, intricate lace. "A glover, your father is a glover."

Shakes laughed, becoming animated. "Yes, yes, he is a glover."

George went back to examining the back of the pamphlet. "At least he lists his credentials and makes passing mention of the Spanish school...always moving their feet." He tossed the pamphlet back down on the pile. "If you ask me, he should have focused on that instead of the tripe about artful tricks."

Field suddenly looked worried, as though he had done something wrong. At the other end of the stall a man was pawing over a particularly large volume. "Richard, looks like you've got a grazer."

Field apologized and left them to try to sell the book.

Shakes leaned in to George and Miao and whispered, just loud enough for them to hear him. "You have to forgive him." He made the imitative motion of making the sign of the cross over his heart. "His family is Catholic, although they no longer practice."

George nodded. "You can take the man from the cross, but not the cross out of the man. I understand."

"What's the main news here today?" asked George.

Shakes shrugged, looking down, pretending to address a book. "The King of Spain gathers his ships at Cadiz, and his agents are preparing the ports for the invasion...good luck with that."

"That sounds serious," said Miao.

Shake's eyes seemed to do a dark little dance. "The thing that Phillip forgets is that while we may be divided in faith, we're still English. Even if Phillip succeeded, who do you think he would've put on the throne? Mary? Even if she still was alive, he wouldn't have. She was more French than Spanish. He wants England for himself, but the problem is he smells of burnt flesh, and of course, he's Spanish."

George nodded. He agreed with Shakes here. He had always suspected that Elizabeth's sister, Bloody Mary, wouldn't have been very bloody without Phillip, her consort, reminding her that she had to atone for the heresies of her father.

Shakes looked up and gave a furtive glance over the crowd of people moving by. The group of men dressed in black and white were in mid progress. The crowd was holding them up.

"You see that group over there." George had been keeping an eye on them ever since they had entered the Walk.

"Can't help but."

They continued to move their way through the flow of traffic, gathering irritating glares from men and miffed expressions from the women.

"It looks like you've been noticed. If you don't mind me asking, why didn't you ask me about the news back at The Theatre earlier?"

"I didn't know you were so well connected," explained Miao.

"Not connected at all, just observant," said Shakes smiling; what she had said excited him. "So, why did you come to one of the most public places in London dressed like that? I suspect there is more going on here than you let on. What do you really want to know? Either you both are very stupid or very smart."

Miao blushed. She had been complimented before, but it had always been about her white hair, or her fair complexion, but when someone complimented her mind, her intelligence, she couldn't help but blush.

"The Lord Mayor's inquisitors are almost through the crowd," grumbled George. "No doubt attracted by your dress. You finish talking with Shakes. I'll go distract them."

"Be careful," said Miao.

"Always am." As George moved off into the crowd he passed by Field and said something in a heavy accent which made him grin.

"What did he say?" asked Miao.

"He said something that doesn't bear repeating in the presence of a Lady. Now, what other questions can I help you with?"

The black ravens were the real problem. Dealing with them would get them a lot closer to gaol than the Court. He had intended to draw attention, but not this type of attention. Sir Water paid him to keep Miao out of trouble not get her into it. One of the main worries of the Devonshire man was that Miao, with her white hair, seemingly pink eyes and strange ways would get herself accused of witchcraft. Even though things under Elizabeth were more liberal, there was a new brand of intolerance fostered by the puritans that tended towards a revival of the Witchcraft Act. The Queen's own mother, having six fingers on her hand was a perfect target for accusation. He wasn't about to let them at Miao.

The other thought he had as he moved to intercept was that of gratefulness, because Shakes was saving them a lot of valuable time. Maybe he would even know something about these murders. The ravens were nearly through the crowd. He had to create a diversion in order to give Miao some more time to ask her questions and for them to make their escape.

George's eyes darted about looking for what he needed, and then he saw it, an Italian fencing master. He had noticed the fellow strutting about in the midst of a knot of some foreigners. From the look of them they were Portuguese of some condescension. Their sharp bearded faces and heavily lidded eyes gave the impression that they were sleepily beyond everything. He noticed the fencing master's impeccable dress; everything from his hose to his lace was strategically contrived for effect. He had to admit, his reading of the pamphlet had gotten his dander up. Perfect, the fencing master would provide the diversion.

He stepped in front of the Italian and turned. George moved his rapier like the rudder on a boat, so that the tip end of the scabbard caught the Italian on the hose tearing it.

"Sirra...you have-a rippeded my hose!" he said with great offence.

George gave a mocking expression of surprise. "I did? Oh, look, so I did." He noticed the vibrant green of the hose. "I'm sorry but I must have mistaken your legs for verdant saplings."

One of the Portuguese snickered, which incensed the Italian. He must have been working this group for future clients.

"I bite-a my-a thumb-a at-a you."

George looked at the Italian as though he was insane. "You bite your what at me?"

"My thumb-a..."

Berto Della Massa, noticed the cool way the Englishman was baiting the Italian fencing master. It was entertaining, much more so than having to endure the prating Italian. He could smell the violence coming, but why, that was the question. He leaned in towards Don Antonio, the Prior of Crato, the disposed King of Portugal and whispered his observation. The exiled king lifted a gloved hand. He too was interested in this confrontation, much more than the Italian's solicitations.

"...I demand-a you pay," finished the Italian his pointed, wax beard vibrating irately.

George put on his apologetic face and reached for his money purse. A ring of people, sensing diversion, had formed around them creating a knot in the flow of walkers. The raven's progress had all but stopped. They couldn't get by the blockage. Good, he thought, now all he had to do was keep them there.

The Italian puffed up and flicked his sword arm forward, drawing his blade. The sword looked to be of reasonable make.

George put his hands up in mock surrender and took a stutter step back. Then in a smooth motion he threw out his own blade.

Della Massa became keenly interested.

"Stick it to him, George," shouted a dirty cut purse from somewhere in the pillars.

The appraisal of the conflict suddenly went higher and others began to stop. Most people knew George Silver by name.

"Georgio Silver?" said the Italian fencing master hesitating. Then his ambition pushed him over his fear. "I wondered where you were hiding." He made a side step slicing his rapier through the air. "It is said you stopped teaching because you lost your edge. Let us see who is the best, eh?"

George shrugged. "That implies a competition and not a lesson."

"A lesson?"

"Yours."

The ravens were now totally bunged up unable to move, and so they would remain until the fight was over.

Della Massa and the exiled king watched as the two combatants began their duel. The scuffling of feet and the clash of steel echoed into the high vaulted ceiling and more of the mumbling conversation that had echoed in the Walk, stopped. Della Massa noticed that the ornate style of the Italian made it look as though the contest would be over soon, but he knew better. He had seen battle. He had seen men slaughtered and knew the cold calm of some who fought. The Englishman had this calmness about him.

The cool, cat like grace that spoke of the predator. Even though it was not apparent to the crowd, he knew that the Englishman was toying with the Italian, leading him, but why? That was when Della Massa began to sort through the faces in the crowd around them looking for something out of the ordinary.

"Stop," shouted a commanding voice. It was one of the ravens. "You are breaking the Lord Mayor's peace."

"Give him a piece of this," shouted a working girl from the pillars. There was a flash of flesh accompanied by raucous laughter.

George was leading the Italian now with workman like efficiency. The problem with the fellow was that he was more interested in impressing his friends than winning the fight. The Italian tried to strike at the shoulder and George slid the blade away with a parry. He turned, dropped the blade so that its tip caught on the man's hose and sliced another rip in it. Laughter echoed in the nave. The Italian spun about and in fury launched a combined attack. It seemed that he threw every pretty move he had into it, but George was able to calmly weather the flurry.

"Here, George," said another rough voice from the pillars. An apple flew through the air. George caught it and took a bite out of it.

Miao didn't bother to watch George's shenanigans. She had seen them all before. It wasn't a surprise that he had friends with actors, because he loved to entertain. Even had she wanted to watch, at this distance she couldn't see very much.

"Aren't you worried he'll get hurt?" asked Shakes.

"George, no, he's just having some fun. We found a girl down at the river last night."

The air about Shakes seemed to constrict, growing darker. She noticed that about people who had secrets.

"I know. She had a drawing," he said quietly, "it was crumpled up in her hand."

"How did you know?"

"You want my advice on this?" said Shakes solemnly.

"Yes."

"All roads lead to the Queen. She can be both benevolent and vindictive. You have fair skin. Do you burn easily, when you are in the sun?"

"Yes."

"The Queen is like the sun; the closer you get the more likely you are to get burned." Shakes looked away. His friend, Richard Field had been drawn away from the book stall and was surrounded by three maids. He was protecting himself by holding a large book against his chest while the maids played with his long, brown hair. His friend was totally unaware of his good looks.

"I have to go, Richard is in troubled again. Women find him irresistible." Many wondered why a wealthy widow like Jacqueline Vautrollier had married a penniless apprentice, but he understood it well. It was lust. He himself had been trapped by a woman eight years his senior. Shakes tried to marry for love, but she had sabotaged that. Well, that was the past and you either forgave or... Shakes was a lot of things, but he would never abandon someone that depended on him. Now he had three children, but he still looked for love. Life was confusing.

Miao reached for her hanky to wave. It had been their prearranged signal for her to tell George she was ready to leave.

Della Massa noticed, as the heat of the fight increased, that George Silver got cooler. While sweat ran down the Italian's face the only thing that betrayed Silver's increased effort was a grim smile, stretched tightly across his face. That would serve him well to incite his enemy into a rash mistake, he noted. There were a half a dozen times when the Englishman could have dispatched his opponent but didn't. Why was he delaying?

Then there was a flash of white off to the right, at one of the book stalls, where some pretty maids were trying to sell something. He saw the white hand of the woman that held the hanky and followed the arm to the pale face and the white hair. Then he noticed the black robed men with the white ruffs. Ah, thought Della Massa putting the three elements together. Silver was delaying for her, which didn't answer what she was about. He had heard it whispered that Sir Walter Raleigh was employing Silver to guard a woman. What made her so valuable?

"The fight has run its course," said Duke Antonio in his characteristic rough voice.

The fight had run its course before it had started. Della Massa nodded. "Where to, my Lord?"

"Away from this place: the usurper gathers his forces. He intends to strike soon."

Della Massa gave Silver a parting glance. If he had to fight this man it would be a close contest. He sensed parity in their skill. He caressed the hilt of his blade. The one thing that Silver did not have was a sword that never failed.

George saw Miao's white hanky, parried the Italian's blade, pulled him close and kneed him between the legs. Just as the little girl had done to the boy. The man's eyes bulged out and his mouth formed an agonizing 'O' before he dropped to the floor.

The crowd groaned in empathy and some booed Silver for his 'ungentlemanly' like behavior. He wasn't waiting because the ravens were on the move. He found Miao waiting patiently.

"Did you have fun?" she asked.

"Did you get anything out of Shakes?"

George took her by the arm and began to guide her towards the closest exit.

"Whoever is doing the killing is close to the Queen, if not the Queen herself."

George felt the blood drain from him and his knees go weak. That rarely happened. "Did he say that?"

"No, it's more what he didn't say."

George gave a groan as they approached the exit. There were men in black standing there. It figured that the blasted ravens would have men at the exits as well. Maybe if they just barged past them... The problem was everyone was watching: the man who made a fool of the Italian sword master and the woman that glowed in the Queen's own colours.

"In the name of the Queen, I command you to halt," said the lanky fellow with baggy fitting hose and morose horse like face. He would have looked almost comedic if it hadn't been for the beefy looking fellows flanking him. They were holding halberds. George thought, in a contest of rapier versus halberds, rapiers lost, every time.

George held his hands up in surrender. "You've got us, what are the charges?"

"George Silver, we've had a very serious complaint and we are constrained to issue a charge."

"On what grounds? I didn't kill him, only wounded his pride, which is a deadly sin, so I think I did him a favour," responded George saucily.

The man squinted meanly at Miao. "No, the complaint is about your...companion."

"My companion?" George looked about and noticed they were attracting another crowd. Miao was staring, as he instructed, imperiously, through the man as though he wasn't there. She was trying hard to keep her eyes from moving about.

"Yes, the law, the colours are not...appropriate for her..."

George and Miao had been ready for this, in fact, they had planned on it.

"Right, silk, purple, gold and crimson, should never be seen except upon a Faerie Queen."

"Don't be impertinent," sneered the man in the baggy hose.

"Forgive me then, I shall make introductions," said George bowing to Miao. "This is the Lady Miao Juzheng, niece to Emperor Wu of the Middle Kingdom, under the protection of Sir Walter Raleigh, Captain of the Queen's Guard."

The man's narrow face blanched, then his eyes squinted suspiciously. George could see that he didn't believe him, but the threat of a noble's wrath had cowed him sufficiently. A mumble, like a rippling wave, went through the crowd that had gathered. The man in the baggy hose gave a stiff bow, and glared at the fellows holding the halberds to do the same.

Miao nodded imperiously and followed George as he led the way out of St. Paul's and back into the street. It was starting to mist and George noticed that the little urchin he had given Miao's robe to was still there. He hadn't run off with it, after all. He flipped the kid another half-angel, as promised. The boy caught it in a filthy hand and vanished down the street.

It felt good to be covered up again, thought Miao. The eyes that had examined her at the Walk had been disconcerting, and the massive motion and the noise in the nave very confusing. Had it not been for Shakes she doubted anything of value would have come about from such an adventure.

"Was that a success?" she whispered.

"Oh, absolutely," said George cheerily. "We should expect an invitation to Court...if not, maybe the Tower."

The idea of being thrown into a prison didn't actually sit well with her, but if they were to solve the murders of the poor girls, they had to get to Court. Then she noticed. The sedan chair was gone as were Leicester's men.

Chapter Nine: Plymouth

The smell of sea salt heightened the scent of sewage and that of marine decomposition. It soaked the port in it. It was enough to make a stranger gag, but then a breeze or outgoing tide would sweep the stench away and make fresh the port.

The harbour was crowded with ships, their hulks sitting black on the night's water, their canvas furled arms and masts making a forest in the sheltered harbour. The fleet should have been sleeping, but not tonight. It was waiting, like some many eyed predatory creature, waiting for the command.

Sir Francis Drake clutched the railing and stared at the sleeping town, his eyes searching. He heard his first mate, stealthily slipping up to his side.

"Looking for someone?" asked Dick in his characteristic rough murmur.

"No," responded Drake, thinking about the command he was about to give. The Queen's indecisiveness had put them all at risk. Yet, web weaving and the politics of courting had kept them safe from invasion for years. But with the death of the Queen of Scots, powers were stirring, powers that could crush England. He was not a man of illusion, Drake. He knew that if Phillip turned his attention from his war with the Turks in the Mediterranean, England would be doomed. All the Duke of Parma needed was transport and his seasoned troops would be at their throats. It used to be that a man's arm and the strength of his sword and lance were all that mattered, but not with the advent of ordinance. A ball of lead was the great equalizer.

"Where are we heading?"

Drake's smile was grim but determined. "We go to singe the old man's whiskers."

Kit learned to ride horses rather late, but once he got the hang of it, he felt liberated. To be in command of a beast bigger than the one inside made him feel more in control of his own passions. It was why he wrote. It certainly wasn't for the money. He touched the envelopes he kept close to his chest. They were so light, but to him they were worth several months of wages he could earn writing: one letter, but two.... Of course it wasn't the letter that was valuable; it was what the old spider had written on them. The second letter was the one that had to make it through. It was better not to know what was in the letters he was delivering. Some dilemmas were useless, like the theological discussion about how many angels can fit on a head of a pin. The dilemma that might be created by knowing the contents of the letters would most likely force him into a situation of life and death. He gently put his heels into the sides of his horse and urged it into a faster gait. The town in its sleepy darkness rose up around him and hung in the air, threatening to fall on him. His horse, hoofs on the stone, echoed against the buildings moved into the dark of the narrow streets and was absorbed. .

The road where Kit had ridden had remained barren for an hour. Then, out of the darkness, riding hard, hoofs splashing through puddles, a second man came. His instructions were to intercept the first messenger and to cancel his delivery. So focused on catching Marlowe he did not see the riders converging on him from the sides. When he did it was too late and his horse was already too tired for him to evade them. In front of him a horse barred the way. He reached for the pistol he kept primed. A terrible weapon for accuracy, but he was hoping the sound might alert others to his plight. At best he might be able to shoot one before being cut down. He reigned in his horse that cantered sideways tossing its head

84

disapprovingly. There were five of them two on each side with one in front.

"What do you want?" shouted out the messenger trying to keep his courage, but he knew in this witching hour, nothing good would happen. He pulled out his pistol. These were demons; papist demons come to drag his soul down to hell. Out in the dark he could hear the heartbeat of the devil. He even thought he could smell the sulfurous reek. "What do you want?" he shouted again. "Come no closer. I warn you."

He squeezed the trigger, but the pistol clicked harmlessly, its prime had become too wet. He threw the pistol at the horseman to the front and tried to draw his sword.

The horses on either side closed and sharp edged metal was thrust into the messenger. With a cry the man fell from his horse into the mud. The horse, in fear, bolted and ran.

"You, after the horse," snapped the man who had faced down the pistol.

One of the horsemen galloped away, while the remaining three circled the dying man in the mud.

Della Massa was irritated by their incompetence. The man should have been quickly and silently killed. This was messy. "Finish him," he snapped.

Three of the men had been from Don Antonio's retinue, the forth he didn't know and therefore he treated him suspiciously. It was this fellow who dismounted to slice the throat of the wounded messenger.

"Search him."

Baines searched the dead man and found the letter where he knew it would be. He handed it up to Della Massa.

He looked at the letter, ran his thumb over the seal; it was still too dark to know for sure, but he knew its touch. He also knew it wasn't the letter he was after.

"You say they sent out two riders?" snapped Della Massa.

"Two riders? There was only one," said Baines cautiously. He knew there had been two, but how had this man known? He had delayed them on purpose to allow Marlowe through. He could almost feel the knowing smirk on the man's face.

"Yes, two couriers. I believe you know him. His name is Marlowe."

"I know him," said Baines grimly. "I will go after him. I know where he will go."

"Do so," said Della Massa. He had known from the beginning that this night's mission was futile. He had suspected that El Draco had already received his orders and that these letters were just a ruse, or maybe not. Who could know with codes and ciphers? He didn't trust this Englishman. He turned his attention back to the other men. "Take the body and secret it off the road. Take any coins. I want it to look like a robbery."

He watched as they dragged the man off into the dark. He felt a sudden kinship with the dead man. Had the pistol fired, it might very well have been his body they were dragging off through the mud. He gave a longing sigh and ran his fingers over the letter's seal again. He had his instructions and where to deliver this, whether it was of use or not. He turned his horse and entered the street where the houses swallowed him up.

Kit wound his way down to the docks, but as he dismounted he realized he was too late. The harbour was nearly empty, devoid of the fleet that should have been there. He gave a longing look out at the water. The clouds had cleared to reveal a waxing moon. There was motion ahead, a man looping up a rope into a coil. Kit dismounted, tied his horse off and approached the man. The man ignored him and kept winding up the hemp rope.

"You've missed him," he said.

"There's no way to get him a message?"

The man looked up. The splinter he was chewing made its migration from left to right as he considered the question. "I can have him chased down. It might succeed, but it might not."

Kit handed him the second letter he had received.

The man tucked it away and gave a terse nod. "I'll find a ship that can fly."

Kit wanted to thank him. He had succeeded, so why was he filled with a feeling of despondency? He needed time to think, to rest. Leading his horse by the reigns, he trudged his way to The White Ship, an Inn that was anything but white.

Entering the empty Inn he looked about. It was a simple place that stank of sour ale and urine. The only redeeming feature of the room was its high ceilings. Other than that it was full of scarred and hacked trestle tables, as though the patrons had taken to using their knives while waiting for their drink. Even at this time of night it wasn't empty. Slouching against the wall, hood pulled over his face was a man. Kit approached him.

"Good morning, Marlowe," said the man sitting up and removing the hood.

Kit was startled, but not surprised; he stopped being surprised awhile back. He felt the instinctual tug to turn and run. Sitting in front of him was Richard Baines.

"Drake sailed early." He almost told him about the second letter, but something told him not to do that. "What are you doing here?" The question was out before he realised the stupidity of it.

Baines ignored it. He was using his dagger to dig something into the thick wood of the table, something that looked like a cross. Kit couldn't be sure, not in the dim light of the Inn.

The Innkeeper, a man with a big, round stomach had come out, glanced at them and then vanished.

"Absolution," said Baines.

"Absolution?" returned Kit. The man was insane. Kit glanced enviously at the exit, wondering if he could reach it before Baines was on him with his dagger. Reach the exit and his horse and he might be able to escape the mad man.

Baines rose to his feet. In the dim light he looked like a priest full of righteous authority. "I'm here to absolve you of your sins, which are many."

"I don't need absolution. I'm not dying."

The grin on Baines' face had the rictus clench of a skull. He pricked his thumb and sucked on the blood that beaded there.

"That remains to be seen," he mumbled. "Your father and mother were followers of the true faith, weren't they? So, as a favour to them I extend this opportunity to you."

Kit felt the blood drain from his face. He had never thought he would die like this. The truth of the matter was that he had never thought of his own death. Perhaps he could make a deal. He had been toying with the idea of a man who makes a deal with the devil, and he wondered if he could deal in like with Baines. What would Baines want so that he might live? Kit reached into his doublet, retrieved the first letter, the one Walsingham had written, and threw it down on the table. It had been a letter retained expressively for this purpose.

Baines glanced down at it, and picked it up gingerly to examine it.

"You're Walsingham's man..." protested Kit. There had to be a way out of this without a fight.

Baines' grin deepened becoming darker, if that was possible. "So I am, but I am also God's. I am also one of the horsemen that John the Beloved spoke of."

The man thought he was one of the horsemen of the apocalypse? Those dark eyes seemed to pull him in. No, this was not a jest, Baines believed in what he was saying, truly believed it, and bizarrely enough, there was a truth in that.

Baines pointed at Kit, his fingers curling into a fist that slammed down onto the table with the sound of judgement.

"If you refuse absolution, there is nothing more I can do for you. The wages earned at Rheims is Hell. Fare well."

Kit reached for his dagger, but Baines was too quick. Again he grabbed him and pulled him close so that their faces were touching. The man looked like a one eyed monster about to eat him. Kit stopped breathing.

"I don't know anything about Rheims," said Kit in frustration. If the man was going to kill him why didn't he do it?

"You lie," spat Baine's, his spittle wetting Kit's face. "You owe me. You owe me your life. I do this for your mother, your father and the true faith."

Instead of the sharp point of the dagger, Kit felt himself being shoved away. Before he could recover from the stagger, Baines was already at the door. In the next moment he was gone. The man was like a nightmare, thought Kit as he sank back down onto the bench and began to breathe, wondering why he was still alive.

Outside, Baines went to the horsemen that was waiting for him in the courtyard. He handed the letter to Della Massa.

"The messenger?"

"I've taken care of him," said Baines who caught the purse of coins tossed to him. Baines turned and walked off into the night to find his horse.

At the door Della Massa knocked: three slow knocks followed by two rapid. The door promptly opened up to let a crack of light out. A breath of garlic escaped on a draft into the warm air around him. The faint light cast by a candle he held revealed part of the servant's face on the other side of the door. The man's nose was purple and the size of a turnip.

"The Holy Spirit of Enterprise..." began Della Massa.

"...will come to fruition," said the man completing the password.

"I have letters."

The door swung in and Della Massa was ushered into the dark house. Their shadows danced along with them as they climbed the narrow stairs. With each step the stairs creaked. It would have made it impossible for anyone to sneak up from below. At the top, in front of a narrow door, they stopped. The servant opened it, and turned sideways in order to get through. He leered back at Della Massa as if he was taking some perverse delight in his discomfort.

One frugal light illuminated the desk and the writer hunched over it. Instead of facing the door, the desk faced a big window that overlooked the moonlit, and empty harbour, so all he saw was the back of the man.

"Thank you, Hugo, for escorting our guest to me. You may go."

The servant, leering treacherously at Della Massa, left the room, shutting the door, which squeaked behind him.

"You must forgive my squeaky servant, stairs and door. I find them very useful when I have unwelcome visitors. Please," continued the man without turning around, "place the letters on the desk and have a seat."

Della Massa, suddenly aware that he had been manipulated by the man behind the desk, shifted uneasily. He did as he was told, placing both letters onto the desk. There was only one other chair, other than the one the man was sitting in, in the room. Was he expected to sit? A crawling sensation went up his neck. He was being watched from somewhere, most likely from a hole in the wall.

"Please, forgive me for not wanting to show my face. These are dangerous times. Just as an aside, Hugo is aiming a crossbow at your back...should you become a threat."

"Poison, he struck me as a poisoner, your man. I misjudged his aptitude for murder."

"Please be so kind as to place the letters in my hand." He held out his hand.

Della Massa picked them from off the desk and place them in the palm of the hand. The fingers closed on them.

Marco Antonio Massia had been called upon to do many difficult things for his Grace, and dealing with men like Berto Della Massa was just one of them. If he was at all really interested he might inquire as to the man's real name. But he wasn't. The man was just another tool, a deadly tool, in which to accomplish an end. He took his letter opener and sliced through the seals, and began to read. His fingers followed the script: a rather hurried affair, yet he could see Walsingham in every letter even though he had never met the man. He placed the first down and began to devour the second. Here the script was entirely different. It was impeccable, flowing with a studied hand and full of substance. It borrowed some loops and flow from the Italian school. It was in the Queen's own hand. When he was done he placed both letters down onto his lap and stared out over the harbour. He liked looking out over water. It gave him a sense of contemplative peace. He mused over these two missives: Two letters that El Draco never got, whether he was meant to get them or not was another issue. He smelled the musty scent of subterfuge in them. No messages in a beer barrel these.

"Amazing, is it not? Orders arrive late, men die and a fleet sails, not necessarily in this order. What am I to surmise?" Massia stood up and turned about suddenly deciding to let Berto Della Massa see his face.

Della Massa instinctively reached for his dagger.

Massia held up his hand. "Do not worry, Hugo will spare you."

Della Massa was tense because he knew his life was forfeit if this man's safety was compromised, and seeing his face might have done so. He forced himself to relax.

"That's better. I always find seeing someone's face is illuminating. It tells me so much about the person. Have you ever seen El Draco?"

"Yes," responded Della Massa the feeling of unease making him itch between his shoulder blades, where the cross bow bolt was aimed. "Once, I saw him at Court."

"At Court? You are either a lucky or unfortunate man. Tell me, what did El Draco's face tell you?"

"That El Draco has a mind of his own."

"Yes, but two letters. One undoubtedly is for me, or maybe both, or maybe neither. If one is for me, then the question is, which one?"

Massia held up the second letter. "The Heretic Queen gives her blessing on his attacks in the area of El Ferrol." Massia held up the second letter. "This, now this is a more interesting missive; it gives a view into the very heart of the Heretic Queen. In it she changes her mind. In this she tells Drake not to attack, only to disrupt trade." But it is in the hand of Walsingham. Which one is for me?"

Della Massa shrugged. He didn't really care. He had taken on this task because his Master Don Antonio had asked him to. While he was cultivating relationships with the Queen, he also wanted the support of the Pope, and this man was the hand of the Pope in England. "I would say the second one, or perhaps both."

"I am of a tendency to agree. Is the Spider's timing so bad that both would miss El Draco's departure?" He held the second letter to the flame of the candle. It caught and flared up causing shadows in the room to jump. After most of it was consumed, he let it fall to the floor where he extinguished it with his foot. "Don't want that one to fall into the wrong hands. So, that leaves us with this." He waved the first letter. "What should I do with it?"

"Warn the governors in the area of El Ferrol?"

Massia waved his finger disapprovingly. He burned this letter also. "Why should I warn Phillip, I am not Phillip's man, nor why should I warn the governors about a dragon who, most likely, will not appear?"

"Then where is he sailing?"

Massia shrugged haplessly and sank back into his chair. "Now that is a good question. A question that only El Draco knows the answer to."

"So, what will you do?"

"Nothing; if El Draco bloodies the King of Spain it will give our Grace a better moral footing to command Phillip to reclaim this lost land from heretics. Now, to matters closer to home: How is the Prior of Crato doing?"

Della Massa was wary of Massia's sudden interest in Duke Antonio, but this is what was wanted, the eyes of the Pope.

"He is well."

"Unfortunately," said Massia shoving a black purse onto his desk. "If it is acceptable to you, his Grace would like to employ you. Duke Antonio has a long history of failure behind him. We would like that to continue."

Chapter Ten: Lotus House

The down strokes were fine, even on the diagonal, but it was the curves that were giving her problems. Miao Juzheng sat at a specially designed table and practiced her calligraphy. The table had been raised and put at a forty five degree angle so that the surface of the rice paper would be brought closer to her eyes. Still, to see clearly, she had to place her nose inches from the paper. She gave a sigh of despondency and sat back.

Old Lao, who was pacing behind her, closed in to give his verdict. He grunted and complimented her down strokes but tapped his finger beside the curves.

"These look like pregnant ducks." His blue veined hands, gnarled yet still with strength, touched her hand with the brush. "It is as I thought; you hold your brush like you were trying to choke someone. You must loosen your fingers. Do not move from the wrist, move the entire arm, be one with the form."

Miao was about to complain when she heard the noises from the room nearby. The walls were very thin, so it was not uncommon when her father had visitors, mostly for some mandarins, working on some policy or another, to come by, to seek his guidance, but those were gentle inquiring voices. The voices she heard now were harsh, demanding and full of the potential of violence. She had always been able to tell the intent of a person through the tone of their voice. True intent always lurked behind the person's language like an animal. The only time she couldn't tell intent was when all life had been drained from the voice. Those were very dangerous voices, voices beyond feeling. The Emperor had a voice like that.

She placed her wolf hair brush down and rose to her feet. The door to the next room had been left open a crack so that she could hear if her father or mother were to call for her. She went to that crack. She had heard those voices before. They were the voices of the men who carried arms. What were they doing here? They never came to see her father.

The voices rose in anger as her father refused them and their demands increased. Then there was the sound of one of the men striking her father. Another voice sounded. It was her mother's voice, a pleading voice.

Miao was about to go to them, when Lao placed his hand on her shoulder. He shook his head and placed his finger to his lips. He collected her, cloaked her, and took her out the back entrance. She had always been a good girl and had never thought to question Lao, still, once outside the building she had the urge to burst back in to help her father, her mother.

"What is happening?" she said in a frightened voice. Even though it was a warm evening, she felt cold and could not help but shiver.

"The Young Dragon is waking," explained Lao. He always called the Emperor, the Young Dragon.

She had always thought of dragons as being benevolent creatures, full of luck and good will, but the dragon in Lao's voice was full of anger and fear.

"What is happening, Lao? I am frightened."

The old man's arm tightened around her shoulders as he guided her away from the building.

"Come," said Lao as he led her down the street. Eventually they found a rickshaw. Lao pressed some money into the man's hand and they climbed up onto the wicker seats. They began to move away from her home.

"Where are we going?" she asked in bewilderment. She still had ink stains on her fingers. "Lao, look my hands have ink on them. I must return to wash."

Again, that old hand, so aged, so strong, covered hers and gave a comforting squeeze.

"There are no stains on your hands. When we get to the sea, you may wash them."

Stains on her hands. She listened to the intent there, in Lao's voice. Along with the word, stain, a sense of great wrong, of great violence followed. She shivered and wanted to ask more questions but found her courage had flown away.

To the wharf, where the ever present sounds of the sea resided, they went. The smells and the sounds filled her with a sense of wellbeing. She understood Lao. This was to be a distraction for her. They would spend some time down at the sea. By the time they returned home, her father and mother would have calmed the angry voices and things would be harmonious again. Everything would be as they had always been. Miao did not believe it, but she was desperately determined to hold onto the hope.

As they stepped down from the rickshaw and began to walk along the wharf bathed in the light of the setting sun, Miao was filled with a sense of dire foreboding. Everything she was seeing, hearing, scenting, seemed to be saying farewell to her. A feeling overwhelmed her, as though she was never going to see these things again. They stopped beside a tall strange looking vessel. She had seen this ship before. It was very distinct. While most ships in port had sails that looked like the fins of fish, these sails, when filled with air, billowed out like great bed sheets. She turned to Old Lao.

"Where are you sending me?" She heard her own voice and the strength in it surprised her, but it seemed so far away.

"I have arranged for you to be taken to Macau, for you to be taken to safety."

"I am frightened."

"Don't be." Old Lao's hands were on her shoulders, pressing strength into her. "I have talked to the captain and have shared with him your gifts. You will be safe."

She did not want to ask the questions, because she knew the answers. She did not want to ask if her father and mother would be all right, because she knew they would not. She did not want to ask about Lao's future, because behind him, all she could see was darkness. When she looked up at the tall ship, images floated around it, but they were not images, or colours of safety. What she did see, however, was a city beneath a heavy pewter sky, perpetually cloaked in mist. The city stank.

**

The door to Lotus House shook with the hammering of fists. Miao panicked. The men who came for her parents were now coming for her. She reached out into the darkness for Old Lao's comforting hand and grabbed, instead a thick forearm. She opened her eyes and gazed pleadingly up at George who was sitting beside her.

"Don't let them take me," she implored.

George had enough wits about him to realize that she had been in the throes of some nightmare, she often was. Usually he would sit in the corner as she tossed and turned. Sometimes she would scream, sit up in bed and begin talking in that strange, sing-song language of hers. And her eyes would be flickering back and forth. At first it had given him the shivers, but now it only frustrated him. He had yet to meet an opponent he could not solve, but this young woman confounded him. He wanted to help, but was clueless how to do so. He patted her shoulder with his big hands.

"I won't," he looked deeply into those strange eyes, "I promise."

Miao came to herself and gave a stiff, embarrassed nod. "A promise is a promise."

George laughed. He had taught her that phrase, and his mother had taught it to him. "Indeed."

A sudden pounding shook the front door. Fear gripped Miao's stomach.

George's eyebrows tensed together to make furrows. "There was no pounding downstairs. It must have been in your dreams. But we do have a guest. I told him he had to wait until you woke, and I wasn't about to wake you."

She swung her legs off the bed. "How long have you made him wait, George?"

He shrugged. "An hour or two: it's good for him. He's an impatient sort."

"George, who is it?" she said in admonition.

"Oh, just that playwright fellow, the one whose play the Burbage brothers are about to show."

"Marlowe? Christopher Marlowe?" She was out of bed now and fumbling through her clothes.

"Kit, yes, that's his name, the fellow with the big pustule on the end of his nose," quipped George.

She hit him with her pillow. George knew that she found Kit attractive and was now teasing her.

"Go down and tell him I'll be there, presently," she pleaded.

Knuckling his forehead, George mumbled something subservient and left with a half-smile on his face. Miao quickly threw on a robe she usually wore around the house. It irritated her because for a moment she thought about the Bel Imperia dress. The part that irritated her wasn't the dress, but her desire to wear it, for Kit. She had seen him about The Theatre and had hoped to be introduced, but George seemed to be keeping them purposely apart. She looked at herself in the mirror and tried to tame her wiry hair. It was white and unmanageable, and her eyes were incorrigible, if she could just find a way to stop them from jittering back and forth, but she couldn't, so she hid them. She pulled on her hooded cloak, took one last look and covered her face up in the deep recess of her hood.

He was sitting down at the small table when Miao came down the stairs.

"Achoo," sneezed Kit.

"God Bless you," said George as a reaction. He didn't really mean it, not until he had made up his mind about the young man.

Kit groaned. He had been wearing the same clothes for several nights.

"I'm not sure it's my soul that needs saving, but I could sure use some help." He noticed Miao coming down the stairs. He stared up at her, his mouth hanging wide open.

"Shut your mouth, boy, before you choke on a fly."

"Lady Juzheng," said Kit. As he went to stand up he banged his leg on the table.

George put his hand on his shoulder and shoved him forcibly back down. "Sit, before you hurt yourself."

"George, could you get our guest some Ch'a."

Miao noticed George hesitating. He didn't trust the playwright, and she wondered why. The man was pleasing to look upon, and his work, although dark and exceedingly violent, was full of the brilliance of words and colour. To her there had always been that connection between the two. Certain words held the pigment of certain colours. Some words could be as black as night, while other contained the brilliance of the sun. Kit, in her opinion, knew how to harness both types and all the gradations in-between

"I'd rather ale," said Kit.

George snapped at him. "If the lady says it's Ch'a, then it's Ch'a. Personally, I don't know why My Lady wants to waste Sir Water's personal stock on you." He stood there glaring at Kit his arms crossed.

"George," said Miao as she sat down.

"Fine, I'm going."

Kit leaned onto the table, trying to see into the hood. "What's Ch'a?"

"It is a common drink from where I come from."

"Oh," said Kit. His hands were in constant motion, neither staying for long on the table or at his side.

"You are bothered by something?" asked Miao her heart naturally going out to him. She wanted to help.

George had returned holding a porcelain pot. He placed three cups down on the table and poured the clear, greenish tinted liquid into the cups. "I didn't think much of it at first, but it kind of grows on you." He sat down heavily at the table and lifted the cup to his lips and sipped. He made a face. Both Miao and Kit were staring down at the table in awkward silence. Oh, lord help us, thought George, I better put a stop to this.

"So, Kit, what do you want from My Lady; it better be good or your arse will be meeting the sole of my boot as you fly through yonder door."

"Oh, right, yes..."

"Drink, first," said Miao.

Kit took up his cup and drank at the same time as Miao did. He put the cup down and looked at it curiously. "Very...different."

George laughed. "I told you he wouldn't like it. It's not up to his boozy tastes."

"Continue," urged Miao.

"No, no, I do like it. It's just so...different."

"Right, right," said George wryly. "Different is as different does. So, what do you want?"

Kit took another sip. "Really, this is quite good. What did you call it?"

"Ch'a," said Miao.

George gave an inward groan. He wasn't about to let Kit get his Miao. "Great, feel better now? So, what was so important that you had to get My Lady out of her bed chamber?"

The nervousness that had been in Kit before he drank returned. "I've lost a letter. It was taken from me."

"You lost a letter," laughed George, "lad, just write another one."

"No, it was taken from me. It was written by Lord Walsingham and was to be given to Sir Francis Drake."

George gave an impressed whistle. "I knew you ran with a dangerous crowd, but..."

"I know, I know, but the money, George..."

"That's not the worst of it. I can explain that to Walsingham. Did you know that Richard and Will and the rest were arrested?"

"Arrested" asked Miao, "when?"

"Yesterday."

George and Miao exchanged a knowing glance.

"What?" asked Kit. "You know something about this? I mean it's a nightmare. How can they perform my play if they're all in the gaol?"

"That's easy enough to fix," returned George. "We just march down there and get them out."

Kit ran his hand nervously through his hair.

"Drink," insisted Miao.

Kit did as he was told and took another sip. The drink, whatever it was, did have some calming properties. He could see where this could become quite a habit. He wished he had some of Sir Water's stink weed to smoke but he was out.

George watched Kit through narrowed eyes. Sometimes he could squeeze the truth out of people by looking at them this way. The letter was a good excuse, but that was only a half-truth, he sensed it. The players in gaol were even better, but that is not why Kit was here. He suspected something else. He liked the lad well enough, but his time with dissimilating folk was making a liar out of him. He cracked his knuckles and glared at Kit. "Out with it, boy."

"I had a secret audience with the Queen," breathed out Kit quickly.

George barked out a laugh. "And good ol' King Henry came back to ask me to fix him up a proper roasted chicken, said he was hungry."

Miao leaned forward. She had seen something float beside Kit's head when he had mentioned the audience with the Queen. It was like a dagger, a dark dagger. "George, he's not lying."

"It's true, that's why I'm really here," said Kit. "Richard told me about your ability."

George growled. "That's the last time I tell that squib anything."

"George," said Miao, "what did you say?" She had warned him about how people responded to finding out about how she '*saw*' things. Most had thought her ability was connected to the devil (whatever that was). Fortunately most people thought actors were also in league with the dark arts anyway.

Her protector looked guiltily down at his cup and then up at Miao. "I only told him that sometimes you can see a person's possibilities."

A light seemed to dance in Kit's eyes.

George knew that the part about the letter was not really an issue. The old spider knew when to send something and when not to. It was probably lost on purpose. As far as the lads being in the gaol, George would have found that out quickly enough. He wasn't about to let them sit there, victim of some puritanical hatred for all things diversionary. Left to the Lord Mayor he'd have everyone working from dawn to dusk and beyond. They did that anyway, so why deny the people a momentary dalliance? He saw that as downright cruel. No, this was about Miao and her abilities. This was what Kit was after. "Kit," he said his voice growing cold, like steel being pulled from a scabbard, "no matter what you say, the answer is, no."

"The Queen is without Dr. Dee. He has been away on the Continent for years and doesn't seem to be coming back, and she needs someone to draw comfort from."

"Let her draw comfort from her puffed up bishops."

"She doesn't want someone like that. She wants someone who can see."

"No, not for sale, best you leave now, while you can," said George matter-of-factly.

"No, it's all right, George. I want to hear him out."

Kit relaxed. "What exactly does it mean when George says you can see?"

Miao hesitated and decided to trust him. "Sometimes I can see things about a person, sometimes around them," explained Miao. She felt a sudden exhilaration that came with telling someone other than George and Sir Water. It felt nice. Yet, she still felt a bit apprehensive. For some reason it mattered what Kit thought.

"Could you, let's say, see things about the Queen?"

"Kit..." warned George.

Miao nodded gravely. "Yes, especially people who have much responsibility." Suddenly she remembered how dangerous this truly was.

She had only been a little girl when she had told her father about the white fish floating over the emperor's head. She had thought it was innocuous at first, but she learned that speaking an ill fortune of someone with power is not always the best thing to do. She suspected it contributed to her family's death.

"If I told the Queen you could read her fortune, would you?" asked Kit.

She could sense his nervousness, and listened to his voice. She liked the sound of his voice. "George, if I did this thing, would it mean we would be invited to Court?"

"Court," said George as if he said gold. "Where the Queen is, so is the Court, but are you sure you want to do this?"

She placed her fingers over Kit's hands to comfort him. Something sprang out from behind him and hovered over his head. It was an ethereal black cat. It regarded her warily with its green eyes. Then something strange happened, something that had never occurred before. A white wisp began to rise from her hands, forming another cat, a white one with pink eyes. This cat immediately spotted the black one and began to stalk it. Springing away the black cat shot off with the white cat in hot pursuit. They dissipated and Miao laughed.

"What are you laughing at?" asked Kit.

"You," barked George. "She's laughing at you. Now let's go get those laggards out of the Lord Mayor's gaol."

Kit looked at George in awe. "You can do that?"

Rising to his feet George slapped his thick chest. "No, I can't but Sir Water can. The mere mention of his name has caused many a man to wet himself. Why do you think they call him Sir Water?"

***

They could tell it was morning, but to extract the exact time from the grey sky was more than difficult. The cobble stones were wet and slick in the narrow streets. Kit led them through the cleaner streets to impress Miao. The buildings, their second stories jutting out over the first, often created a narrow passage much like a tunnel for them to traverse. George hated walking in streets like this. He preferred the open sky, when he could find it.

Miao was wrapped up in her black cloak, giving her the impression that she was either the Oracle of Delphi or a witch. She felt herself jerked suddenly beneath one of the overhangs as a torrent of night soil came sloshing down onto the street.

"Hey," yelled George up at the person, "watch where you're throwing that stuff."

"Hey," came the characteristic plucky voice of a Londoner, "watch out, you're in the way of my leavings."

"Obstreperous wench," grumbled George. Then he saw Kit's closeness to Miao and he inserted himself between them. "Well, isn't this nice, at least we know what time it is in the morning," he glared at Kit. "It's time when admiral brown makes an appearance."

Kit looked awkward. "Yes, well. We're not far."

"I know," said George. "Let's keep it that way."

Kit led them up the street, around a few more corners until they arrived at a big stone faced building. Through the iron barred windows in the double door, they could see an open courtyard beyond. George stepped up to the door, grabbed the knocker, which was a big iron ring, and started smashing it against the wood. He didn't stop until a bleary eyed man appeared on the other side of the door. The man had a long beard with bits of bread in it. Apparently his breakfast had been interrupted. His mouth, which was missing several key teeth, was busy moving the food he was chewing around his gums.

"Go away, unless you want a room," he said spitting food. He was sure the petitioners weren't worth his time.

"A group of players were arrested yesterday," said Kit.

"Players? Players?" the man ruminated. "No, there are no Table Players here." The man laughed at his own jape, spitting food out at them.

"Leicester's men, the actors?" said George impatiently.

The gaoler squinted suspiciously, "Now, who did you say you were?" His eyes darted from the dark form of Miao, to Kit and then back to George.

"I'm George Silver..." he was about to introduce Kit and Miao, but the gaoler stopped him.

"George Silver?" his tone rose perceptively with excitement. "George Silver, of course, sorry, sorry..."

Keys jangled on the other side of the door as the proper one was inserted into the lock and turned. The doors swung in and the man ushered them in enthusiastically. He stood back and brushed off the crumbs from his doublet and held out his arms to display himself.

"Don't you recognize me? Barley Buttercorn. "You knocked out my front teeth with a staff, remember?" He pulled his lips away from his puffy gums.

Miao examined the man closely. He actually seemed happy about losing his front teeth.

"Barley?" He had knocked out a lot of men's teeth. Then George remembered. Once he had to train some plough boys to fight so that they could be some service as soldiers when called up. He remembered a burly lad, full of braggadocio, bullying some spindly lads. He had taught him a lesson with a staff and in the process, accidentally, knocked a few teeth out. The man in front of him was bearded and scrawny, but he recognized the eyes. "Yes, I remember you. You've changed."

"Got sick, but Barley wasn't destined for the pits. Though they thought I was dead, came and got me, even threw me on the wagons. Surrounded by bodies I was. Dumped me in the mass grave. They were about to heave me into the pit, when I woke up and asked for a pint. The fellow pissed himself," laughed Barley. "So, I've come up in station. I'm a gaoler now. They figured since the dead couldn't keep me, I'd be best at keeping the living."

"That's great, Barley," George said giving him the praise he wanted. "We need your help. Leicester's Men, we're here to release them."

Barley frowned, thought about it and shook his head. "I'm sorry, George, truly I am, but without the proper papers. It would mean my job, it would."

George touched his breast pocket. "Would a letter from the Captain of the Queen's Guard turn your mind?"

Anxious for the approval of his old instructor, Barley nodded. "It would, it would at that, Knave outranks Mayor. Pardon me, but could I see it?"

George frowned disapprovingly, and made a slow show of reaching for the letter, but as he was pulling a piece of paper from his pocket, Barley stopped him.

"No need, Mister Silver," he winked at George, "I can now say without a shadow of a doubt, that I have seen the letter, and can in good conscience, recommend them to Lord Water."

He led the way through the cells until they came to a large one that was crammed full of men. Instead of the mindless lethargy that often occupied the imprisoned, the inmates behind the bars seemed to be having a rather good time.

A malleable voice rose high and dipped low in imitation as a story was told.

"And he's quaking and shivering, saying he's going to raise me up in the Papist rights.' Then the landlord spies him through the keyhole and he's praying, crossing himself and splashing holy water every which way. My head was drenched.

What do you think the Innkeeper does? He runs off, fetches the constable and drags us off to London for hanging. Of course everyone recognizes Tarlton's ugly face. And they say, this is no Papist priest, this is a fool and his fool. And Tarlton says: 'more fool the

Innkeep who lost the due owed for a night's rest and feast.' And with that he thanks the constable for the free ride, and we walk away."

The cell burst out in laughter. A big red faced man with a bulbous nose clapped Will on the back appreciatively.

"Tell us the one about the three maids from Cheapside," he said.

"I hear they weren't so cheap," laughed another.

"Oh, I've got one better, lads," said Will puffing up for another story. "This one is about Black Luce and Lord Liver Warts."

Richard noticed the gaoler and Kit and George and Miao at the lock and gave a weak, exhausted smile. Ned threw himself at the bars his hands in prayerful supplication. "Please, for all that is Holy get us out of here before he tells another dirty story."

Barley ran his stick over the bars to remove their fingers. "Back please. Leicester's men, please present. It seems that this is your most fortunate day. You are to be released."

As the door opened Ned slipped out through the door followed by Richard, George, Augsy and Tom. Last to follow was a fellow with the big, red face and round nose. Barley put his stick against his chest to stop him. "Will, Will Kemp?"

"I, I will have you know, I am Will, the mighty Will who will have my freedom," he said through gap toothed grin.

Ned groaned. "Will, stop playing around."

Richard walked away. "Let's just leave him. This fellow is probably a better actor."

Barley was about to agree when Will bounded through the crowd and slipped out of the cell. He looked apologetically at the man with the rubicund nose.

"Sorry, lads, I'll have to expound on the size of my wit some other time."

108

Barley shut the bars and turned the key.

Miao couldn't help but feel compassion for the men behind the bars, who now, without Will's good nature, seemed rather forlorn.

"What are these men being held for?" she asked.

"Don't worry about this lot," mumbled Barley. "Most of them broke the Mayor's peace with their drunken howls. Their wives will be showing up shortly to collect them."

"May the Lord have mercy upon their souls," said Will in his best priestly voice as he crossed himself.

Chapter Eleven: Another Death

It had the taste of the present: her memories, so substantial that they replaced reality and left her standing amazed. Some things she did not desire to remember, but they came back nevertheless. Sometimes, it could be the type of sunlight, the sound of a voice, a certain smell. This time it was the flapping of a kite's wings as it landed on a midden pile. The bird began to peck through it, looking for food. George touched her on the arm to guide her and she slipped into her waking dream.

***

She was taken by the arm and led down into the belly of the ship. The hatch was closed leaving her in darkness. It was then that she felt the full weight of being torn from kin, from her mother, father and Old Lao. The hold stank with the scent of crowded humanity.

Although she couldn't see them, she could hear them breathing. They must be sleeping. She curled up into a ball not to disturb them and then began to sob. She felt a body draw close to hers but that didn't help.

When the dim light of the hold during day finally came she was able to see her fellow sufferers. Unlike herself they were chained: an entire hold of

109

despondent faces looking at her. What was the purpose of keeping people chained on a ship? Once a day they were fed by the hairy faced men with the harsh, unforgiving eyes. Once a day her keeper, a man who limped and had a face that looked as though it had been partially melted, came down and placed slop like food in a trough. They tried not to act like they were treated, like animals. She kept track of the number of times they were fed to tie it to the days so she could keep track of time, but she failed.

Most of her companions had become sick with the heave and roll of the ship. The hold smelled of vomit and feces. There were twenty of them, but half of them died. In time she began to feel that the belly of the ship was the belly of some great beast that had devoured them and was slowly digesting them, one by one. The oldest and the youngest died first. Miao could see their spirits leaving their bodies. They seemed happy to be departing. Some of the spirits even clapped their hands for joy. That was a good thing.

There were storms where the ship heaved and rolled and salt water poured down on top of them. There were times of intense heat where parched lips searched desperately for foul water given to them in miserly sips. There were days and nights unending, and she began to feel envious of those who died. Slowly she forgot to count the days and slipped into the mindless numbness of lethargy.

Then the heavens opened with ear shattering detonations and the boards above their heads groaned as something great and ponderous moved about. Men were yelling, and screaming. There was a great whistling outside and then a portion of the ship's hull exploded just above the water line. Wood splinters and water sprayed everywhere; fortunately none of the wood fragments hit Miao, but something wet ran down her head and into her mouth. It had a salty, coppery taste to it. There were more explosions, more shouts and then the clashing of metal on metal. More screams and cries, until a merciful silence settled about the ship. She was shivering uncontrollably. Then there was light. It blazed down through the hatch that had been fully thrown back, and air, even though tainted by the smell of burnt wood and powder, flowed down into the hold. Up until this point their captors had only opened the hold a little bit at a time, just enough to permit the passage of the man with food. Miao, barely conscious and in a delirium, squinted up into the light. For a moment it looked as though a dragon, a glorious white dragon writhed about in the light. The dragon suddenly grew legs and arms. Another man came down the stairs into the hold in front of the dragon.

"What's in the hold?" said the man who was the dragon of death, for white was the colour of death. His voice was strong and full of authority as though used to bellowing commands into the wind.

The sailor on the stairs shouted back. "Naught but some poor devils; the slavers have been about their trade."

The white dragon with the big voice descended the steps to get a better view. He made their way through the grim cargo. Almost all of her companions in suffering were motionless. The man ahead of the white dragon moved through the dead. He bent down to examine the hunched over form of one of the slaves. "They're dead, or soon to be dead. Probably the bloody flux, best we burn this ship before it spreads."

The white dragon let out a great sigh. "Try to salvage any of its stores and then put her to the torch." He was standing so close to Miao that she could feel the dragon's steam coming from his mouth. He was not happy. She continued to shiver in her sickness. "Poor devils."

It was impossible to understand what they were saying, but Miao could tell what the mannerism in their stance said. It spoke of compassion and pity. Still, that would not have made her reveal herself. Her decision was decided by the image of the white dragon that was preparing to breathe fire into the hold. She knew they were going to burn the ship. Summoning all the strength she had left, she lifted a pale arm.

"Captain, it's a ghost," said Dick, his voice quavering.

Drake groaned at the man's superstition. He walked over to the arm that had fallen back down amidst the corpses of the others. It was a tiny, emaciated girl. Despite her filth, her skin and hair seemed to be as white as snow, or so it seemed in the half light of the hold. Odd, he thought, the dead had the features of those from the Middle Kingdom. They all had dark hair with a yellowish hue to their skin, but this girl was different. Words came to him, words which made all the difference to his pious mind:

"A body white as snow, hair white as wool and eyes that are like the rays of the sun," quoted Drake.

"Sounds scriptural," said the sailor not knowing what to do with the ghost like girl. Maybe she had been the cause of the sickness that had killed everyone in the hold.

"It's the book of Enoch, Dick, the book of Enoch. Noah, did you know, Dick, this is how the scriptures described Noah."

"Not so dirty," said Dick, "or sick." He hesitated. It was one thing to show Christian compassion to someone, but it was quite another thing to take someone who was sick onto a ship where everyone was without the flux.

"No, not so dirty, but her filth is the filth of the slavers. Let's clean her up."

"The flux, captain," said Dick cautiously.

"I will not abandon one of Noah's children here in the belly of the whale."

Somewhere off in the distance Miao felt a blanket being thrown about her as she rose into the air cradled in the arms of the white dragon.

***

Beneath the Southwark Gatehouse the black water of the Thames slid smoothly by, reflecting the rare, clear moon in broken shards of light. It was the hour after midnight, the early hours of a new day, but the hope of light was still far away, leaving the secrets of the night to rule. Around the perimeter of the gatehouse's top were the heads. They were the heads of traitors impaled on long poles and hung out for anyone passing below to see. For those entering the city it was a pellucid message: the Queen's law of the realm was supreme, defy it at your own risk.

Shadows detached themselves from the areas where the moon's light could not touch. These men moved about, carrying heavy burdens. Two of the men carried a backless chair and placed it close to the edge. It all happened quietly, like a scene change for a production. Then the shadow men were gone and the night took a deep breath waiting for the Act to begin.

Della Massa walked towards the backless throne; on his arm was a woman. Her head, as usual, was covered in a black veil. She took her seat and Della Massa backed away bowing. Royalty must have its due, he thought. It was a poisonous thing, this royal blood, spreading throughout the body until it infected the mind. If he had royal blood in his veins, he would have opened them to drain it out. Still, he must bend before power, and the lady was powerful. She was powerful enough to give his master Don Antonio audience to the very source of power he desired, The Queen. Who knows who this woman was? Some of the nobility had their own peculiarities. He remembered the story of a Sultan and two slaves.

Both slaves were given a feast. After the feast, one was set on a rigorous march, the other was forced to rest all day. When the one on the march returned, they were both killed and opened up. The Sultan wanted to see which one had best digested his food. Royalty had their peculiarities.

One of the black shadows returned, bringing a drawing board. On it was stretched an expensive piece of paper. The shadow vanished. The woman picked up a piece of chalk in her long fingers and readied herself.

"You may present her," she whispered to Della Massa, who with a slight bow vanished into the shadows.

Della Massa escorted the woman before the Veiled Lady. He was glad he didn't really know who she was, which was ironic because he killed for her, an act, in his mind, of intimacy.

It had been a strange interview, their first meeting. She had sat there, veiled in black and asked him questions while she drew him. It made him nervous, which intrigued him; because the tremors of nervousness were inspired by fear and he had, until that point, been free from fear. Perhaps it was not fear; perhaps it was something more intimate. Let her touch him with her eyes, he was beyond the intimacy a man could show a woman anyways. That part of him had been removed by a knife years ago. And afterward, after his portrait had been sketched, he had felt himself bonded to her, more so than in any other way possible. They were husband and wife in murder.

"My Lady," he said presenting the poor woman to her.

The woman was a sad thing. Her hair was pell mell and dirt was so embedded in the pores of her skin that it would have taken much washing to clean her. Yet, still, there was nobility about the woman, a straightness in her posture that said she still had some sense of self. Although it was hard to tell colour beneath the light of the moon, he knew her hair was flaming red, like the Queen's. It was one of the requirements of the Veiled Lady: all the subjects must have hair, like the Queen's.

The Veiled Lady nodded her approval.

"Please, sit," said Della Massa placing a hand on her shoulder and guiding her down onto the chair. There was no shortage of women in London with flame coloured hair, and there was no shortage of the poor. Come to London in hopes of a better life, many found a quick end to that life. Give them a few coins and they would listen, offer them more and they would do anything. He had expressly told this woman that there would be gold in it if she did not speak. My Lady was not pleased when the last one had spoken.

The veiled woman worked busily, her gentle fingers making deft, confident moves across the paper. It was engrossing to watch her work. He admired the technique, how something could go from nothing to something in a few moments. It seemed like a mere instant while the Lady drew, but it must have been a good hour before she was finished. So entranced had he been that he thought he was under a spell where time had no sway. He gasped when the Lady finished and motioned him forward.

The drawing, as usual, was amazing. He glanced at the poor woman. They always looked drained, somewhat lesser in substance after she had drawn them. Maybe that was it: after the Lady had pulled their souls into the drawing, there was naught left but a dried husk of humanity. He was doing them a favour by killing them. It was an act of ultimate compassion.

"It is nearly done," said the Veiled Lady.

Della Massa nodded and placed his hand on the woman's shoulder. She flinched at the touch and could no longer remain silent. He instructed her to rise.

"Is it over?" she said.

Della Massa gave an inward groan, the lady would not like her voice; it was much too high. But it didn't matter. Whether she spoke or was silent, she would still have to die. All died. He was, in a sense, doing her a favour. He motioned her to move over to the side of the roof of the guardhouse where the gruesome heads hung on their poles.

"Come."

"Where are we going?" she asked, a quaver of uncertainty in her voice.

"It is as the Lady instructs, before you are paid in full."

"I did well, didn't I? I never flinched. I was as still as stone," she said.

Della Massa felt melancholic. What was she doing, asking for approval? He shook his head. He had killed so many people, what was one more. Everyone died.

"I must show you something."

He led her to the edge where the poles slanted out to stare down at the river below. She took a tentative look over the side and then skittered back.

"I'm not so good with heights. I get queasy when I go up steps." She tried a carefree laugh but it came out strained.

One of the things that Della Massa had learned, about killing, was that intent mattered. This was especially important in duels, or murder. If the combatant or victim was at ease, or deceived, the killing was much quicker. Duels could be quickly ended with a feigned injury; just enough to surprise, to throw your opponent off his rhythm. As for murder... "I did not bring you here to view the river, but the heads. Do you know why they are without body?"

The girl made a big 'O' with her mouth. "I wouldn't be telling anyone of this. I swear," and she spit on the ground.

"That's good," said Della Massa, "very good." He smoothly slid his dagger out from its hidden place. This would be close work. "Take a look at that head there, third over from the left."

She squinted. It was hard to see in the dark. "I can't see."

"Lean forward."

She leaned forward and as she did so his left hand fastened over her mouth and he drew the blade quickly across her throat. He held her while she struggled, bled and went limp. He gently placed her on the stones. She had a peculiar look on her face that startled him: almost a look of peace. Reaching down he closed her eyes. This night's work had not pleased him. He had wanted to use his beads, but the Veiled Lady had forbidden it.

"The head, remove the head," commanded the Veiled Lady.

He hesitated. He thought of denying her, of turning away and telling her to do it herself. There was blood on his hands, on his clothes, but there was more on her clean, white hands. Her hands had been in swirling vats of blood. Taking a deep breath he let the urge pass. He preferred battle to this, even duels. He had always hoped for death in battle, but it had never come.

"Well," said the woman imperiously, waiting.

Della Massa turned and walked away. Let the shadows remove her head for her.

Chapter Twelve: Southwark Gatehouse

It was still about an hour before dawn. Miao hurried through the streets while George, still in the act of dressing, struggled to follow along. He hopped into his boot while his shirt hung out from his unbuttoned doublet like a treaty flag.

"Could you wait a second," pleaded George. The girl had surprised him out of the depths of sleep. It was a trick he had learned, the ability to sleep deeply when it suited him. Normally, when he suspected danger, he could wake in a moment, but when there was no danger, he slept as the dead. She was always surprizing him. She would've gotten out of the house without him noticing had she not kicked over the pot he had left outside her door. It had clattered and banged all the way down the stairs. That had barely slowed her. Stuffing his shirt into his trousers he caught up with her.

"Maybe it was just a bad dream," he offered moving his rapier around so that it wasn't trying to trip him by hanging between his legs: Will would have laughed at that, some bawdy jape. He stomped his foot down hard into his boot making sure it was fully in.

Miao shook her head adamantly. "I saw the man this time. He became distinct, separate from the act."

George had a tendency to worry about dreams that were real. The girl was no witch, he knew that, not that he had met many; in fact he hadn't met any. He had met some women he would call witches, but they weren't. He knew the troubles that an accusation of witchcraft brought.

He had grown up in a little town in Somersetshire, and when he was a child, he knew of a widow woman who lived in a little hovel who practiced healing. There was a particular bad fire where everyone in the house perished. Couple this with a bad harvest, and the good people started looking around for someone to blame. The widow was unfortunate to be a widow. Her being a witch would explain everything including why she was a widow.

During the trial at the assize she had explained she used herbs like belladonna, hemlock, mandrake and cannabis to heal. That didn't matter; it was obvious evidence that she had made a pact with the devil. The woman was promptly hung, since torture in these cases was disallowed. Her neighbours, the ones who brought the charges against her, got her land. If the Queen couldn't protect Doctor Dee (his house had been ransacked after he had fled) how could Water protect Miao Juzheng, a woman who fit perfectly the mold of witch?

"What do you mean, a man separate from the act?" George asked as he struggled to keep pace with Miao as she hurried through the streets. For a little thing she certainly could move when she wanted to.

"In my dreams, I've seen the victim, and sometimes the killer or what seemed to be the killer," explained Miao.

"You never told me that," said George.

"It was never a face, just a presence, behind a veil with a blue sword...together."

"A blue sword?" He was suddenly keenly interested.

"Yes, but not tonight. Tonight I saw a man detach himself from a veiled woman. We've been thinking that there was one murderer, now we know there are two: a man and a woman."

"That's interesting." It did add another crucial bit of information, vital, not too many men walked about London with a blue sword. Find the man and they find the woman...maybe. "Where are we going?"

"Southwark Gatehouse, we will find the body there, or part of it."

They approached London Bridge now. After the boat shaped starlings, the twenty large pillars and the bridge were built, it had become prime real estate and had been enthusiastically built upon. Nonsuch House, built in the Lowlands, had been taken apart, shipped across the channel and reassembled right in the middle of the bridge. There were sections on the bridge that were open, but most of it had become so built up that it was, in effect a tunnel with a medium for coming and going traffic. It was the only street in London that was clean; everyone's latrine opened over the river. As a result the smell was not half as bad as London proper. George should have felt good about crossing over in the night, maybe a whiff of good air from the country, but he didn't. He approached the bridge with a growing sensation of terror. There were not too many things that frightened George Silver, but this was one of them. He hated tunnels and confined spaces with a passion. If he could only keep them from closing in on him.

"Southwark Gatehouse, that's on the other side of the bridge," he said watching the dark, yawning entrance of the north gate house opening before them like a mouth.

"Yes," said Miao not pausing to consider how he felt. She was too focused on her vision.

"And where did the killing take place?" asked George feeling his heart racing a bit faster as they passed into the tunnel. On this side there were no guards, because there were no heads. It would be different on the Southwark side.

"On the roof, the murder took place on the roof. I saw heads and the heads were staring back at me."

"Wonderful," he muttered following her onto the bridge. Its construction was firm enough; it had to be in order to hold the weight of the buildings. The tunnel closed in around him with such force that he had to exert all his will on the rushing river below to survive. He felt his balance go and the firmness of the bridge began to melt beneath his feet. "So," he said trying not to feel the weight of the buildings pressing down on him, "do you have a plan? You know the guard house is guarded, that's why they call it a guard house."

"I was hoping you would come up with something," said Miao, surging ahead of him through the dark.

120

"Sure," lamented George, "I'll just come up with something."

Actually he was grateful for the puzzle to keep his mind off the walls that were starting to bend in on him. The bridge wasn't narrow at all, it was quite broad, built for wagon traffic from Bankside, but in the dark his mind made it small. What really helped was to focus on his charge and just her. If he did that, then everything would be all right and they would get to the other end of the bridge. Unable to hold back anymore, he pushed past Miao out into an open area where he stood gasping by the railing. There places on the bridge that could be lifted to allow tall ships through. He felt a light comforting hand on his back as he gasped for air.

"George, are you all right?"

"Oh, me? Never been better...just needed some fresh air."

"George, what's the matter?"

He paused looking down at the river. It was a beautiful sight, the flowing water and the numerous ships waiting for the morning's business to begin. He took a shallow breath and began to tell her something he had never told anyone else ever before:

"It's nothing. It's just, when I was a kid I got stuck in a hole."

"How old were you?" she asked compassionately.

"Six. I was there for two days, until they found me." He tried to laugh. "I just never got over being in close, if you know what I mean."

"George," she admonished him. "You should have told me."

"You were in a bit of a hurry."

"Oh, I am so sorry. What do we do now?" she said looking at the end of the bridge where the tunnel waited for them.

George shrugged. "Don't know, in for a penny, in for a pound. Maybe if we run?"

She reached out took his hand and squeezed it. "We will take a wherry back when we get to the other side."

"I'd like that very much," but he knew that no self-respecting wherryman would be plying his trade at this time. He closed his hands with Miao, glad that it was dark. What would they say if they could see George Silver holding hands with a little girl so that he wouldn't be afraid? Funny that, he thought, when he was down that hole, to stop from despairing, he had created a friend. "On three."

One doorway followed another until a blur of them added together until they stood at the far end of the bridge, at the Southwark Gatehouse.

More substantial than the other buildings it was indeed guarded. George didn't hesitate when he recognized one of the guards. Being George Silver was turning out to be quite fortuitous – unless he was in a tunnel. He strode up to the two guards. They held their long halberds casually and were surprised to see anyone at this time of night. George knew that those halberds, in an instant, could become an impenetrable barrier.

"You still know how to use that, James," said George.

Miao was constantly amazed at the number of people George seemingly knew. Who in London didn't he know?

"George, George Silver, is that you?" said the young man squinting and relaxing his grip on the halberd. "You two gave us a bit of a start, coming at us out of the dark like that. Why were you running? I was afraid I'd have to cut you up into little pieces and feed you to the fishes."

His companion, a man with cruel, tiny eyes and a square block head laughed.

"No, just out for a little walk with my charge. Let me introduce you. My Lady this is Jim Witherspoon, Jim this is the Lady, Miao Juzheng."

The guards looked suddenly awkward as they gave her stiff bows. "We don't get many visits by the gentry down here at night."

"Watch your tongue, she's a Peer of the Middle Kingdom, with title."

The man looked confused. "I haven't heard of no Middle Kingdom. You wouldn't be pulling a fast one on me, now would you?"

"She takes precedence over a Marchioness," said George. "It's almost dawn. Any chance we can go up?"

The indecisions in the guards became hard with resolve and their duty snapped in. "Any chance you could grow wings?"

He remembered Jim Witherspoon, a young man who thought he was terribly witty. Kemp and the boys would've whittled his sparse wit away and left him shivering, naked in the cold. He would have to take a different tack with this one.

"Were you two on guard here all night?" asked George.

The other guard squinted, his eyes, if possible, becoming meaner. "Here, what's this about?"

"So," continued George, "when your relief does its inspection and they discover something up there, something that's not supposed to be there, you'll be fine with it?"

He finally had Jim's attention although the other guard just looked confused.

"And you know what this something is?" asked Jim warily.

"Yes, we do, that's why we're here."

"It would help," said Jim slyly, "if you crossed my palm with your namesake."

"Here," said the other guard offended. "You want him to give you a snake? That's just creepy that is."

"No, you dolt," said Jim. "I want him to give me some silver."

"Oh, yeah, no coin, no admittance," spat out the mean looking guard.

George placed the coins quickly into the guard's palm. "There, can we go up?"

"We'll have to escort you," said Jim. "To find out what this thing is."

"Suit yourself," said George letting the guards lead the way up the dark stairs. At first, because of Miao's aversion to light, he had thought she could see better than most in the dark, but she had corrected him in this. The reason it seemed she could see better was because she had used her other senses, like touch and sound. He could appreciate that. He used touch and sound and smell when he fought. Fear had a particularly pissy smell to it.

The top of the Southwark Gatehouse was expansive, but the two chairs at the far end of the flat roof made them feel that some preternatural event had happened here.

"That's not supposed to be up there," mumbled Jim in surprise. He turned to his fellow guard and said accusingly. "You didn't put that there did you?"

The fellow with the mean eyes shook his head.

Miao went directly to the chairs. The day was not far from dawning. They had a few moments before the sun rose up over the cusp of the horizon and illuminated the sky. From the amount of stars they could still see, it would be a rare, cloudless sky. Miao ran a hand over the chair.

"Don't you think we should leave those alone," warned Jim.

"Why? So your relief can ask you questions how these things got here on your last watch," said George.

"Last watch?"

He left the guards behind and followed after Miao. They needed something to think about. While they

124

were doing this, then they could investigate. Miao was standing there gazing down at the stool. George joined her.

"She sat here," said George, "didn't she?"

"And the woman who did the drawing, sat over there," said Miao moving to the throne. She lowered herself onto the throne like chair and let out a small gasp. It was full of spite, the chair: spite and hatred and envy. For a moment she was looking out through the eyes of the woman who was responsible for the killings.

"What do you see?" asked George.

"I see," said Miao, "a head without a body."

Just then one of the guards called out from the edge of the guard house. "Silver, you better come here."

Both Miao and George joined the guards, their gob smacked faces stared at one particular head pinioned on a steel pole. Unlike the others it had not been dipped in tar, but was fresh. It gazed glassily out over the river, long, red hair draping down. A slight breeze sprung up and the hair moved.

"You better get that down," said George.

Even now the streets were beginning to come alive all over London. One thing they didn't need was someone noticing the new head from below.

The guards struggled to retrieve the head. When they had it Miao was able to closely examine it. Something was sticking out of the head's mouth, a rolled up piece of paper. She knew what it was, but wondered what fury would have thrust it into the head's mouth. Slowly, tenderly she pulled out the drawing from between the woman's lips.

Although the guards had seen much death, and indeed been entertained by the various forms of execution, they both felt sickened. Then, from below came the sound of men. The guards gave a panicked look at each other. It would be impossible for them to explain the head or why two people who seemed to know about it were up on the roof of the guard house, unless – they arrested Silver and the Lady and blamed them.

George read their thoughts. "You, throw the head and pole into the water."

"How will we explain those," said Jim motioning towards the chairs.

"Throw them too," suggested Jim.

"But there's blood..."

George hit Jim in the nose. It wasn't much of a punch, just enough to get the nose bleeding but not enough to break it.

"Why did you do that?"

"Bleed over there. Tell your relief that you had a nose bleed."

"That's a lot of blood," complained the mean-eyed guard indicating the spot where the girl had been murdered.

With that George poked him too. "Tell them you heard something up here, you investigated, found that one of the heads had rotted off the pole, then you had a disagreement, had a fight, and bled.

George took Miao, who was holding the paper gently in her hands, by the arm and made to escort her off the roof. The guard's relief, from the amount of noise they were making, were coming up the stairs. There would be no way of getting past them. He watched as the two guards threw the chairs off the building's roof. Now, he had to think of a good story to explain why they were there.

"We should leave," said Miao.

"That's the problem," said George, "we can't go down the way we came up; we'll be seen."

"They'll think we're involved?"

"Yes."

George turned back to the guards who were just finishing throwing the last of the objects from the

126

tower. "Are there any other ways out of here?" said George.

Jim was still attempting to staunch the flow of blood from his nose.

"I say we tell them it was them who killed the girl," said Mean Eyes glaring at them and we caught them in the act of disposing the evidence."

"You must be as stupid as you look," said George. "Who is going to take your word over the word of a Lady?"

Mean Eyes fixed Miao with a withering gaze.

"He's right," said Jim. "There's an exit over there, only Lords and Ladies if you please."

George nodded. "I owe you one, Jim."

The guard nodded still trying to staunch the flow of blood. "I owe you one too."

They found the exit just as the guard's relief came rushing up onto the roof. They heard them demanding to know why they had abandoned their post. It was in the midst of the guard's demands, explanations and protestations that they took the narrow, secret steps down the Southwark Gatehouse and back to the bridge.

Chapter Thirteen: Tamburlaine The Great

The Theatre was the big attraction in Shoreditch. With its oval design, thatched roof, dark beams and white plaster, it was the model of respectability. The Burbages were committed to quality entertainment and a quality viewing experience. It was a shame that the puritan fathers of London proper, and their own patrons, were of different minds. To the Mayor all theatre was the breeding ground of diseases both carnal and plague.

Richard had to take a peak before getting himself ready. It made the others nervous, especially Ned. Ned was a creature of ritual and habit. Seeing the house for him was strictly taboo, but Richard had to see. It gave him a rough estimate of what the take would be. They were still pouring in, filling up the galleries and the dirt floor in front of the stage that would be occupied by the groundlings. It was going to be a full house. He hoped the lads at the gate were getting payment from everyone. Kit's play, and its promise of blood and conflict, were certainly drawing them in.

At the front gate, people were swirling about, waiting for their chance to enter the play house. Most were waiting patiently, some were not. A dark knot of nobles moved through the crowd with impunity, making the crowd part like the red sea before Moses. The common man moved aside because, first of all, the men in the knot were above them in station and second, they were foreigners, and everyone knew foreigners carried diseases.

Don Antonio, the claimant to the Portuguese throne, the Prior of Crato, the King without a throne, was the centre of the dark knot. Most men of his station wore clothes of a more flamboyant colour, but he would not permit it. Until he regained his throne, he and those who served him would wear black, because black was the absence of all colour. When he regained the throne, he would regain colour. At his side strode Berto Della Massa.

"Look," chuckled the young man on his other side. He had followed his king into exile in the hopes of finding adventure and fortune. So far, the young fop had only found genteel poverty. While his lord had some of the crown jewels there was hope. His lord had given up some of those jewels and the colony of Brazil to Catherine Di Medici for a French fleet. It had sailed forth in hope and full of the adventurers' lust for lucre and ended in the Azores with utter failure. Now, they were soliciting the Heretic Queen for another fleet, but she was turning out to be more parsimonious.

"I will handle this, your Highness." The young lord strode up to the big man standing at the gate taking fees and looked down his nose as one would look at something just dumped on the street, which was a trick because the purse man was a good head taller. "May I introduce, Don Antonio, the Prior of Crato, the King of Portugal. We are here to pleasure his Highness with your performance." The young lord waited expectantly.

Jack twisted his nose at the perfumed scent coming from the man. His dad always told him that sauces were invented to disguise the taste of rotten meat. He grunted, catching the eye of Jill, who guarded the other side of the gate. His name wasn't Jill, it was some ungodly Irish name, but Jack liked the humour in calling him Jill, and the big man didn't mind. Jill towered over everyone and provided the muscle to encourage payment. He also carried a cudgel about the size of a small tree. They would have let a real lord in post haste, but these ones were just pretenders, and they weren't even English.

"You can pleasure my palm with payment, if you don't mind, M'Lord," growled Jack.

The young lord was offended. "This is Don Antonio," he said in a shrill, sing-song voice. "He is the Prior of Crato, the King of Portugal!" He looked about waiting for it to matter. It didn't.

Jack gave a jerking pull with his head and Jill took a couple steps in their direction. He was caressing his cudgel tenderly. How the Irishman ended up in London nobody ever asked. He just showed up one day at The Theatre looking for work and just stood there waiting for it. He didn't say a word, just stood there, staring at them with those icy blue eyes from beneath that greasy black hair. Will Kemp liked him immediately and persuaded James Burbage to take him on, so they did, and their take at the gate improved precipitously.

"I suppose his Highness wants a private box in the galleries, complete with girls," said Jack. He really wasn't serious about the girls, although there was some talk that Henslowe and the grocer Cholmley were building a theatre on Bankside that would be connected to a brothel and a pastry shop that specialized in tarts. It was all about appetite, wasn't it? "That will be fifteen pence," he said making a quick count of the exiled kings' entourage.

The offended lordling brooded as deep as he could. "The Queen shall hear of this."

"I'm sure she will," said Jack holding out his hand. "You're holding up the queue. There are four of you, so that will be a groat a person, please and thank you."

There was some grumbling behind them. A true lord or lady would have never condescended to come in through the common gate.

Don Antonio whispered into Della Massa's ear and he nodded. It was in his job and nature to assess threat and danger, and the big black haired fellow with the cudgel set him ill at ease. In this crowd it would be nigh impossible to check a swing from that tree he carried.

"His Highness will take seats on stage," he whispered to the young lord. "Pay the man."

Some of the arrogance drained from his face, but there was pride in the request for the best seats in The Theatre.

"We will take seats on stage."

Jack gave an approving nod. "Very good; that usually costs a crown, but for you a quarter angel will do, please and thank you."

The young lord's face widened in disbelief; a world not possible had opened up before him. No commoner would ever cheat a lord back home. Before he could say anything Della Massa nudged him.

"Pay the man." To him it didn't really matter how much or how little was paid. The Theatre was an important place for Don Antonio to be seen. It would get him closer to the Queen, in a roundabout way. Even though they had been invited to Court, they were still only one of hundreds. They needed to move up on the hierarchical list and attain an audience.

Entrance paid, they moved past the big fellow with the cudgel and made their way to the stage.

Kit had seen the entire interaction between Jack and the men in black. They had caught his attention because, at first, he had thought they were some of the Lord Mayor's puritanical minions come to cause trouble with the opening of his play. That idea was dispelled when he was able to hear their accents through the rumble of the crowd.

The Don, he knew his face anyways; it was the man who stood beside Don Antonio that caused his fingers to grow cold. He had seen that face before. It was a face one wouldn't soon forget. The man had the face of predator, a hawk, whose stare gave the impression that he was deciding whether to kill you or disregard you. He had met many unsavory individuals, but this man interested him. There was a power there, a similar power he had tried to capture in Tamburlaine's ruthlessness. Maybe he had seen him when he was last in the Low Country.

Jack, seeing Kit, waved him over. "Clear the way, clear the way. Master Marlowe wants to get into the house."

"Who's Master Marlowe?" said a rough looking fellow with a tight fitting peasant cap on his head. He was next in line at the gate and his tone was resentful after being pushed aside by the Don and his entourage.

"Who's Master Marlowe?" said Jack in disbelief. "Jill, I do believe this bloke needs a bop on the head."

Jill smiled, not a pretty thing because of the scar rippled on the side of his face.

"Oh, Marlowe, of course, he's the playwright. By all means," said the fellow giving a little bow and patting Kit on the shoulder. "After you, by all means."

"That's better," said Jack pleasantly.

"I hope there's some violence in this one," complained a woman. "I saw one of Greene's plays...what was it?"

"Friar bung bottom and a side of bacon," laughed a man.

"It was about as entertaining as watching bacon fry," said another.

"Are they serving bacon? I heard someone say bacon," shouted a voice from a man who only heard part of what was said.

Soon the crowd was rumbling hungrily about the buns and bacon that were going to be served up during the performance.

Kit could imagine Richard's face going white. The last time they sold food, half of it ended up on stage. It was almost impossible for the actors to say their lines while being pelted by tomatoes. He had seen a French troop almost covered in salad, but they had asked for it. Who ever heard something as stupid as putting a woman on stage to play a woman.

"Is Kemp going to Jig?" shouted another woman lustily. "I do so enjoy his jigging."

The crowd laughed.

"Better get inside, quick," whispered Jack through his teeth. "This lot is going to turn ugly when I tell them the house is near full."

Kit ducked inside as if they had already started to throw food. "Thanks, Jack," and as he passed the big Irishman he said to him, "thanks Jill."

He couldn't help it but the lines leapt into his mind: 'Jack and Jill went to the gate to fetch a pail of coins, Jack stole them and Jill broke his crown with that tree he carried.' He would have to work on the idea later...second thought, maybe not. The last thing he needed was Will capering around with bells and a cudgel sabotaging his play.

Turning back to Jack, he said, "Have you seen George, George Silver and the Lady he accompanies?"

"He's inside. They say the Lady's face was burned in a fire, that's why she keeps it covered. Is it true?"

Kit thought about correcting him and was about to explain that she was anything but deformed, but thought better of it. She kept her face from the world for her own reasons and that was good enough for him, although their escapade at the Walk had all of London talking. He found her faerie like face strangely appealing.

He made his way up into the galleries to have a better look. From there he might be able to better locate George and Miao. He was used to crowds, but the press was making it difficult to move through. They really wanted to see his play, which thrilled him and at the same time terrified him.

"Meat Pies! Meat Pies!" came a shout from below. So, Richard had decided to sell food again. Then he saw them: George and Miao were sitting on stage. George was buying a pie. The man's appetite was legendary. It was a wonder he didn't weigh over five stone. The gentry and nobles sitting on the stage were buying nuts: not a good sign, because they often used them to pelt the groundlings who would then yell back at them, terribly distracting for the players. He also noticed that they were close to Don Antonio and his retinue. Kit made his way across the gallery and down the stairs that would bring him to the stage. He was about to step onto the stage when Ned and Richard, arguing as usual, saw him. They immediately closed on him.

Ned was dressed magnificently in the martial costume of Tamburlaine. He scowled at Kit. "Be gone with you! You know it's bad luck..."

"You don't need luck, Ned," laughed Kit knowing that the way to calm the actor down was through his hubris.

"No," responded Richard, "he just needs to stop bellowing all the time. I was just telling him that Tamburlaine needs nuances, depth."

Kit gave an inner groan. The only reason Richard was bringing this up now was to irritate Ned. Richard had wanted Ned's role, but James had decided (and Kit agreed) on a more seasoned actor.

"It's called projection. All must hear the pathos in my voice. It's the pathos that is heard above the curses of the groundlings and the condescension of the ones on the elevated stage. It's pathos that turns the day that makes a man a king. Don't you think so, Kit?

Ned was in good form, and he agreed with him, to a certain degree, but he also agreed with Richard. Ned could go over the top sometimes. Right now he needed to get on stage, close to George and Miao and he needed someone to get him there, and these two weren't going to do it.

"Richard, Ned, have you seen Shakes?"

Richard looked consigned to give Ned the argument for the sake of the play, which was good. "I think he's in the shadows with the spear holders. Have you ever read any of his stuff; he's quite good you know. I think we better be careful or Lord Strange may nab him. I hear the Queen's Men have raided him again."

Kit slipped off back stage. He couldn't count the number of times someone had tried to get him to read something they had written. He hated it, because mostly what he read, when he deigned to read at all, was rubbish. However, there was some truth to the Lord Strange bit. The Earl of Derby had not only been trying to get him to come over, but also Ned and Will. The Earle paid a lot more. It was something to seriously think about. The spear holders must have moved around to the other side because he couldn't find them. It did, however, provide him with an excellent view of George, Miao and the exiled king's entourage.

"Seems to be a full house."

The voice made him jump. It was Shakes appearing as if a trap door had just sprung him. How did he do that? He should be the one running messages. The man was full of surprizes, maybe he should read some of his work.

"Richard said you were looking for me?" Shakes was dressed in gold and black armour and held a round shield and a long spear. His eyes danced lively from behind the nose piece on his half helm.

Kit touched the pouch of coins he kept inside his doublet. He knew that Shakes was from Stratford, that he had a wife that had forced him into wedlock, that he had three children, one girl around five and twins only two years old, although he couldn't remember their names. He also knew Shakes had a keen eye. He also had the ability to fade into the background so that no one would notice him. His anonymity was a rare skill.

"Shakes, it occurs to me we have a lot in common. Your father is a glover while mine is a cobbler. We are the leather of our father's hands. Could you do me a favour?"

"Absolutely," responded Shakes when he felt the money Kit handed him.

"Can you get me onto the stage, a seat right beside George and Miao?"

Shakes twisted about and picked up a backless chair. He shrugged. "You're not the only one who wants last minute seating. Don't tell Cuthbert."

Kit hesitated.

"Come on. Do you want me to put you between our displaced Don and George?"

"Yes, are you sure there's enough space?"

Shakes winked at him. "When I set up the chairs I space them a little wide. Cuthbert hates it, but I tell him that it keeps tempers down if the wrong Lords get seated close to each other."

"Does it work?"

"I don't know. It sounded good when I made it up. It just gives me extra space to sell."

"You're not worried that I'll tell Cuthbert?"

Shakes seemed to be assessing him. He smiled again. "Not in the least." He held out the stool. "Shall we? The sooner I get you seated, the sooner I can sell another space."

Kit followed him onto the stage. They reached a space between Don Antonio and George. Shakes cleared his voice. His stage armour creaked when he bowed.

"Your Highness, I hope it is propitious to seat the playwright beside you?" asked Shakes.

This caught Don Antonio's ear and he turned his long, aristocratic face to regard Shakes. There was a flicker of interest in his eyes.

"The playwright...Christopher Marlowe? This is he? Yes, yes, it would indeed be propitious."

Kit sat down on the chair and Shakes withdrew into the shadows. If he handled a quill as well as he made money, his writing would bare consideration. If Richard thought the writing was good, maybe it was. He was now at shoulders with George and Don Antonio.

"Good day, Kit," said George finishing off his meat pie and wiping the crumbs out of his beard. He kept it neatly trimmed. "Lady, look it's our favourite playwright."

"I'm the only playwright you know," said Kit wryly.

George laughed.

Miao leaned across George and extended a pale hand to touch Kit's. "Good to see you, Kit."

Kit felt an electric shock when her fingers made contact with his hand, and a momentary sense of sadness when she withdrew. She had her hood up to hide her features. He also noticed that none of the gentry on the stage had said anything about it. George's reputation went before him.

"I want to thank you," said Kit.

"For what?"

"For stopping Kemp from turning my play into a farce of rude jokes, songs and jigs."

"He's still going to do that anyways; the crowd loves it."

"In the epilogue, I don't really care, but if they let him, he'd do it throughout the entire play."

"I could see where that could become a problem. I'm partial to sword play when you want attention. Sometimes I miss instructing."

"You're going back to teaching?" asked Kit.

"No, I'm done with that."

Kit noticed that Don Antonio was listening keenly to their conversation even though he pretended he wasn't. This couldn't have worked out better. He reached into his doublet, pulled out a long, white letter and handed it to Miao.

"My Lady."

Miao took the letter and looked at the seal on the back. It was the Queen's own royal mark. She broke it and began to read. It was in the hand of Lord Burghley and was cordially inviting them to Court after the Queen was back from the Maundy Ceremony at Windsor Castle. She handed the letter to George.

"It seems that the Walk at St. Paul's has garnered royal attention."

"Hah," laughed George, "and you thought we were going to get arrested."

"Everyone who helped us was," reminded Miao.

"Yes, well, we got them out didn't we?"

Don Antonio could not maintain his aristocratic reserve any more. Here, beside him was not only the contentious playwright, but the couple that had caused such a stir at The Walk. He had seen the duel with the Italian sword master (if duel it could be called), and had also been entranced by the white Lady who had accompanied him. Like the centre piece in the crown jewels, she outshone the rest of the women at the Walk. The colours she had chosen to wear had created a stir at Court. Perhaps, if he got closer to these two his diplomatic value would rise in the eyes of the Queen: value through association.

"Might I introduce myself," began Don Antonio in a slow lazy drawl of his best English. "I am Don Antonio, the Prior of Crato, the rightful King of Portugal." He did not extend his hand. He might have done so to the Lady, but the two men beside him were from common, although exceptional, stock.

George, always a bull with etiquette, reached over and grabbed the Don's hand anyways. He pumped the hand vigorously. Kit sat back as to not get in the way but failed. Their arms bumped against his chest.

"Pleased to meet you, your Highness. May I introduce you to Lady Juzheng, cousin to the Emperor of the Middle Kingdom."

Since they were still seated they exchanged polite nods.

"I must apologize," said Antonio to Miao, "for the dreadful weather of this place. Back in my realm, I could introduce you to the brilliance of a golden sun."

Miao smiled grimly inside her hood. She was not amused because the images of dead slaves were standing before her eyes. "I know something of the hospitality of the Portuguese, and the sun burns those who are not wary."

Don Antonio looked confused, but soon figured out that she was insulting him.

Della Massa's hand slipped down to the hilt guard of his sword. He began to caress it. When he found out that the playwright was also the messenger, he had become alert. Baines had not necessarily lied to him. He had said he would 'take care' of the messenger. Double agents could be lethal to both sides.

George had instinctively noticed the man's smooth, lethal motion. Behind the cool exterior he could smell a man who had killed. He also let his hand fall to his blade. This could turn violent very quickly. He had never seen Miao so angry.

Kit felt as though he was caught between two thunder clouds ready to collide, but there was no rumbling. That was its nature, when it was the quietest it was the most lethal. One part of him was terrified, the other, fascinated. How, if possible, could he portray that in a play? Richard was right; the bombast of Ned would only go so far, just as far as the vulgar songs of Will. There was depth here yet to plumb. Then Kit's survival instincts kicked in.

"Your Highness, you must forgive, the Lady comes to this land via the circuitous route of a Portuguese slaver."

The tightness in Don Antonio's neck relaxed and he gave an understanding nod.

Della Massa's hand fell away from the guard of his sword to caress the leg of his chair.

George also relaxed. The moment was past and would likely not return. The future was a different thing.

"Yes, slavery is a pernicious habit that I find offensive. It is a trade I promise to end when I regain my crown."

Miao read the Don as his ethereal symbols appeared. Around his head were burning ships, men dying and drowning, a staff of a pilgrim and the ratty cloak of the dispossessed. She knew with a surety

139

then that Don Antonio, the Prior of Crato, the exiled King of Portugal, would never regain his throne.

"Thank you," was all she said, because what do you tell a man who is doomed to fail.

George felt the need to find out more about the man he had almost fought. It was his soldier's instincts: get to know your enemy before your enemy kills you.

"Your man there, your Highness, I could not help but notice his sword." George wanted to make sure that he had been aware. He had noticed a peculiar design on the hilt and the blue hue to the tiny section of the blade he had seen. "Is it Damascus steel?"

Miao shifted.

Don Antonio betrayed a flicker of interest beyond the wall of formality and status. "I have noticed that you have not introduced yourself."

"Oh," laughed George, "I'm just George, George Silver, no title, no lands, just a humble old soldier."

The tremulous beginnings of a smile threatened to break the thin line of the Don's mouth. "Indeed, I saw you duel at The Walk."

"Duel? That wasn't a duel, your Highness. A true duel is where the outcome is undecided."

"I think you boast?" said the young fop on the other side of Della Massa.

"He does not boast," corrected Della Massa speaking coldly. It was obvious he held the young man in no esteem whatsoever. "He merely tells it as it is." He looked indifferently at George with the lazy glare of a predator.

There it is, thought George. He wants me to know that he is doing exactly what I am doing. He is beginning to explore for my weaknesses. Miao had mentioned a blue blade in her vision belonging to one of the murderers.

"Do you wish to see the blade?" offered Della Massa.

On the surface it seemed a polite question, but what he was really saying was: 'do you want to see the sword I will kill you with.' It was the common tongue of the soldier. He had just been issued a challenge, in a very friendly way, but still, a challenge. George would indeed like to have a look at a blade made from the fabled Damascus steel. It was a rare thing to see a sword made from that material. The best European smiths could do was imitate the look of the metal by imbedding filigree work onto the blade, but those were just etchings and did not imbue the steel with any of the fabled strength or sharpness.

"Don't mind if I do."

Della Massa stood up and pulled the sword out in a forward motion. For a moment the point of the sword hovered before George's chest. Then the weapon was reversed and he took the sword by the hilt.

George examined the beautiful banding and mottling reminiscent of flowing water in the blade. That was the thing; it was in the blade, not scratched on it. The blade held an edge better than any he had seen. He noticed that the sword was not specifically a rapier, although it had the long characteristics of one. It was more of a cross between a rapier and a long sword, but while a long sword required two hands to wield it, this sword needed only one. This made it all the more dangerous. Any attempts by European smiths to duplicate Damascus steel had failed. The lives of men taken were written into the wave pattern. He handed the blade back. There was something about the blade he couldn't put his finger on, but strangely enough, the sight of it was familiar to him.

"An amazing sword, wootz steel I take it?"

Della Massa gave a respectful nod, and took the sword back, but it was obvious the man did not want to talk anymore.

"Alcazarquivir, the battle of the Three Kings," said Don Antonio gravely. "There is the answer where the blade comes from."

"I am not familiar with that battle," lied George. Most soldiers were familiar with the debacle.

Distaste touched Don Antonio's face. "I curse the name of Abu Abdallah Mohammad. I curse his murderous, usurping uncle Abd Al-Malik, but I loved King Sebastian, may he return."

"May he return," murmured Della Massa and the other two Portuguese lords that were listening intently. There was still a strong sentiment that the youthful, charismatic Sebastian would return and put all pretenders to rout.

"Sebastian," said Don Antonio, "is how do you say...he is our King Arthur."

"I'm not Welsh," said George not bothering to tell him that he was descended from Angle-Saxon peasantry, although he wondered what expression that would evoke on the Don's face. He saw how he ignored the groundlings, as though they were the stuff to be scraped from the bottom of his foot. It was just as well, because Don Antonio continued.

"I was taken prisoner."

George's opinion of Antonio increased precipitously. He had always admired survivors of battles. It got him thinking of the position of luck and skill, which one truly mattered. Some very skillful men were killed moments into an engagement, while those with little skill lived, seemingly immune to the flying balls propelled by flashing ordinance and the slash and jabs of sharpened steel. He surmised that the Don's man, Berto, like him, was a rare creature of both. Before George could respond, Miao did.

She bowed her head forward as in acknowledgement for the man's suffering. "I am sorry for that."

The apology broke Don Antonio out of his melancholy reverie and he laughed. "I escaped by pretending I was a knight with only a papal promise, with no lands to support me. Had the truth been known, I most likely would still be in Morocco or the guest of the most gracious Turks." He shifted his focus to Kit. "This Tamburlaine, I am he."

That caught Kit a little off balance. He ran through his mind a quick comparison. No, Don Antonio wasn't Tamburlaine. The only likeness was that Don Antonio had a taste of being king, while his Tamburlaine rose to become emperor. Perhaps Don Antonio should have said he had the ambition of Tamburlaine, or the delusion of Tamburlaine, but no, he was not Tamburlaine. Instead he said: "Your Highness honours me by saying so."

A blast of a horn announced that the players were ready to begin the play. They needed something loud to get the groundlings and the stagelords to settle down. Will wanted to use a blast of cannon fire, but the Burbage brothers nixed him saying that one spark on the thatch roofing would mark an end to them all.

George Bryan and Philippe Augustine strode onto stage and the play started, their voices ringing out over the crowd. Kit noticed Richard still trying to count heads, figuring out what the show's take was: each groundling was a penny and each stagelord was a groat...the greatest worry Kit had was that if his play was keeping and holding the attention of the audience.

Then about half-way through, the interlude came. George and Richard met at centre stage with swords drawn. Don Antonio leaned forward into Kit's space and whispered.

"What is this? It does not fit within the context of the play..."

"We needed to give Ned's voice a break," explained Kit, "so we worked in this interlude."

"Ah," said Don Antonio. "Ingenious."

"Actually," continued Kit. "It's a bit I'm working on for another play. I wanted to see if it was possible for two men to kill each other simultaneously on stage and for it to look real."

"A Senecan blood bath?" suggested Don Antonio.

"No, not really; the actors live."

"Too bad," said Della Massa with a cold, agitated voice. Obviously he didn't like theatre.

George decided to take the bait. "The play offends you, sir?"

Della Massa regarded George with cold eyes. "The waste of my time offends me – sir."

Don Antonio laughed. "I wish to watch this duel first, please. You say this has not been done?"

Kit felt the tension between Della Massa and George abate slightly. Being between the two swordsmen was not such a great place to be.

Kit tried to ignore them. "Yes, dueling on stage...most action, as you have noticed takes place off stage. The actors try to relay the conflict through their language, but I wanted to see how the audience would respond to real engagement."

"Good, good. I despise jigs."

Kit felt a sudden kinship with the exiled King. "So do I, although the groundlings love them."

"Corp Di Dio," swore Don Antonio passionately, "does one mix the sweet with the sour?"

Miao entered the conversation again. She had been listening very closely and had noticed the tenseness in George. Even though he remained nearly stationary, she had never seen him so agitated. He definitely did not like the man named Della Massa; neither did she, especially since he was one of the murderers they were hunting. He could be no other. The owner of the blue sword was one of the murderers. Death was a natural thing, ending a person's course of life, but she sensed a different type of death around him. It was as

144

though he had become death, which was an offence to the Way. "Only one very skilled does that, mixes the sweet with the sour."

Don Antonio gave Miao a pensive look; then after a moment said: "Yes, my mistake, you are right. We will examine this work."

Richard and George began their duel and the clash of metal on metal rang out over the silence of the audience. This would be good, thought Kit – or bad. Either they would cheer or they would rain down a shower of rotten produce smuggled into the theatre. James Burbage didn't care what they brought into his theatre, as long as they paid.

Kit felt the fleshy prickles on the back of his neck and he reached up to rub the chill away. That was when he noticed someone behind George, stooping to whisper something in his ear. It was Shakes, no longer dressed in his armour; he was attired in plain, black hose and doublet. George was saying something back to him because there was a hesitation, but then a very slight nod.

The duel reached its climatic point where both combatants skewered each other. They both fell like boneless fishes onto the stage, twitched a bit and then were still. Kit waited for the whistles and the shouts, and the flying, rotten produce, but instead came a tumult of cheers.

Shakes and a couple other stagehands moved between Don Antonio and Della Massa to fetch the bodies from off the stage as the crowd continued to cheer. In the process, Shakes did something uncharacteristic of him; he was usually very agile, but he bumped up against Della Massa. Instinctively, the man reached for his sword and stood up turning on the bewildered Shakes.

"Fool!"

Don Antonio gave his man his characteristic bored look. "Berto, sit down. He is just going to retrieve the bodies."

Della Massa gave a terse nod and slammed the blade back into its scabbard. It gave an ominous 'snicking' sound, as he sat back down, a calm coolness replacing the sudden, mercurial response.

As they struggled to pull the bodies to the back of the stage someone shouted. "Are they really dead?" The crowd laughed in response.

Another responded, "Hope so."

Death was such a common occurrence that it was sometimes deemed the subject of much humour.

George leaned into Kit and whispered. "I think we should leave."

Kit nodded and made to rise.

"What, you are leaving?" came the cool voice of the Don. "You have not seen the finish."

"I know how it ends," replied Kit not wanting to sound too glib. "I just wanted to be assured it was received well. Now, I can be at rest."

Don Antonio noticed that George and Miao had also risen. His eyebrows rose questioningly, but he didn't say anything. He turned his attention back to the stage where the play had picked up again. Ned was doing his best to bellow down the groundlings who were still juiced up from the duel.

Kit met George and Miao in the tiring room surrounded by costumes. It was the one place that they could be sure to be alone.

"Are you insane," began Kit, "telling Shakes to bump into that lying killer?"

Miao reached up and pulled her hood off. She tilted her head to the side to get a better image of Kit. "That was me."

Shakes bustled into the room where the three stood, the costumes hanging about them. His face was flushed with excitement. He fumbled at something in his doublet and pulled out a crumpled piece of paper. He handed it to George.

"You were right, that fellow had something in his pocket."

"You're all mad," ejaculated Kit. "The man is a killer."

"In more ways than name," said Miao taking the drawing. She looked at the charcoal drawing of not a young woman, but of the Queen. She showed George, Kit and Shakes.

"That's the Queen," said Kit in bewilderment.

Every drawing in the collection at Lotus House resembled the Queen. The murdered women had looked like the Queen at different ages, some young, some middle aged, but this drawing was as the Queen was now.

"I'm afraid it is," said Miao.

"What's that Berto fellow doing with it?" asked Shakes.

Kit looked irritated. "His name isn't Berto Della Massa."

George didn't look surprised. "I didn't think so."

"No," continued Kit. "That name was invented by Giovanni Boccaccio. It's from the Decameron, a book of stories, much like the Canterbury tales except more bawdy."

"Who is Berto?" asked Shakes.

Kit shrugged. "I don't know, but he is definitely not the monk who disguises himself as the angel Gabriel to seduce a Lady."

Miao shook her head. "No, he is not, but he is an angel, an angel of death; it is written on him."

They had identified one of the murderers; the problem was they still had to find the other.

Chapter Fourteen: Meeting the Spider

Kit led George and Miao down the familiar dark hallway. He had been down it a number of times and each time it was like taking a passage to another world, a world where it was difficult, if not impossible, to know the truth from designed lies. One thing was sure, at the far end of the hall there would be manipulation.

"Are you sure this is necessary?" growled George. He was feeling the threat in the hall.

"If you want to get into Court, you have to pass the final test."

"Test?" asked Miao.

Kit kept taking covert glances at her. In the dark, with her hood down, she looked rather luminescent. It was her white hair and pale complexion that transfixed him, the exotic nature of her features, as though she was not of this world, but of the Court of Faerie. That was usually Edmund Spencer's thing; Kit was more interested in heaven and hell, of things divine and profane. That was it; she was divine almost like an angel. Doctor Dee, with his scryer Edward Kelly, believed he could talk to angels. He had met the man only once, but he had seen some ideas that he had been kicking around. He wondered what would happen if a mortal made a pact with a being supernatural.

"Yes, well, more approval. Sir Francis Walsingham, he is the master puppeteer. With one hand he makes half the night dance."

"And with his other hand?" asked Miao.

"He waves it and the gold appears to pay his puppets."

George gave his characteristic barking laugh. "Now that's a hand I'd like to shake."

Miao had noticed something about Kit as they walked down the hall. There were lines coming from him, ethereal lines connected to him but waving off into the air.

"And does he pull your strings?" she asked.

Kit averted his eyes afraid that she might not see the truth in them. At times, because she seemed never to be looking directly at anyone, she gave the impression that she wasn't examining them. But it was the things she said, which indicated otherwise. Fortunately they reached the end of the hall.

"Look," he said, "we're here."

"Appears so," said George relishing Kit's awkwardness around Miao.

He rapped on the door – two short and one long. The door opened and the gimlet eyes of Arthur Gregory emerged in the door's crack to examine them. He gave a grunt and the door swung in.

Arthur's little weasel like face was split in a brown toothed grin. "Ah, the young lady is here, with her escort, excellent. Please come in."

Miao stepped into the room but Arthur held up his hand to stop Kit and George. "Only the young lady, please."

"I go where she goes," growled George.

"Not this time, I am sorry," said Arthur sincerely compassionate but nevertheless shutting the door on them.

George looked at Kit. "So, what would happen if I broke the door down?"

Kit cleared his throat. "Imagine the worst fight you've ever been in: now, imagine not being able to see your assailants."

"Right, I think we'll wait out here."

Miao found herself in the presence of one of the most formidable men she had ever met. Arthur melted away, but the thickness of energy around the form seated at the paper festooned desk was palpable. She felt the urge to reach out and touch it, but thought better of it. There were also colours there, a myriad of them swirling in a dynamic aura about the man. She also knew that he was nearing the end of his life. Whether it was one, or two or three years he had left, she didn't know, but she could see it about him. She forcibly shut the vision away and focused on the physicality of the man. He reminded her of Old Lao.

Walsingham stuck the quill he was using into the apple on his desk and stood up. There was a congeniality about him that made her immediately at ease.

"Please, please," he smiled, a smile of honesty, totally devoid of guile. "Arthur, could you please get the Lady Juzheng a chair."

Miao had thought that Arthur had gone, but he had not. So great her focus had been on Walsingham that the little man had disappeared from her mind. She heard the chair scraping as it was dragged across the floor and she sat down without looking.

"No man's head should be above that of the Emperor," she said.

Walsingham sat down and laughed. "Emperor, heaven forbid. Me? I am just a servant intent on the security of the realm."

Miao sensed truth in the man and decided to be equally direct. "Why do you have no chairs, other than yours?"

"Ah, yes. You know you are the first person to ask me that. Most people are too afraid, or are too embroiled in the game."

"The game?"

"The game of shadows, of secrecy, of information, or too focused on the gold I'm going to dole out. I find people tend to be terrible liars if they have to stand," explained Walsingham.

"And you are not afraid of me lying?"

"No, no, not at all; as soon as I saw you I knew you would be truthful."

Miao shook her shoulders and bowed her head slightly. "You do me a great honour by saying so."

"No, no, the honour is all mine. Now, down to business, if you don't mind. I understand you have been invited to Court by Lord Burghley and therefore the Queen herself." It was more a statement than a question.

"Yes."

"It is also said that you can see the future?" Even though his voice still maintained a grandfatherly timbre, the question was meant to dig.

Miao shifted, feeling the beginnings of discomfort. This man was indeed like Old Lao and could see into the very soul. "I see directions and sometimes symbols."

"Directions, symbols, that is very good. Some say the future is the dominion of God and to tamper with such is the work of witchcraft."

Even though the voice was still friendly, there was possible danger here, depending on how she answered.

"I know nothing of these witches. Are they creatures so fearsome?"

"There is less danger in fearing too much than too little," explained Walsingham.

"I do not think I am a witch."

"No doubt you are not. However, you are a very special young woman, and these abilities, which I have no doubt are very real, may put you in grave danger at Court."

"How?" asked Miao moving to the edge of her seat.

"There are those at Court, as in the Privy Council who see witchcraft in the very air we breathe. Have you heard of the esteemed Doctor John Dee?"

"Yes, Kit has mentioned him."

"Yes, I see. Well, before he fled to the continent, he was the Queen's astrologer, and friend. Even with her favour the libel of witchcraft reached him. I warned him to flee. He took my advice and is still alive. Let me give you my advice, because I am inclined to permit you access to Court."

"I thought it was the Queen who did that."

"She does," however, "she often asks me what I think, and I am brutally honest with my thoughts, as is her fool, as is Lord Burghley." Walsingham gave himself a self-deprecating smile.

"No, you are mistaken. You are no fool."

"Nevertheless, while at Court do not reveal your ability to anyone, except the Queen. In this little moment I have decided to like you."

"And I you." He was indeed a likeable man, however, there was a ruthlessness to his aura that made her wary. She did not like to think about what would happen if she disappointed this man.

Walsingham rubbed his hands together excitedly. "Perfect, perfect. If you should accept, you will be placed under the protection of the Queen herself."

Miao hesitated. She was already under the protection of Sir Water. Did this new acceptance mean she would have to leave Lotus House and live at Court? What would happen to George? Would he be allowed to come to Court as well? She had not thought things would go so quickly, but she was grateful that they had, because there was a murderer to catch, and she suspected this woman was at Court.

"You hesitate," said Walsingham.

"I do. I am not sure what being under the Queen's protection means? What roll will my benefactor play in this?"

Walsingham gave a terse, commanding nod. "Sir Walter Raleigh's benefactor is also the Queen, without her he would be nothing more than a philandering adventurer."

Miao felt suddenly silly. Here was a man offering her everything she needed in order to catch the killer and here she was indecisive as a sunny, London day.

Still, she felt she needed an anchor. "Will I be able to remain at Lotus House?"

"Lotus...oh, you mean the little town house Raleigh has you boarded up in, down by the Three Cranes? Of course, Doctor Dee lived at his cottage at Mort Lake. In fact I would recommend it, separating yourself physically form Court; your mind will need it."

"Then I will accept. When do I go to Court?"

"Well, the Queen has the Maundy ceremony to conduct at Windsor. I would say she would be happy to receive you after she comes back to London. Usually she proceeds to her other palaces, but times being the way they are...she does not want to be far from London."

Then he looked at her soberly, as though he had just remembered something he had forgotten. "You understand who the Queen is, don't you?"

She considered the question and the mentored words of Old Lao came into her head: "It is said, 'Of old, these came to be in the possession of the One: Heaven in the virtue of the One is Limpid; Earth in the virtue of the One is settled; Gods in the virtue of the One have their potencies; The Valley in the virtue of the One is full; The myriad creatures in the virtue of the One are alive; Lords and princes in virtue of the One become leaders in the empire.'"

Walsingham stared at her in quiet shock. He pursed his lips. He had been afraid of this. The girl's understanding of Western Monarchy was distinctly lacking, or perhaps his understanding of Eastern Mysticism was; either way, he needed to provide some clarification on this before someone started crying 'witch, burn the witch!'

"Right," he began, folding his hands. "The Queen is the Supreme Governor of the Church of England; her father was the Supreme Head. She may require you to take an oath. If you do not, you can be charged with treason, which may, at the very least, mean your head. Do you understand?"

Miao nodded gravely. The English seemed to be particularly fond of removing heads from their owner's necks. "A young woman lost her head on the Southwark Gatehouse the other night, a woman who bore a likeness to the Queen."

Walsingham shook his head gravely. "I know; this is another reason why I am permitting personal access to the Queen. You see, you are chasing a murderer whom I believe is ensconced within the Queen's own Privy Chamber."

"One of her ladies in waiting?"

"Perhaps, but I am not sure. The Queen holds each one of her Ladies with extreme care, and the fact that they all come from great houses, makes it very hard to broach the idea with her Highness. You can understand my predicament."

"I do." It was then that Miao decided that if she needed to take an oath, she would, but before doing so, she had to express her own personal belief. "There is a thing in the Middle Kingdom called the Mandate of Heaven: It gives the people the right to depose a ruler if the ruler does not follow the rule of good government."

Walsingham's sudden concern showed in the tightness of his face as he considered her words. Then the tension deflated with a sigh. "In all the years of service, The Queen has held the care and dedication to her people above all else. She is without reproach."

"I do not believe in many things that you believe," explained Miao. For some reason she wanted to be perfectly clear before she committed to this man. "Do you understand the Tao?" It was a test question, to explore the depths of his soul: to see if he could suspend his belief. If he could, then maybe she could trust him.

154

His face brightened markedly as though he had just been presented with a favourite puzzle. "Yes, the Tao. I have read the work, the Tao de Ching, by Lao Tzu. There is some debate whether he even existed."

"Did you understand his writings?" she probed.

"I don't think they were meant to be understood, not with the mind anyways," said Walsingham.

For Miao that was the right answer. "If your Queen asks me, I will swear, but what I will be swearing to will be more than she might understand."

He rubbed his hands again. "She might surprise you. Excellent. Now, to a more practical topic: do you practice the mystical science of astrology?"

"No, I am not skilled that way." She found the animals and planets befuddling. "Sometimes, when I look, I can see things around the person, indications of what may happen. It is not always reliable."

"Not reliable?" he suddenly looked worried.

"But I can also tell things when I touch a person's face." This had come to her in a moment of play, when she had been touching a girl's face. Suddenly she saw things that had scared her.

"Will you touch mine?" asked Walsingham.

"Yes," she said.

Walsingham moved his chair around to the front of his desk so that he could be closer to her.

Miao extended her fingers and began to feel his face. "You will have to remove your hat."

Walsingham removed the black cap he characteristically wore.

She felt his face, starting at the top and working down to the bottom. There were things there, hidden in the creases, caused by worry and care. There were also, as with anyone's life, things intensely private. It didn't matter if the bottom of his face was covered in a beard; she could feel through it. She took a deep, calming breath and began to tell him what she felt.

"In the lines of the top part of your face are written the days of your youth. You were one of seven. Your father died when you were young and this scared your soul. There is much sadness there. The middle part is for your middle age: Law was important to you, but you had to flee. There is a terrible woman. You learn the art of protest and then you return and dedicate your life to service. There is much, much more, but you love your children whether of your body or not. The lower part is for your old age..." Miao couldn't help herself so she laughed.

"What, what's so funny?"

"Your whiskers, they feel like the bristles of a broom."

"Sometimes I feel that I sweep the floor with my face."

She continued to feel his face through his beard. "I notice that most men hide their deeds by wearing beards: the more deeds, the thicker the beard."

"The Queen likes beards," explained Walsingham. "I suppose if this was Rome then we all would be sans beards. Lead on, what do you see?"

"I do not think you are led by anyone except by your love for your Queen. You prepare for war, for an arrival of a great fleet. One word comes up – Cadiz." She suddenly withdrew her hands from the old man she was becoming quickly fond of. She found it hard to imagine why so many people were so terrified of him. "I will not speak of your death."

Walsingham bolted out of his chair and began to pace furiously through the room, hands clasped tightly behind his back. He was obviously disturbed.

He talked more to himself than her. "The facts of my youth, my middle age, even my old age can be found out, or guessed at, but not Cadiz. No one but Drake and I know about Cadiz." He turned on her. "So, the question is, what and how do you know about Cadiz?" There was a fierce intensity in his voice that promised wrath and she began to understand the respect this man garnered.

"Of Cadiz I know nothing except the name. I don't even know what it is. I just sense that the future hinges on this word," explained Miao so succinctly that it calmed Walsingham's obvious agitation.

He gazed at her so searchingly that it again made her uneasy. Then after what seemed a long while, he gave an approving humph. "I have never met one like the Queen until today. I will do something with you that I have an exceeding rarity of doing – I will trust you."

"I thank you."

"I would not be so quick to thank. This game of shadows does not lend itself to friendship, but in you, I perceive a friend. You will no doubt make an impression on the Queen, and she on you."

Chapter Fifteen: Shooting the bridge

George felt the keen edge of hunger. He had spent a lot of his life hungry. When he was a child, it seemed he was hungry all the time. As a man, when he had wealth, he forced himself to go hungry when he could afford to eat his choice of foods. He was wise to recognize in himself that his hunger was for discipline and not consumables. In the end, the waiting did make everything so much more enjoyable.

He sliced through a nice piece of Stinking Bishop cheese and tore off a big chunk of bread from a loaf. Warm vapour rose up from the bread. He liked it that way, nice and hot. He examined the big jug of beer on the table with relish. He noticed that his charge showed no such excitement. She was stooped over the small trestle table examining the pictures they had taken from the dead girls. He took a bite of the cheese and then the bread and chewed.

"How can you see anything like that? Your nose is almost touching the paper."

Miao continued to examine one picture after the other. She would touch each one tenderly as if trying to summon the identity of the artist with her fingers. "Chew before you talk, George; you're easier to understand that way."

George took a big swig of beer. "Ah, that's good. You should eat. You're wasting away to nothing. A stiff breeze might knock you over."

"I thought you knew I was made of sterner stuff," she said trying not to be distracted from examining the pictures.

He continued to chew and talk. "That you are, that you are. Listen, the Old Raven told you that he suspects one of the Ladies attending the Queen."

"He suspects. Even Sir Francis Walsingham can be wrong."

"You're not going to find the killer looking at those pictures."

Miao looked up irritated, consternation on her features. "Well, what do you suggest I do? I won't be able to go to Court until after the Maundy Ceremony."

George waved his fingers, summoning a drawing to his side of the table. He licked his fingers before smoothing it out. "Let me have a look at this." It was the last drawing that had been scrunched up and thrust into the victim's mouth. There was a bit of dried blood on it. So, what do we know?"

"All were women," offered Miao.

"All had stunning red hair, like the Queen," added George.

"Walsingham has a suspicion that the one responsible for the murders was a woman close to the Queen," commented Miao.

George gave a characteristic humph, shoved the drawing back across the table and took another pull on his beer. He belched.

158

"More's the reason for us to go about this surreptitiously: offend one of the great families and we will be wearing our guts for garters."

Miao had become used to George's Bacchus tendencies while eating; indeed she almost didn't notice them. "The question I want answered is why?"

George barked out a laugh. "Don't expect the killer to think like you. You might say oh, how terrible, these killings, but in the killers' minds they are justified. There's a deep seated hatred in the killings, an almost tender intimacy. Through the eyes, the artist touches the very soul of the subject."

"Who said that? It sounds almost poetic," said Miao rather surprised at George's words.

"I did, just now," laughed George stuffing some more cheese into his mouth.

Miao winced and crinkled her nose. "The man does the killing, but the woman, she organizes it. She is as guilty, if not more guilty than the man. I just have a hard time believing a woman is capable of this."

"I've known some pretty bloody women. Did I ever tell you about the girl who disguised herself as a man? I trained her. I saw her fight in the Low Country. We called him, or I should say, her, Sweet Bloody Robin. Hand to hand she was as ruthless as any man. She went right for the knackers."

"Who of the Queen's Glories would do this? And why?"

George ruminated over this while he chewed. "Good question." An idea lit up his face. "Since we know that one of the killers is that Portuguese bugger, maybe he'll lead us to her."

"The man you almost dueled at the play?"

George nodded continuing to chew. "Wouldn't have come to that; we were just feeling each other out."

"Berto Della Massa? I've had my thoughts about him."

Then an icy draft seemed to blow into the room in which they were sitting. Miao looked up, her eyes wide in disbelief of the idea she had just awoken to. "Do you think it was any of her Glories? Or maybe even the Queen herself."

George let drop the piece of cheese he had in his fingers to the table. He gaped at her. "No, no, don't even consider that. If it was then why would Walsingham let us into Court?"

Miao shrugged. "I don't know, but what if he knows that the woman behind the killing is the Queen. George, would Walsingham sacrifice someone to protect the Queen?"

A wide owl like expression dominated George's face. "In a trice. He would sacrifice an entire legion of red haired women for the Queen, even us. But sorry, I just don't see the Queen teaming up with someone like Della Massa. Her taste in men tends towards men like Sir Water. They can be ruthless, but they're fair men, no guile in them."

"Everything leads to Court," ruminated Miao.

"All right, then, let's just entertain this unreasonable assumption of yours. If the Queen is the killer, then why would you get invited to Court?"

Miao shrugged. It was a rather strange assumption. "But the red hair..."

"Have you ever seen the Queen's Glories? Half of them have red hair. It's almost as if she picks them because of their hair..." he stopped because she was giving him an 'I told you so,' look.

Their argument was broken up by the sharp pounding at the front door. George gave her a quick look. Miao froze, but George silently guided her. Quickly she gathered up the drawings on the table and stuffed them under the table where there was a hidden ledge. George ever resourceful, ever ready, had planned for this. He immediately knew the intent in the pounding at the door, and knew that the men outside were not their friends.

"Just follow my lead. Do exactly as I tell you. Go to the stairs, just out of sight."

Miao gave him a frightened nod of her head.

In one hand, George, grabbed what was left of the cheese and in the other, the stein of beer. While on campaign on the continent, he had gotten into the habit of drinking his beer out of a stein. Not only could it hold a lot, it could also be a formidable weapon. He had even taught Miao a few lessons in close quarters Inn brawling, just for fun. George swung the door in just as the man's fist was descending on the door again. This caught the man by surprise. There were five of them, and by their dark, feral looks, their intent wasn't good. They were also armed with daggers and swords. He eyed them jovially.

"Lady Juzheng," he called out, it's the Queen's men, and I don't think Tarlton is with them. We've been expecting you, come in, come in."

The men who had been tense with the intent of violence became suddenly confused by George's congeniality and entered cautiously.

"Lady, please, you'll have to dress accordingly for Court. Gentlemen, would you consider a drink. I have some nice, brown ale: ale in a pot to fortify you against the night."

George ushered the villainous men to the table where he quickly dished out a wooden pot and sloshed some ale onto them. Had he been a bit slower it would not have worked, but his speed was startling. He apologized for the Lady's tardiness and leapt up the stairs to fetch her.

Miao knowing something was wrong had prepared herself to leave and was cloaked. The grim look on George's face when he entered the room confirmed her suspicions.

161

"They're not here to take us to Court, are they?"

George shook his head. "At this hour, no, and those aren't the Queen's men. I don't know who they are, but they mean us ill. I've amused them for a moment. I suggest we make our departure out the front window."

Always one for contingency plans, George moved stealthily to the window, opened it and tossed the knotted rope out. In the beginning, when George first began to ward her, she had thought George was just of a nervous nature, but she soon realized his preparedness was an ingrained way of survival. His axiom was 'never go into a place without at least two exits.'

George slipped out the window and down to the street where he waited for Miao. Along with sword play, he had also taught her to climb ropes and found her an apt student. No sooner had Miao's feet touched the cobble stones then the twisted face of one of the men peered out the window and yelled something down at them in Portuguese.

George slid to the side of the doorway, and as the door opened, he hit the first man to burst out into the street, rapier drawn, on the back of the head with the hilt of his dagger. The man fell causing the second to stumble over him. Dealing with one assailant was easy, but there were four of them, and those were odds he didn't fancy. Grabbing Miao by the arm they ran off into the night.

Down the street they ran. Miao had practiced this route many times until George was satisfied that she could make it with her eyes closed. George was quite fastidious and exacting in his training. The fact that they had been forced to flee this way concerned her. It smelled wrong. She knew her protector would have preferred to have stayed and fought, but he was doing this for her. They turned left, then right, made a long slog down a filth laden street to the river, and eventually came to the wharf where (they hoped) there were still a few boats still working. Most wherrys at this time of night had been taken out of the water.

"We could have fought," she said.

"We could have," grunted George. "Where's your sword?"

She felt her side and of course it wasn't there.

He looked at her reproachfully. "Exactly, and when you can remember to have your weapons on you all the time, we will fight, all right?"

Miao took the reproof to heart and nodded. "All right; do you think there will be any boats?"

"Plenty," said George. There were plenty of boats of all types on the river, waiting for the business of the next day. They were all moored, some at dock, but there were no wherrys: the little personal transportation boats that effectively plied the water during the day. "Just not the right type."

Around the corner they were able to see the crib work for one of the Quays. A despondent feeling took them as they searched, but then their emotions leaped. Someone had left a wherry gently pulled up on the bank. It was as though the owner had just arrived and left it there for someone to steal. Who would do that? George reached the wherry first to see if it had oars. Then someone stepped out of the shadows of a building and waved his arms at them.

Even at that distance, Miao could recognize Kit; she had memorized his mannerisms. He waved his hand in a very particular way where he twisted his wrist and dipped his arm. He ran up to them panting. He looked over his shoulder and another man limping on a wooden leg came hobbling out of the shadows. The wherryman directed them into the boat and pushed it free from the bank. Slipping onto his seat, he began to row them out onto the river and amongst the wooden hulks of the stationary boats.

"I followed them," said Kit heatedly. "Walsingham had given me intelligence that Don Antonio's men were up to something tonight."

George nodded. "That's a little more than delivering messages, Kit."

Kit shrugged glancing at Miao. "We all have something vested in this."

"Don Antonio," said Miao. "Why would he do this?"

Kit shook his head. "I don't think Don Antonio knows anything about this."

"Who then?" snapped George. It was beginning to irk him that he had fled without a fight. He knew, he could feel Berto Della Massa behind this.

Kit shrugged. "Don't know. The Pope, The King of Spain...some Lord in the Privy Council."

"The Privy Council? Aren't they on our side?" protested Miao.

Kit glanced at Miao. "Sides are very hard to tell in the dark. Some of them have a thing for witches."

With the wherryman pulling strongly, they passed the last moored boats and were out on the clear part of the river. They could just make out the distant shore of Bankside.

"We're safe, right?" asked Miao. George had warned her about her looks and ability. It seems that those warnings were coming to fruition.

Kit shook his head. "They came by water. That's how I followed them. With the four of them pulling we couldn't keep up. When we got to shore they were well ahead of us. We went after them, but then I saw you two go by and turned around. It's good we found you."

"Glad you did," said George. "It would have been better, if we had kicked a hole in their boat." He swivelled about. Close enough to see them, a larger wherry came speeding out around the last boat, pulling strongly. It was four oars to two. He also noticed that the wherryman was also fatigued. He shifted position, rocking the boat and slid in beside the man. "You mind if I take an oar?"

The wherryman gave a terse nod. "I wouldn't mind if both of ye took over."

Kit and George scrambled into position while the wherryman moved to the stern and began fumbling with something in the bottom of the boat.

Kit grabbed the oar and began to pull awkwardly. George told him to calm down and follow his lead. The worst thing he could do was to panic.

"Sorry, writing doesn't really prepare me to do anything physical," apologized Kit.

After a few moments of flailing about, Kit was able to match the cadence set by George. Even so, the larger boat was still closing on them.

"The best we can do," said the wherryman through his exertion "is to delay them. They will catch us; four against two isn't good fortune. Who are they?"

"I think they're Portuguese," said George.

The wherryman hocked and spit a large gob of phlegm over the side of the boat.

Miao noticed, for the first time that the wherryman had one leg. The other culminated in a wooden peg, just below the knee. That's why he was so far behind Kit when they had appeared on the street.

"I hates them Portuguese," he ejaculated. He was now fitting something into the stern of the wherry. "It was a Portuguese ball that took off me leg." He glanced nervously at the speedily approaching boat. "They'll have us within fifty pulls or more."

They were a lot closer to the bridge then Kit wanted to be. No sane person would go close to the bridge's starlings when the tide was running out. The night was dark, but clear. The moon and stars were able to shed enough light on the river for them to get a sense of reference. They could see the cut waters ripping the water into foam and above, on top of the great, arching pillars was an almost continuous line of buildings. Holborne House stood out on the bridge with its peculiar architecture. Some of the windows glowed with the amber light cast by candles, and it was that light that germinated the grains of Miao's genius.

"Let's make for the bridge," said Miao.

"Shoot the bridge?" gasped Kit through his exertion. "Nobody shoots the bridge in the day let alone at night."

The wherryman gave a hacking laugh as he moved the tiller on the portable rudder he had installed on the wherry. "You must have read my mind. Let's give those devils something to really think about." With that he leaned on the tiller and the wherry swung downstream and towards the sharp cutwaters.

"You've done this before?" asked George. There were five men in the other boat: four of them were bending and straightening rhythmically while the fifth leaned over the bow of the boat. He thought it might be Della Massa, but then changed his mind. He was too cautious for that. The man was probably waiting in some dark room, waiting for the arrival of the white witch who his mistress would most likely draw and kill. His teeth clenched together in suppressed fury.

"Do it all the time."

"At night?"

"There's always a first." The wherryman gave a wicked grin.

"Never thought it would end like this," moaned Kit.

"Quit your whining," snapped the wherryman. "If the Sir can have faith in me, you should."

"Hope you don't mind if I pray," mumbled Kit.

"Not at all" laughed the wherryman. "This is going to be fun."

The pursuit boat was almost on them, when the current seemed to catch them and pull them forward. Had it not, the quarrel that thunked into the gunnel between Kit and the wherryman would have taken one of them.

"They've got a crossbow," lamented Kit.

"I would say so," said George between his teeth. "We've got a few seconds while he reloads, so put those precious fingers of yours to work and pull."

Briefly, they pulled away from the other boat. The crossbowman in the bow of the other boat reloaded and was trying to set himself for another shot. He cursed and stumbled as the boat attempted to turn to follow their course, but without a rudder they were finding it difficult to navigate in the current. At least that bought them a few seconds.

The sounds of the water coursing around the starlings roared up around them. It had always been in the background, but now it demanded eminence. Another bolt was loosed but it splashed harmlessly into the water on the port side. Miao felt their boat surge forward, and suddenly she wondered if her idea had been such a bright one after all. It was likely, as not, to get them killed.

"Oars in," yelled the wherryman trying to out shout the noise of the foaming water. "I'll take it from here, lads!"

The massive boat shaped starlings that formed the base upon which the bridge's great pillars sat on leapt out of the dark at them. The weight and span of the bridge and closeness of the stone was all about them, yelling at them, threatening them with white water destruction. Suddenly, the boat was plummeted downwards and Miao screamed. She had not thought that 'shooting the bridge' actually meant they would be shooting a waterfall, but that's what it felt like. She felt Kit's arms around her. He said something, but the roar of the water drowned him out. And then, as suddenly as it had come upon them, it was over. They were floating down river of the bridge, with the peace of having survived about them. The wherryman gave a whoop as he pointed at the wrecked hull of the other boat bobbing in the water.

"Well done," said George in admiration.

The wherryman's voice became suddenly sober: "I think it's them that are done."

The damaged boat floated by them, no sign of life, only glistening water. Something bumped against their hull. George reached over and picked up a piece of broken plank. He examined it before throwing it back into the water.

"Like my leg, after the Portuguese got through with me, smashed. A fair return, I think," said the wherryman grimly who slid back onto his bench and took up the oars by himself. "Where to?" he said matter of fact, as though nothing had just happened. "Can I suggest Southbank? I'll have to wait for the tide to change before I can get back above the bridge."

The little wherry slid soberly up onto the river bank and they disembarked. Miao, grateful to be alive, thanked him.

She took the wherryman's hand in hers as he helped her out of the wherry. For a moment she saw something around him, two boats crushing his small wherry. "Can I make a suggestion?"

"You would like to shoot the bridge again?"

"No, take tomorrow off."

"Off? Would that I could, but I have children to feed."

"George, how much does a wherryman make in a day?"

George pressed money into the wherryman's palm.

"Take the day off," she said, "don't be greedy."

He bit the money before it disappeared. "I will."

They made their way up to the closest street.

"What was that about?" asked Kit.

"I saw him die, tomorrow, on the water."

"So you figured he should take the day off?"

"Do you think it will work? I mean you think your advice will save him?" asked Kit.

"I hope so."

Fate, while it can be delayed cannot be cheated. George knew that better than anyone. He watched the two and shook his head sadly. He also knew that it was only time before he and Berto Della Massa would meet; that was fate.

Chapter Sixteen: In a Brothel

Much to George's chagrin, it took them awhile to get back over the bridge to Clerkenwell, but with Kit trying to get close to Miao, he had his incentive. Eventually, after a journey through a number of stinking streets, they arrived at their destination.

Kit rapped his fist gently on the door, and it swung inward revealing a light inside. Miao had never been to a brothel before and did not know what to expect. To be perfectly honest, she had never thought about the carnal part of her being. To her, sexuality was something to be ignored, overcome. It represented danger. So many women died in childbirth, love or lust brought death, and while she was not averse to death, it being the balance to life, she did not feel the need to dance with desire. They were pulled inside by a number of arms and giggles. A blonde girl with delicate features wrapped her arms around Kit and gave him a familiar kiss. Miao felt an odd sensation in the pit of her stomach.

"I was going to say, we're closed, but since it's you..." said the blonde girl.

"Thanks," said Kit awkwardly. "These are my friends."

"Three?" Her eyes ran up and down George's body, then they leapt to Miao: "A man's man and a monk?"

Miao felt her temper rise and she resented Kit for being the author of it. She reached up and pulled back her hood and glared at the girl, trying not to let her eyes flicker.

"A child?" said the blonde, "and her eyes are pink."

"Isolde?" came a strong, feminine voice from inside. It was a rich voice, rounded with strong vowels and perfectly finished consonants. "Did you tell them we're closed?"

George pushed past the girl who made to protest and embraced the beautiful, black woman. Eventually they parted. "Long time, Luce."

Miao frowned. It seemed that most of the men in her life were familiar with brothels.

"George, George Silver, my, my, what brings you back to my waiting arms? How long has it been?" Luce held him at arm's length to survey him with pride.

"Since I left for the Low Country," said George.

"You look the same," said Luce.

George laughed. "No, there's more grey hair, but you, you look as beautiful as ever."

She pursed her sensuous lips. Everything about the woman seemed to be sensuous; she exuded it from her pores. It was her perfume. Her black hair was tightly pulled back, adding to her wide, attractive features. Her smile flashed white against her chocolate hued skin, and her deep, brown eyes seemed to emanate warmth. "It's almost dawn, and we have had a rough night..."

"No, no," said George blushing. Miao couldn't believe it was possible to make George blush. "We're not here for that. Kit says you sometimes deal in...information. You see, we were attacked tonight."

They must have had a secret look, the abbess and the whore, because Isolde left the room. Luce gave a jerk of her head and led them away to the back of the building. It was a small room skirted by benches that were covered in plush pillows. In the centre was a small table.

"Please, sit," she said formally. When everyone was seated, she leaned over the table, exposing the depth of her cleavage. "So, our kitty-cat says you're going to court? I am impressed." She smiled her blinding smile. "I have been waiting for an invite for ages. I know enough lords to make me noble by association."

Isolde re-entered and placed four silver goblets onto the table. Before Miao could say she didn't drink wine, she had filled them and left.

"Please," continued Luce, "drink. You say you were attacked."

"Yes," said George, "we believe it was Don Antonio's men."

Luce whistled and then she hesitated. "That is rather brave of him, considering his position."

"Too brave, if you ask me," blurted George draining the goblet. "They almost skewered us with a cross bow bolt."

Luce reached across the table and placed her hand over George's. It seemed to calm him down.

"Given his position here, I would hazard to guess far too brave," continued Luce.

"What do you mean, his position?" asked Miao.

"He is a king without a country, dependant on a foreign monarch for any hope to retrieve his land. Why would he attack someone under the personal protection of the Captain of the Queen's Guard?"

"He's mad?" offered Kit.

"No, I know Don Antonio, he is one of my best customers. He is many things, but he still believes in honour. He would not send men to kill you in the night. If he wanted you dead, you would know who held the sword."

Miao noticed that Luce's fingers were playing artfully over George's knuckles.

"He is a knight of the ancient order, almost as ancient as our knight here," she said indicating George.

George growled with disgust but didn't remove his hand from beneath hers. "I've never been knighted, nor do I want to be. You won't see me parading down the street with a garter wrapped around my leg!"

"Then who?" asked Kit wanting to find out who was behind the men that had just tried to kill them.

Isolde entered the room again and refilled their goblets. Miao noticed how she hovered around Kit, brushing against him. She placed her hand over the goblet to keep Isolde from filling it. She would not accept drink from this woman. As it was, after a few sips, her head was beginning to spin.

Luce shrugged. "I don't know, most likely the Pope, or the King of Spain, or someone slighted at court, but definitely not Antonio." She looked knowingly at George. "Have you offended someone recently?"

George drank again and shrugged innocently. "I kicked an Italian Sword Master in the oysters the other day."

Luce laughed. "Oh, George, I have missed you -- dearly."

There was pain in George's face, but when Miao looked to Luce, she noticed the dark woman staring back at her, in an unflinching, knowing gaze. A shiver ran down her spine. She was saying something to her, something with her mind, and immediately she felt a kinship with the woman. It was as though she knew that Miao could 'see' things, but that was impossible.

Around Luce's head swirled a mass of colours, none of them slowing enough for Miao to see any type of solid image. The images were in constant flux, something she had never seen before. When images formed they were almost always in a definable object. And most of all, it seemed that Luce was aware that Miao was seeing something.

Luce removed her fingers from George's hand and took a shallow breath. "I think you should leave, now."

"Luce..." began George, but she cut him off.

"No, really, Kit and you should leave. But not her, I need to talk to her, in private." And then she added, "Please."

George gave a terse but confused nod and rose to leave. Kit followed. Isolde looped a friendly arm through his and led him out of the room. When they were gone, Luce reached across the table and placed her hand on Miao's.

When she did that, she knew how Luce was able to know that she was 'seeing' things. She was like her, except she knew things, instinctively through touch. Then she thought about the woman's profession.

"It must be difficult," said Miao blushing. "To 'touch' so many men."

"Yes, it was, in the beginning, but now, as the Abbess of this fine brothel, I only 'touch' whom I will." Then the expression on her face became serious. "You can see me, can't you?"

Miao felt the apprehension toward this woman slip away. "Yes, but nothing definite. I just see colours around you, undetermined images that are trying to form out of the colours."

A worried expression pinched Luce's face. "Is that bad?"

"I don't know. What do you see about me?" asked Miao.

"That's why I asked the others to leave: the fewer who know the better. I see danger, but I also see strength. Your fate is bound up with George Silver's. It would not be good to be separate from him. I know this from experience."

"You and him?"

Her face illuminated with a bright but painful smile and her eyes sparkled tragically. "Do you know what the fool asked of me, before he ran off to fight in the Low Country?"

"No."

"He asked me to marry him."

"Why did you refuse him?"

Her laugh was deep and rich and full of life. "Me? Oh, you are an innocent aren't you? I am a whore, and no matter where I go, I shall always be a base borne whore. Besides I do not think that giving up power would suit me. You see, I, like you, was once a slave."

"You saw that when you touched me?"

Luce shrugged. "Also, I too, like you are partial to actors. I would not have lived long had not Phillipe Henslowe freed me." She waved her hand. "He gave me this palatial surrounding, giving me girls to manage and allowed me to function independently." She took a drink. "As long as I make a profit, all is well."

She leaned forward staring intently into Miao's eyes. "What has George taught you?"

Miao hesitated and then realized what she was referring to. She blushed again. She was beginning to feel that if she didn't leave the brothel she would be a permanent tone of pink. "No, no," she rushed on trying to find a way out of the question. "He taught me how to use a rapier," she said offering it up to the Abbess.

Luce laughed again. "Everybody knows George's sword; he is famous for it." She sat back satisfied. "And now, down to business. I also wanted you alone, because passing information is a tricky thing. It could mean my life. You see if one woman talks to another, it is not as treasonous as if I talk to a man. Now, what do you know about these men?"

"The men who tried to kill us...I don't know if they really wanted us dead," explained Miao.

"What do you mean?"

"Well, George was able to trick them into thinking we were going with them...they waited. I mean, if they wanted to kill us, wouldn't they have stabbed George right away?"

"I would have," ruminated Luce. "He's a perfect terror once his blade is unsheathed." She drummed her fingers on the table. "You may have something here. Maybe they wanted to take you somewhere first."

"I was thinking that, but where?"

"That is the question, isn't it? If we could find them, maybe we could ask them."

Miao told her about shooting the bridge and what happened to the pursuit boat.

"That's too bad. Well, at least that's five less villains to worry about."

"Why don't you think Don Antonio is behind this?" asked Miao.

"I have 'touched,' him, multiple times." From deep within her cleavage, she pulled out a large diamond which dangled on the end of a long gold necklace. "And he in return has shared with me one of Portugal's crown jewels." Tucking it back away, she went on. "Don Antonio has a sensitive soul, not one for this world, I am afraid."

"You don't think he is capable of having us killed?"

"Not without telling you first. The King of Spain, or the Pope, or even our dearest Queen, would have your throat slit before you could think. No, I don't think Don Antonio knew what his men were doing, nor do I think they were out to kill you. The accident on the water was unfortunate for them, but fortunate for you."

"What will Don Antonio do when he finds his men missing?" asked Miao.

"Get new men. These ones didn't seem too competent."

"Will you tell Don Antonio?"

Luce smiled. "I may take chances, my dear Lady Juzheng, but I'm not a fool."

"You know my name?"

"Yes, of course, after your escapade at the Walk, half of London knows your name now. It is going to be very hard to keep your hood up."

Luce reached and took Miao's hands into hers. She examined them in silence and when she was done, she looked up. "You two, Don Antonio and you, are very similar. You are both exiles, and are destined for greatness. You will be a great success, but Don Antonio will be a great failure."

"You can see that?" asked Miao feeling a kinship with this woman. "I saw Don Antonio's failure also."

"Do you believe in fate?"

"I believe that there is greatness beyond our understanding."

"Fate favourable will not court the beggar king. Twenty days was the time he ruled after declaring himself king. You see, Phillip, the King of Spain also coveted Portugal."

"He said he lost when he followed Sebastian into Morocco," said Miao remembering the strange encounter with Don Antonio on the stage at The Theatre.

"You see, how the fates wind our lives together. This is not happenstance, you, me and Don Antonio. This was meant to be, but I'm afraid that our Don lost, spectacularly, again, in Portugal."

"Yet, he still dreams," said Miao.

"He still dreams. Just don't say the word Alcantar."

"It does not end there?" asked Miao.

"No, it does not. In our world, our little world, we must fear three women, well two, for now, after one lost her head, compliments of our gracious Queen."

"Mary Stuart?" said Miao. Just a few months ago, the Queen had submitted to the pleading of her counsellors to put away the matter of treason with a stroke of an axe.

"Even so, poor Mary, but still an indomitable woman, gone; so that leaves us with two: the Queen and Catherine di' Medici. A vacancy waits to be filled."

"What do you mean?"

"There was a Greek writer, Hesoid. In his Theogony were many groupings of triads or trinities. The children of Chronos and Rhea are Zeus, Poseidon and Hades. In Aristotle's Rhetoric he writes of three types. Also, Evander fought with one endowed with three lives and had to kill him three times," as Luce went on she became more visibly excited. The excitement was working up through her entire body manifesting it in words. She was indeed the oddest of the odd, a literate whore. "Even Caesar, when taking a seat in a carriage was in the habit of repeating a certain formula three times to secure safety on the journey." Her eyes were now shining with a fervent glimmer. "Even the Christian God is in the trinity form, whether three in one or three separate, it does not matter. What matters is the number three. So, who is now the third?"

Miao was trying hard to understand what Luce was saying. Many of the references were strange to her, but she did have the feel that the number three was the right number. She hated it when she had to tell George something more than three times. "Who is the third?"

Luce leaned forward, the intensity in her eyes threatening to burn. "The killer you seek is that woman."

"You know who it is?" asked Miao.

Luce shook her head her eyes darting about the room as though she suddenly feared the shadows there. "No, if I did, I doubt I would be alive. But the three are toying with our dear friend Don Antonio."

"How?" asked Miao.

"After Don Antonio was deposed, the only thing left to him was to take the crown jewels and flee to France. With some of those jewels and the promise of the colony of Brazil, Catherine di Medici raised a fleet of adventurers for him. It was a way for her to strike at Phillip without declaring war."

"War is a waste of life," said Miao.

"A man would not think like that," said Luce pensively. "War is a man's opportunity for glory and a quick exit. Yet a woman must strike through her agents, she must strike from the shadows."

Miao didn't need to ask the question, because Don Antonio's presence in London meant that his adventure had failed. Yet there was something that bothered her, something that Luce had said. "This thing about the number three fascinates me. But one thing I don't understand is why you want to help us?"

"I could say that it is because I still love George, but you would see the lie. All I will say is that one of my girls had red hair. She was one of the murdered. I treat my girls as my own daughters. Now, tell me, what are you going to do with this knowledge?"

"Do you think the third woman was behind these men attacking us?"

Luce remained silent, but shrugged her shoulders. It was a motion of agreement. "Might I advise something?"

"Please."

"When you go to Court, be careful. You will be going into the den full of lionesses. She will have her Glories about her. Look for death amidst her Glories. Look for a woman with red hair. Now, I think I should return you to your men, before they start to bother my girls."

Miao and Luce walked in on them, and it was their turn to blush, which surprised Miao very much. Isolde was sitting on Kit's lap, while a pair of dark haired twins were on either side of George. They were playing with his beard and he was in the middle of one of his stories. He abruptly cut it short when he saw Miao and Luce and stood up dumping the twins from his lap. Kit also struggled to rise, but Isolde wasn't giving up her seat so easily. George's girls pouted sulkily.

178

"So, we're off?" George said, but Miao could tell he didn't really want to leave.

"I'm afraid so," said Luce dispersing the girls with a look. She stepped into George and kissed him on the cheek. "Don't stay away too long, this time."

Luce turned to Kit and gave his cheek a motherly pat. "You be careful."

Kit smiled wanly. He had heard this admonition before. "I always am, Luce," he lied.

Outside in the street, Kit, George and Miao bade them farewell and they headed back to Lotus House. Miao, after the night's adventure, was suddenly exhausted. Her head was swimming. It was worth it though, because they were one step closer to identifying the murderer.

"So, what did she say?" asked George.

Miao didn't want to talk in the streets, because people were beginning to move about. All she wanted to do was get back to the house and her bed that waited. But she knew George, and knew he wouldn't wait. "She said the killer has red hair and is one of the Glories at Court. George, what is a Glory?"

George stopped in the street. Miao checked herself and turned back to him. "The Glories are the noble women that the Queen surrounds herself with. She commands them herself."

Chapter Seventeen: Dream

Miao's dream was different this time. It was not a dream of her past, or present, perhaps it was a dream about her future, but she was unsure. One thing she was sure of, and that was she was seeing through someone else's eyes.

There were women all around her. There was an anxious excitement in the group. They must be going somewhere important because their homespun clothing, although worn, was clean. Men dressed in glimmering armour and holding long halberds were escorting them. The great curtain wall of a stone castle rose up in front of them. The dream was so real she could almost feel the paving stones beneath her feet. Narrow sounds echoed off the walls as they passed through a gate. It all added to the gravity of what seemed like a ceremony.

Ceremony: the words pulled a deep cord within her mind. She was involved in some type of ceremony. Miao's mind spun and she closed her eyes, yet she still felt the body she was in, moving along. Around her was the rustle of fabric and excitement. When she opened her eyes they were in a room. They were instructed to sit.

There was a cool, wet sensation against her feet and she looked down. A woman was bent over washing her feet in a wooden basin, washing the dirt from her bare feet. The washerwoman looked up, but then she was busy again drying her feet with a deft, forceful rubbing. She saw something in her eyes and that frightened her. It was a nervous fear. What did the washer woman know?

Feet washed and dried, they were all now standing. Another woman, a younger one, had given her something. Her hands were holding a nosegay of flowers. Their scent rose up and masked the body odour of the women. How could she smell this? It was said the Queen had a sensitive nose. Different guards moved about them now, in more sumptuous livery and less armour.

Through a series of rooms they were led, until they final came to stand in front of large, deep oak doors. The doors opened on a world of light, and people dressed in bright colours. There were ladies in silk and taffeta, in fur and gems, and men in tall, plumed hats. They were standing on either side of the long carpet that led to...

And then she saw her at the far end of the audience, the Queen. Gone were the sumptuous clothes, the gems, and the dresses wide enough to consume the world. In their place she was wearing a simple dress a maid might wear. The only thing that remained, to accentuate the Queen's beauty, was a wig of youthful, red hair. It was piled high in an elaborate show. The hair, thought Miao, it was the hair that drew her attention. She felt that somehow there was a kinship between the hair of the murdered women and the wig, because it was the same colour.

On either side of the Queen stood her Glories, dressed in the homespun clothing of the work maid. They seemed to be all cut from the same cloth, younger versions of the Queen. It was as though, Elizabeth, had paired off pieces of herself in an attempt to make images of her that would last forever. They were her children who created the light in which the Queen bathed. Without them the cult of the Virgin Queen would have faded into the darkness and dotage of age, but with them around her she seemed to glow. In front of the Queen, on the floor, were a number of simple stools waiting for the women who clutched the nosegays protectively to their chests as though they could ward off evil with them.

Miao felt herself whisked along the carpet to the stools, where she followed the example of all the other women and took a seat. When they were all assembled before the Queen, a hint of a smile touched the Queen's lips. The toothy smile had gone when her teeth had been pulled. Her love for sweets and of fashion had caused the decay: sweets, because they created the caries in her mouth, and fashion, because the clothes hid the self-promoting lies at Court. Yet, in the aging Queen's eyes, Miao saw a trapped woman, trapped by the cult she had created for herself. She also saw a hardness that made her flinch when those dark, amber eyes settled on her.

Suddenly, the Queen's arms opened as though she was about to embrace them as a mother embraces her children. With grace the Queen knelt down before them. Two of her Glories, one on either side of her, held a cloth and a basin of water. The Queen began to wash and dry the feet of the women. When she was done, she gave each a little velvet purse with something in it. Miao noticed that the Queen was slowly working her way to the middle from the right. She was working her way to where she was seated. Miao felt the apprehension that something terrible would happen as soon as the Queen reached her.

As the Queen approached, Miao could feel her heart begin to beat rapidly. She felt a clammy, cold sweat on her forehead. There was no way she could control the dream. The bad event that was intended to happen would happen. The Queen went to wash Miao's feet.

Again there was the cool sensation of her feet being washed, and then the comforting feel of the cloth rubbing against her feet drying them. Miao sensed the base emotion of the woman she inhabited. It came surging up into her mind, so strong that it threatened to entirely cast her away. She fought to remain in the dream. The emotion was a blend of anger, hatred and violence. It was bathed in the colour red, not the red of luck that she had known in her childhood; it was the red of vengeance, the red of blood.

Miao felt her hand tighten around the cold metal of the dagger's hilt that she had secreted away in her skirt. Then, as the Queen handed her the velvet purse, she thrust her dagger forward. There was a look of surprised shock on the Queen's face.

And suddenly Miao was screaming and sitting up in bed.

George backed away from the screaming woman in his charge. Her arms and fists were flailing about. She may be small, but she certainly packed a punch. All he had been doing was shaking her by the shoulder in an attempt to wake her up. It was what she had instructed him to do when she showed no signs of waking from a dream. She was afraid that if he didn't wake her, she might not ever wake. It was a fear of hers, and he believed it.

"Miao, Miao," he called forcefully moving back to her and swatting the flying fists aside. He sat down on the edge of the bed and pulled the sobbing girl to him wrapping his arms around her. Suddenly, she clung to him as though he was the only thing keeping her afloat and safe from drowning. "Are you all right, girl?"

She clung to him and then pushed away. Horrified she said: "I've killed the Queen."

"You what?"

"I've killed the Queen, well, I saw the Queen killed, no, no...the Queen is going to be killed."

It was then that she saw the faces of the two actors standing in the doorway. She couldn't see them clearly, but she knew who they were by the way they stood. Will slouched forward on bent legs as though he was about to break into a dance at any moment, while Richard stood more erect, more proper. They both exhibited the confident movement of those who knew how to move well. It was the same fluidity that George had.

"George, is there anything we can do?" asked a concerned Will.

"You said the Queen is going to be killed?" asked Richard. "Are you sure?"

George gave him a withering look. "Of course she's sure. Miao, tell us what you saw."

"I saw the Queen washing the feet of some women. One of those women, after her feet were washed, stabbed the Queen"

"It's the Maundy Ceremony," said Richard hoarsely.

"Has it happened?" asked Miao desperately.

"No," answered Will. "Tomorrow, the ceremony happens tomorrow."

"Then we still have time." Miao jumped out of bed and began to dress. She didn't pay any attention to the obvious discomfort she caused the men in the room.

George stood back. He knew that determined look on her face. It meant 'tunnels' and danger. While he didn't mind the danger, the tunnels he abhorred. "Time for what?"

"Time to stop the woman from killing the Queen," she said tersely. "Will, hand me that."

Will took the corset that Miao had pointed to and handed it gingerly to her.

She snatched it and pulled it over her head. "Seriously," she said, "don't stand there, help me dress. It's not as though you haven't dressed Ed up in women's clothes before. Will, tie me up."

Will began fumbling with the strings on the corset. She had just pulled it over her head. It was an affair with strings on the back. "Yeah, well, Ed's not a Lady now is he?"

"Please," lamented Miao turning and slapping his hands away. "Richard, you try. Am I the only woman you've dressed?"

Richard blushed no more successful at lacing her up than Will.

George stepped in and took over. He had done this before, many times. "The women they've dressed weren't ladies."

"Where's the Maundy Ceremony?" she demanded.

"Windsor, Windsor Castle," stuttered Richard.

"Then that's where we need to be," said Miao beginning to slip into her outer clothes.

"You can't just stroll into Windsor Castle," explained George, "after all, it's a castle."

"We could always storm the walls, beat off the guards with a bit of humour, and dance past a few hundred courtiers and guards surrounding the Queen."

Richard turned to Will. "Could you be serious?"

"Absolutely, not," responded Will.

Miao was now pulling on her sleeves. They were detachable from the dress and had to be tied on. She held out her arms and glared at them. "Well?"

Richard and Will realised that she was waiting for them and leapt into action.

George had been thinking. Miao was going to get into Windsor Castle one way or another, she was so determined. It was now up to him to figure out the how of it.

"You could send a message to Lord Water," said Richard.

"No, it's too late for that," responded George. "We'll have to come up with a plan ourselves."

Will became suddenly cheery. "We're good with plans. All we need is a script, one that allows us passage."

"Right," responded Richard skeptically. "And where are we going to get someone to write a script that can get us into one of the best protected places in England?"

"Kit," answered Miao finishing her dress, "Kit Marlowe."

Chapter Eighteen: Absolution

Those who watched Berto Della Massa thought it was Don Antonio he served, but that was just a ruse. True, both he and Don Antonio had followed Sebastian to Morocco and defeat, but he had not fought under Don Antonio's flag. His story about how he had acquired the steel he now wore was somewhat accurate, but no one would ever know the real story. He would keep that to his grave. No, this was a question of his soul and only Pope Sixtus V and his agent Marco Antonio Massia could save his soul now. This was why he served the Veiled Woman, why he killed for her, because they had commanded it. How innocent he had been when he had followed Sebastian. Then he was under the command of Thomas Stukley and went blithely into Morocco.

The only thing orderly about the battle of Three Kings was how they all lined up. Sebastian was a fool, riding around on his horse in front of them, encouraging them, waving his sword. Half the Moors on their side couldn't understand him. While Sebastian rode Della Massa's eyes had swept the opposite field, watched, as the Moroccans, ten thousand horses strong, moving to flank them. He smelled defeat even before the first shot was fired. He also recognized the hardened Moors that the Sultan had placed in the centre to face them, all of them men who had been dispossessed of their lands in Spain.

Stukley, an excellent commander, may have been able to turn the day, may have been able to smash their centre before they were encircled, but maybe implied opportunity. When the musketry and artillery opened up, a ball took Stukley's head off. Fate was that way. If it was your time, it didn't matter; with a crook of her finger, you would go, whether you were great or not. The ten thousand horse men that had encircled them charged and the world turned to blood and screams and dying.

Berto Della Massa – that wasn't his name then. It was something else, something that died that day. He fought on with what was left of Stukley's personal guard. He knew, as soon as Stukley's headless corpse toppled to the ground that the battle was lost. So they formed a wedge and went head on into the melee.

One by one they killed and died. In the end, when they had pushed beyond the battle, or the battle had flowed past them, he was left alone. Inexplicably fate had let him live. Wounded in a dozen places, and weak from the loss of blood, he found him, the flower of Portuguese nobility, his honourable Highness, Sebastian. He was stuck beneath his horse, half crushed, but he was still alive. Every struggling breath he took was accompanied by bubbling blood. Della Massa dropped to his knees. That was when he saw it, the sword, gripped in the hand of a dead Turk. He didn't know whether Sebastian had killed him or he had killed Sebastian, but it didn't matter, not really. He reached out and cut the sword from the dead fingers of the Turk. That was when Sebastian opened his eyes.

"Water…" was all he said.

The king was dying, and Della Massa, without flinching took the blade of Damascus steel and cut Sebastian's throat. A foolish king deserved to be a dead king; after that killing became easy.

Did he enjoy killing the women the Lady sketched? He did not know. It had been so long since he permitted himself to feel emotion the way a normal person might. His killing of the women had been like a workman in an abattoir. People had to eat, the nobles had to play their game of thrones, and he had been instructed to kill, so he killed. For many of them his blade had been the kiss of mercy. This was an ugly world ruled by the ugly and he was the ugliest. So it was, so it is, so it will be. Still, he wanted his soul back.

He opened the door for the Veiled Lady and she entered. In her wake flowed the perfumed scent of a lily. In France they had made incredible advances in the realm of scent. If he was curious he would speculate that this was where the Lady was from. To him the scent of lily was the scent of death.

"Berto," said Massia standing, his back to them, looking out the large window onto Plymouth's harbour, "would you be as kind as to invite the Lady to sit."

There were two plush chairs in front of Massia's desk. The Lady claimed one and sat on it as though she was sitting on a throne. That was very interesting. She was French and noble...someone close to the Medici's. He was about to sit in the second chair.

"Berto, you will stand."

Della Massa felt the warning prickles on the nape of his neck again. Was Hugo aiming at him with his cross bow? The feeling was often the precursor to violence, to an attack. His hand fell instinctively to his side where his sword was.

Massia, for an old man, moved quickly and fluidly from where he was standing. He spun around the desk and lunged at him. The slap was totally unexpected and took Della Massa entirely by surprise. It stung, but no more than a fly might bite. What made him wary was the cold, lethal look in Massia's eyes. He was a man who was well versed in the death of others. Then the flint like hardness was gone and he slumped back to his window, hands clasped behind his back.

"I am sorry you had to see that," apologised Massia to the Veiled Lady. "Tell me, how five men, five good men are dead, dead without their last rights, and how Silver and his Witch are not?"

Della Massa now understood the cause of the slap and his hand moved away from his sword. "The order came from Don Antonio. They were to bring Silver and his Witch to him."

"What did our illustrious beggar King want with them?"

Della Massa shrugged. "He was interested in the woman and Silver. They have been invited to Court and perhaps he wanted to ride on their sudden fame. Perhaps it would get him closer to his goal."

"So, why are these men dead?"

"Silver and the Witch ran, and the men chased."

"And they died."

188

"And they died," confirmed Della Massa.

"What colour is this Witch's hair?" asked the Veiled Lady suddenly interested. There was a thickness to her voice that indicated a rising passion.

A mischievous light leapt into Massia's eyes as he wagged an admonishing finger at the woman. "There shall be no more killings. We are too close to the fruition of our intrigue."

"The hair?" there was something else in the woman's voice, something fueled by a pathological hatred.

"White, it is white," said Della Massa.

The woman sighed. "That is too bad."

"Berto," he said sympathetically, "I understand that Don Antonio is a fool, even a king in exile, but still a fool. Let us not have any more accidents."

Della Massa gave an assenting nod. He may have despised Massia, but he had to acknowledge the man's power, and he had plenty of that. He had both the ecclesiastical and secular power of the Vatican behind him. He was, in fact, at the present, one of the most powerful men in the world. Massia had not given him permission to sit, so he kept standing. "Your Grace."

Massia moved to his customary place behind his desk and slid back down onto the bone hard chair. It was uncomfortable on purpose as it was a reminder that comfort often equalled complacency and complacency killed.

"Now, My Lady, everything is in place, as you have requested."

Della Massa noticed the familiarity with which Massia addressed the woman. He knew her. The roots of this man's connections went deep into the Court.

"Is the woman truly capable?" she asked.

Instead of answering, Massia, having anticipated the question, gave two sharp claps. A hidden door in the wall opened and another cloaked woman stepped into the room escorted by the ugly Hugo.

Interesting, thought Massia, how so many women took the precaution of cloaking themselves, but then, women by the weaker nature of their sex had taken to the shadows. Was not the Veiled Lady, in essence, an assassin who used puppets instead of wielding the knife herself?

To the order of Massia, the woman pulled back her hood revealing her features. There was nothing exceptional about her. Her features were bland even plain: nose, overly large, and mouth too broad and thin. Her hair, thick and tangled looked as though it had never seen a brush. But it was red, a vibrant, and luxuriously red.

"May I introduce Mary Donohue," said Massia. "She comes from a good family of noble parentage, of dispossessed land, of a murdered mother and father, compliments of the Heretic Queen."

Even though the woman's features were plain, there was a sharp, cutting intelligence in her eyes. She went down on her knees before the seated woman.

Apparently, mused Della Massa, the girl had manners even though she was from Ireland.

The Veiled Lady rose from her chair, reached out and took a lock of hair between her thumb and forefinger and rolled it. "Your hair," she said, passion heating up her English accent, letting the true cadence and timbre of her French voice rise to the surface. "It is most beautiful."

Mary Donohue's response was one of intense discomfort. She looked pleadingly at Massia.

Massia placed his hand over the Veiled Lady's and gently moved it away. He was most tender with the woman. "I think what you desire to know is if she has the strength to do the deed?"

"Yes, indeed, I do," she responded.

190

Della Massa noticed that the French accent was gone and the cold steel of her English had reasserted itself.

"Mary, child," said Massia taking the young woman by both shoulders and raising her up so that they stood facing each other. It was as though he was pouring his strength into the woman. "Do you swear," began Massia, "by your immortal soul, by his Holy Grace, Pope Sixtus, by the very wounds of Christ, that you will act as the hand of God?"

Mary Donohue's chin quivered with emotion. "I will." She went to fall on her knees again, but he continued to hold her up.

"Then by the Grace of God and the power that has been afforded me by the Holy Church, I bless this venture to its glorious success: In the name of the Father, the Son and the Holy Ghost." Massia made the sign of the cross, and kissed her on the forehead. "You may go, child."

Mary turned and was ushered out of the room by Hugo through the secret door. Della Massa wondered how many secrets Massia had tucked away.

"Tell me how the deed is to be done," said the Veiled Lady. Her voice thick with the hint of a French accent again.

The Maundy Ceremony, it will happen then. As the Heretic Queen is washing Mary's feet, she will take her hidden dagger and stab her through the heart. Rather a simple, direct approach."

"They search all the women who participate in the Maundy Ceremony," said Della Massa immediately recognizing the problem with the plan.

"We have friends in high places. The women assigned to do the searching are faithful."

"If it fails, her retribution will be swift and harsh," warned the Veiled Lady.

There was something with the plan that bothered Della Massa, something that they had overlooked, some fault. "If this should fail..."

"Has not Don Antonio been invited to the Maundy Ceremony to witness the Heretic Queen's most humble, pious devotion? And will you not be beside our beggar King?"

"As I will be," said the Veiled Lady.

"So," Massia's hands were open as though he was revealing the explanation therein. "You two must make sure that Mary does not fail."

"I am satisfied," whispered the Veiled Lady, but Della Massa noticed a slight hesitance in her voice. He had been her killer for long enough to notice her mannerisms. She was still furious with him for refusing to remove the head of their last victim. It had not been a unique experience, being told no. He also doubted that if things went wrong, she would put herself at risk.

He was also not satisfied. He had been promised his soul and now he wanted deliverance. He felt the web being tightened about him, but that did not concern him. In fact he was rather relieved; he felt the end of things coming. The battles he had fought, the men, and women, he had killed, had stained his soul dark, yet he also stood on the edge of freedom and this invigorated his entire being. Absolution...Freedom.

"The promised Absolution..." began Berto.

Massia smiled and spread his arms, in a benevolent crucifixion pose, "Of course, my children. Both of you kneel."

The Veiled Lady unexpectedly pulled back her veil, revealing her face, and knelt obediently.

Della Massa had known for a while that she had been one of the Queen's Glories, but still it surprised him to learn which one. She had fooled everyone. As he sank down to his knees beside her, he had an odd feeling. He had never been married, and he wondered if this was what it was like...to be united with someone before God in Holy purpose; but instead of being bonded to each other in the white of life, they were chained in the black of death. Interesting, he smiled at his poetic thought.

Massia stood in front of them, a fully ordained priest, prepared to do God's work, as were they. Even so, he had never met two people who deserved perdition more than these two. God moved in mysterious ways.

"Dominus noster Jesus Christus te absolvat..." began Massia as he absolved them of their sins, past, present and future. God moved in mysterious ways.

Chapter Nineteen: Cadiz and Windsor

The morning promised to be bright and sunny, no sign of cloud in the sky. There would be no way to hide from the Spanish, but that was all right. Had they been looking they would have raised the alarm by now. They were complacent in the belief of the 'Great Enterprise.' Besides they believed God was a Spaniard, but Drake knew something they did not know, that God was an Englishman. He felt a slight breeze against his face as he stared into the satchel mouth bay of Cadiz. The wind was still with them. He moved his glass, scanning the clogged shipping in the bay. It was packed, full of ships preparing to embark, to hoist their colours in the cause of the King of Spain. At long last Phillip would return to the land he despised so much, England; not if Drake had anything to say about it.

He handed his glass to his first mate. "Clear the decks."

There was some scurrying about on some of the ships in the bay that indicated they had finally been seen. There was nothing they would be able to do, packed in the way they were.

"Slight to port," shouted Drake, as the pilot took the Elizabeth Bonaventure in at the point. Off in her wake, leading the rest of the fleet were the Golden Lion, Rainbow and Dreadnought. Behind the four galleons sailed about twenty merchantmen and a number of armed pinnaces. "We've caught them napping, Dick!" exalted Drake.

He saw the puffs of smoke from the onshore battery and waited until the cannon balls dropped ineffectually into the water. A few more moments and they would be past the danger from the battery and in amongst the Spanish ships.

"A lion amongst the sheep!" shouted Dick, "A lion amongst the sheep!"

"No, Dick, a Rose amongst the sheep, and this Rose has thorns!"

Drake had picked his target well, a big Spanish galleon that towered above the Elizabeth Bonaventure. The enemy ships gun ports were still closed. They were so near now that he could see the panicked expressions on the men's faces as they came about, broadside to broadside. He would have never taken a ship on this large. Out in the open he would have used their speed and the superior range of the English guns and harried them incessantly. Normally it would have been suicide to board one of the Spanish behemoths. In Phillip's Mediterranean war with the Ottoman Turks, ships were used as mere platforms to create a land battle situation on the water. A large Spanish galleon would be packed with soldiers; they would get in close with the enemy, grapple with them and hold them fast. Then they would board and slaughter everyone on the other ship. The Spanish were very good at slaughter, but Drake had caught their ships before they were crammed with soldiers. This was a battle they could win.

There was a flash of oars off to the starboard side and he noticed that the Spanish weren't entirely asleep. Armed galleys, banks of oars flashing in the morning sun, dipped and rose. With the wind in their favour, he felt no threat from the galleys. He had foreseen this and had assigned the pinnaces orders to intercept them. Dip in and harry them, but under no circumstances were they to board a vessel with superior numbers. Drake had no intention of playing the Spanish game. He would hit this port hard, burn everything he could and then run.

The entire port side guns of Elizabeth Bonaventure opened up with a deafening report. Smoke and splinters filled the air, and when it cleared the grappling hooks flew pulling them tight to the larger galleon. Men, dangling from the rat lines swung onto the Spanish deck. When Drake finally boarded, the fight was mostly over: a cue that the Spanish captain failed to take.

The captain, a big burly fellow, with a great black beard, came storming out on deck and began to rally the remnants of his men. Drake knew that the only way to truly take the ship was to take its captain, or kill him. With a bellow, Drake ran at the Spaniard.

Conflict always seemed surreal to Drake, almost dream like. The guns firing, the screams, the blood, the smell, all of it seemed to be a vision, and he was always outside of it staring in. Even though as a combatant he always felt like an observer. This did not mean he had any delusions. A sword or a ball could as easily cut him down as anyone else. He wondered at his seeming immunity. One day it would end and he would die. He hoped it would be fatal and not the lingering agony of a wound turned septic as the poison spread slowly through the body. Or even worse, he would be crippled with the loss of a limb. He had seen cripples in the streets before, and the best they could hope for was a slow, protracted death, sometimes through starvation.

Drake felt the wind of a sword slash as it grazed his shoulder. He twisted away. Deftly, he brought up his sword to meet the Spaniard's. The man was desperate, most of his men had surrendered or were down, yet he fought on. Their swords clashed again and Drake reached out and tangled up the man's arms so he couldn't break away. They stood like that staring into each other's eyes, champion wrestlers looking for an advantage. There was desperation and fury there, but beneath it was the glimmer of thought. Drake could hear his men running about the galleon carrying about his orders. They knew what had to be done and sought anxiously to do it. He saw the flicker of a sword behind the Spanish Captain. He recognized the sailor who was about to run the Captain through.

"No," shouted Drake. "Captain, your ship is lost, your men defeated. Might I suggest you surrender your sword." He had no idea whether the man understood English or not. If he persisted in resisting, he just might have to have him killed. It would be a waste.

The fury in the man's eyes went out, extinguished by his dawning awareness. He gave a terse grunt. "I surrender."

The resistance was gone.

All about them flames were springing up, licking hungrily at the ship's wood. He moved away from the Spaniard who just stood there in a bewildered state. "I recommend you abandon your ship, Captain, before the flames reach the magazine."

The Spanish Captain slowly translated what El Draco had said. Then he turned and ran for the side of the ship.

Drake withdrew, along with his men back to the Elizabeth Bonaventure. They had more ships to scuttle, a good day's work lay ahead of them. They cut the lines that held them fast and pushed away from the galleon.

"I saw what you did for that black devil," said Dick coming up beside Drake. A blast within the bowels of the galleon caused it to shiver. The ship began to list to the starboard side. Some of the Spaniards dropped into the water like so much over ripe fruit. "Do you think they know how to swim?" asked Dick. His face was smeared with black and red.

"Probably not."

Drake noticed that now all over the harbour flames were racing up the masts of the Spanish ships. Nothing would put that out. He counted at least thirty. It was a good count.

"Do you think we've done it, sir?" asked Dick as the Elizabeth Bonaventure began to look for a new victim.

Drake gave a shrug. He knew that the fleet at Cadiz was mostly supply ships. "At best, we've only singed The King of Spain's beard."

***

Cuthbert Burbage had complained about the cost of the barge rental, he even threatened to go to their father, James, but James would be away a fortnight, so it was a bluff. In the end, Cuthbert consented after Richard expressed the vast potential of the venture. If they pulled it off, they would most likely become the favourite acting troupe at Elizabeth's Court. If they didn't (and he didn't tell Cuthbert this) they could all end up dead.

"What of the Queen's Men?" Cuthbert had put up obstinately, not willing to go down without a fight.

"The Queen's Men," chirped in Will, "are nothing more than a bunch of booze sodden mimics whose days are past. It's paltry fare they only put on, to create good, loyal citizens. It's why they're drunk all the time, so they can stomach it. It's not good for a man, you know, the Queen's Passion Plays. Even the Queen can't stand them."

Cuthbert had opened up his purse and sprung for the barge; nothing else would do, because of their numbers.

With the wind and the water lapping at the side of the barge, Kit sat in the corner in isolation. He watched the tow lines that connected the horses to the barge as they were pulled up river. He didn't like being responsible for others. His fingers moved unceasingly, drumming out a beat on the broad wooden rail that functioned as a gunnel. He really didn't know what to do and they were depending on him to come up with something. Walsingham must have seen something in him, or he wouldn't have hired him to run messages, to slip in and out of shadows, but this was entirely different and he didn't like it. With the messages, he was alone, now, others depended on him.

George sat down beside Kit. He had left Miao in the care of Luce on the other side of the barge. Strange, Luce and her girls had been the first ones that Miao insisted on coming along. It turned out that Luce's girls were even better body guards than he was. They had taken to her as a hen takes to a chick. Whenever someone approached Miao their collective stares were enough to make any man wary. Circumstance does indeed make strange bed fellows. The pastoral greenery of the river bank was gliding by peacefully. It was nice to be away from London and into fresh air.

"Can I sit?" asked George.

Kit looked up at him and slid over on the bench nervously. "No, I mean, yes, I don't mind, not at all."

"So," George glanced up at the other members of their party. There was Will, Richard, Ned, Augsy, Tom and George Bryan. Ed was still livid with being left out. They told him he wasn't needed because they had women to play women. "The only ones left behind were the spear holders."

Kit gave a nervous laugh. "I wish I had something to drink. No, we will have plenty of spear holders when we get to the castle. The place will be full of spear holders. I just hope the tips won't be embedded in our bodies."

Will and Richard had noticed George's movements over to Kit and had followed.

"So, the little lady," said Will in his usual tactless way, "said you could write us in to the Maundy Ceremony. How about sharing with us some lines, so we can work on them?"

"We're pretty close," warned Richard. At first, he had been adventurous, but was now looking a bit pale. He glanced enviously over at Ned who was laughing heartily and slapping Bryan on the back. Their roles had changed. Before a play it was Ned who was sick, now that it was real, he was the one feeling sick. His voice was dry and cracked when he spoke. "I mean, you can't just march up there and demand to see the Queen..." He was good at reading expressions and he didn't like the expression on Kit's face. "Oh, by the bodice of Queen Boudicca, that's exactly what you want us to do, isn't it?"

"Give the lad a chance to explain," defended George. "Often, the most direct approach is the best."

Everyone had now gathered around Kit where they were staring expectantly at him. Kit took them all in, friends all. He finally rested on the two faces that were the most important to him: Kit's and Luce's: the white and the black. It seemed strange that the two should be so linked together, but it felt like fate.

"We heard that Kit's ready to tell us what to do," said Ned loudly. "So, what's the plan?"

"Ned, for once," hissed Richard, "could you keep it down. The entire crew of the barge doesn't need to know what we're up to, do they?"

"Like George says, the direct way is the best," began Kit. "A lot of this is going to depend on the Queen's Fool."

"Tarlton," said Richard the pitch of his voice going up a couple octaves. "Our lives are going to depend on a drunk?"

Bryan was toying with a coin in his hand. "Oh, he will be in his cups, for sure. He loves ceremonies."

"I'm...we're depending on it," said Kit. "Now gather in and listen. A lot of this will also depend on our strengths and what we are good at doing. Luce..." he glanced at Miao and hesitated. Why was it that whenever he was around her he became ashamed of his past?

"You want us to make...merry?" Luce said.

"Yeah, well, yes, sort of."

"So, let's get this straight. Your idea is that you slip one of the guards a note to take to Tarlton, while Luce and the girls make merry with the guards?"

"So, what do you want us to do?" chirped Ned.

"Probably let the other guards, who don't have a girl, stick the pointy end of their halberds into us," despaired Richard.

Augsy was rubbing his hands. "So, after he gets the letter, Tarlton comes out and welcomes us into the ceremony?"

There was an awkward silence as everyone tried to understand Kit's improbable plan. There had to be some nuance tucked in somewhere. They just weren't seeing it.

"You understand, Kit," said Ned gravely, "that the success of this plan hinges entirely on the dependable nature of a drunk."

"So, all right," continued Richard his scepticism growing in the pit of his stomach, "what if Tarlton comes out and sees us. Who says he's going to let us in."

George cleared his voice. "Richard Tarlton owes me a favour, or two, or three. He was a pretty good swordsman in his day, but he was constantly getting into trouble."

"Right," continued Kit. "Then I, and George and Lady Juzheng slip into the ceremony."

"All right," said Richard, "then what do you do? How are you going to make your way to the Queen? I mean you can't just say, sorry, sorry, make way, the Queen's about to be stabbed through the heart, and I'm here to save her. They're likely to think that you're the one that is trying to top her." His voice was becoming higher, shriller.

Ned put his arm around Richard's shoulders. "Easy, lad, take deep breaths. Everything will work out. It always does, doesn't it? Remember when you got that tomato in the face during the love scene with Ed and a sword fight broke out in the stools?"

Richard nodded trying to take deep, calming breaths.

"Sure, sure," said Will giving Augsy silent instructions with his eyes and a sideways nod of his head. "Everything is going to be all right."

Augsy led Richard away from the discussion.

"He's very excitable," said Tom excusing Richard. "So, that's the overall structure. Any details?"

Kit looked apologetic. "Well, it depends what we run into and how we make it up."

The silence accompanied by the gliding barge and the slow movements of its crew was startling.

Then Will clapped his hands together and brought them out of the trance. "Right, we'll make it up as we go along then."

Kit seemed to be in the middle of an agonized thought. "Right...of course."

Will clapped Kit on the shoulder. "All right. You heard the man. We'll make it up as we go along." With that, the group dispersed to their areas on the barge leaving Kit, Miao and George alone. George hesitated a bit and then seeing that Miao wanted to talk to Kit decided to give them some privacy.

Kit shifted uncomfortably. "Can I ask you a question?"

"Of course," responded Miao not wanting to sound too eager.

"Why did you ask me to do this? I mean they don't need me to tell them to make things up. I mean, really, I'm dispensable."

Miao took Kit's hands in hers. "No, no you're not." She knew that Kit was many things, but one thing he was not was dispensable. "I don't know why, but for us to succeed, we need you. I've seen it."

"You need me?" His throat suddenly became dry and a frightful sensation began to grip him. He liked her, and he was beginning to suspect that she liked him, but there was a part of him that needed not to be needed. He found it hard to explain, but he had always known he would die young. Therefore he found it rather selfish to develop a relationship where people depended on each other, like his father and mother did. Kit stood up and apologised. "I'm sorry, but I have to go."

George watched Kit move away from Miao. He noticed how she pulled up her hood. She was shutting everything out. When he sat down beside her, he also noticed how she didn't move. He cleared his voice.

"He's a nice enough fellow..."

She turned on him. "He is necessary for the success of our venture that is all."

George knew that when she used her imperious voice it was time to leave alone and not pry. She was a very polite person, but the strength buried beneath the slight frame was as strong as any well-tempered steel, even stronger.

"George, do you believe in destiny?" she finally asked with a soft, vulnerable voice.

He shrugged. He tried, at the best of times, not to think too much; it clouded up the present. "I believe when it's your time, it's your time and no matter what we say, or do, or cry about can change things. When fate, or death calls your name, you have to go."

"Then I am truly cursed, because often I can see destiny."

"But you can't see your own, now can you?" He figured she needed cheering up.

"No, I can't see my own," she paused, "thank you for that."

"So, you like Kit don't you?"

"He will die young, and without a woman in his life."

George wrapped a big, burly arm around his ward. "I don't think so; he's got you to watch over him, doesn't he? We really didn't need him on this little venture, did we?"

"Am I that transparent?"

"Only to me, my dear, only to me."

"I try not to play with the things I see, because whenever I do, things tend to turn out worse. But I knew that if I didn't involve Kit in this, he would die sooner than later, which would be a shame."

George thought about the playwright and nodded. "It's a shame when anyone goes before their time, but it's especially a shame for a person of note. Oh, look, there's the Castle."

The round tower was plainly visible from the river, the highest point on the ridge where the castle walls loomed. Its great, sprawling size gave a sense of foreboding.

"All right, people," shouted Ned clapping his hands together. "We all know our places (which wasn't necessarily true), and we know what to do (which was sketchy at best), so let's do it."

"You ever get the feeling that Ned would be perfect in leading a doomed charge?" asked George wryly.

"Do you think Tarlton will help us out?" asked Miao with sudden doubt in her voice.

"Dick? Of course he will. We both had the same sword master. If he doesn't I'll skewer him and serve him up as meat on a stick."

The barge pulled up to the dock and Richard paid the barge men half the agreed upon price. They would receive the second half on the return trip. If there was a return trip, thought Richard.

Chapter Twenty: Getting into the Castle

"Hey, you," shouted a guard from the bank "You can't put that thing there."

"We won't be long," yelled Kit back. "We'll move along after we've disembarked."

Kit had hoped that there would only be hired security down at the docks, not the Castle guards, but he was wrong. The four guards looked impressive in their clean livery. One of the fellows, with a rough, hard face must have been the sergeant by the way he handled authority. He was holding his long halberd more like a staff than a weapon. On closer inspection he noticed Luce and her girls and his eyes squinted suspiciously.

"Disembark? You're barking mad that's what you are. This is the Queen's spot and it has to be kept clear. Disembark somewhere else."

Kit noticed the interest in the guard's eyes as they kept flitting back to Luce and her girls. "Oh, but we're on the Queen's business, aren't we Richard?"

Richard was fine now. After emptying the contents of his stomach over the side of the barge, his nerves had settled and the paleness had left his face replaced by his more natural ruddy colour. He gave a flourishing bow. "May I introduce, the first Earle of Leicester's Men," and began to do so as they stepped off the barge.

The mere mention of Robert Dudley's title and the implied knowledge that they were under the Lord's license caused the guards to hesitate. But when Luce and the girls went to step on shore, his tongue became untied.

"Here, here. It may have been a while since I've seen a show, but there are no female players. It isn't lawful. This isn't some French trick is it?"

Some of the girls giggled playfully.

"Not at all, my good man," bellowed Ned pushing past Richard. "The ladies will only be providing the Greek Chorus: voices that would make the very spheres sing songs of praise."

One of the guards pointed at Luce. "Hey, wait a moment. I know you. You're the Abbess of one of Henslowe's bawdy houses."

The sergeant gave the other a perturbed look. "Is this true?"

When all seemed about to fall apart, Will stepped up. He had tied on his bells so that every step was accompanied by a merry, jingling sound.

The expressions from the guards' faces went from promising violence to one of pleasant surprise. The sergeant's face was transformed from a brooding scowl into exciting grin. "I know you! You're Will Kemp! No doubt about them now. These are definitely Leicester's men, whores or no whores. Will, I don't mean to be presumptuous, but could you give us a jig, just a little one."

Ned looked crestfallen. "You don't know me?" he questioned in his best oratory form.

The Captain shook his head slowly. "Sorry, can't say I do. So, Will, what's this all about? You know, it's pretty tight up there at the castle with ceremony."

Kemp did a little hop and turn. "Well, that's why we're here: A command performance to end the pious soberness of this most noble Thursday."

The painful expression on the sergeant's face indicated the internal struggle he was having. He scratched his head. "Oh, Will, I wish I could let you up, at least to the lower ward, but…"

George thought maybe he could break the impasse. He was clothed in one of Lord Water's used suits that combined pearls and shiny bits of armour: useless for combat, but attractive enough for ravens.

"Lord Raleigh is expecting us," he said in his best 'down your nose,' voice.

Will had softened him up, and now with the sergeant's defences about to crumble, George pulled him aside and slipped a purse of coins into his hand. "Listen, you see the cloaked Lady? She has been commanded to appear at court by the Queen herself. I wouldn't like to be the one that has to explain why the Lady Juzheng missed the Ceremony."

"Yeah, but what about the others? I love Will and all, but I can't let them up."

"They're not going in," said George. "They're the entertainment, for after. You wouldn't think I'd take them into the Ceremony without being invited, would you?"

"All right, fine. You can go up, but I have to send a couple of my lads with you as far as the Lower Ward and the Gate House."

"Done!"

Viewed from the water, the Castle crouched on a large ridge like a great behemoth. It had been used as Henry VIII's southern base when he was threatened by the doomed March of Grace that left Aske rotting away in his chains as he dangled from the tower wall in York. Soon they had made their way through the town and were making their way up to the Henry VII gateway and the Lower Ward. There would be no need to approach the round tower or the Middle or Upper wards because the Maundy Ceremony was being held at St. George's Chapel.

The hike up to Windsor Castle gave them time to contemplate their actions. The massive size of the reddish-pink stone of the castle brought to mind blood. The great curtain wall that surrounded the wards were intersected at intervals by both round and square towers. Some of the walls were buttressed to give them extra strength. At the lower end of the castle complex, rising above it, were the spires of St. George's Chapel.

"I always wanted to see Windsor Castle," said Will, his bells jingling merrily with each step.

Richard gave him a perturbed look. "Could you take those things off? They're really irritating me. You'd probably wear them to your own execution."

"Sure, why not?" quipped Will, "life is too short and ugly not to go through it without some cheer." He took a couple of steps and did a leap.

"Now, now," said Ned his voice booming. "No need to argue. Augsy, why don't you and the girls give us a little song. Come on give us a Morley. Tom, Tom, you have your pipe and tabor?"

Augsy fitted himself between two of the girls.

"You know 'Now is the Month of Maying?'

"Who doesn't?"

"Right," he beamed, and they began to sing. The four girls that Luce had brought joined in while Will and Tom danced about with each other. Ned, always an awkward dancer, stomped along. Even Richard, momentarily forgetting his stress, smiled. Miao couldn't help herself and she began to walk in time to the music. George and Kit, along with the guards, joined the singing. They made a pretty troupe marching up to the Henry VII gate.

> When merry lads are playing, fa la,
> Each with his bonny lass
> Upon the greeny grass. Fa la.
>
> The Spring, clad all in gladness,
> Doth laugh at Winter's sadness, fa la,

And to the bagpipe's sound
The nymphs tread out their ground. Fa la.

Fie then! why sit we musing,
 Youth's sweet delight refusing? Fa la.
 Say, dainty nymphs, and speak,
 Shall we play at barley-break? Fa la.

The guards at the gate didn't know what to make of them, but when they saw their fellows singing along, they visibly relaxed. It had been, up until now, a grim, sober affair. The winter had been long. The execution of a Queen hadn't helped matters any, especially since a good portion of the guards were closet Catholics. They were employed to be stiff, formal and professional, so when the Lords and Ladies, all dressed in such finery, had passed by them, they hadn't batted an eye lash. But these, these made them smile.

One of the guards with them shouted out. "These are Lord Leicester's men, come to provide the Lords and Ladies with some diversion after the ceremony."

One of the men looked confused. "I didn't know that women were made part of any troupe."

Ned stepped forward, in his element now. "They're not, they're not, my good man. They are maidens fair for our impromptu choir. You heard us singing on the approach?"

"That was some choir, but I'm afraid you won't be able to go in," said the guard soberly. "The Ceremony has already started."

"But we must, we were specifically told that upon the cessation of the ceremony we were to give the Queen her entertainment in the yard outside St. George's."

The guard hesitated. "On the order of the Queen? Why weren't we told? Is this some surprise or something? We don't like surprises."

"That's the part of it," jingled Will with a big, open moon face, "it's a surprise."

"We weren't told of this 'surprise,'" said the guard stubbornly.

"A surprise known is not a surprise at all," retorted Tom. "Now would it be, Will?"

"That's right a surprise is something that is rather 'surprising.'"

"But I wasn't told..." said the guard digging in.

"Of course you wasn't told." Will put his arm around him and pulled him into his confidence. "You know how the Queen washes the feet of poor women on Maundy Thursday, the day before Good Friday?"

"Of course, everyone knows that."

"Well, this is also Lord Leicester's thank you to the great men of the Castle Guard. To wash their souls with song and wit."

The guard's frown deepened. "Isn't Lord Leicester in the Low Countries?" he asked one of the other guards.

"He is, everyone knows that," said another.

"Oh, yes, he is," remonstrated Will, "but his reach is long, and we just received a letter the other day with our instructions, our orders," his voice became that of a conspirator, "they were almost held up, nearly intercepted by some Spanish agents."

The guard stroked his whiskers pensively. "You have this letter?"

"Indeed, we do."

"Kit, you brought the letter. The good guard wishes to see it."

Kit came forward, reached into his chest pocket and just as he was about to pull the letter for Tarlton out, the guard waved him down.

"No need for me to see it. I trust you will not object to some of my men accompanying you?"

Will threw his arm back around the man's brawny shoulders and gave him a bracing hug. "A man after my own heart. We welcome your men into our company."

The guard gave a shy, self-effacing grin. "My pleasure, Mr. Kemp, my pleasure. Off you go, then."

As they left the gate house behind, Kit sidled up to Will. "How did you know he wouldn't want to read the letter?"

Will laughed. "I didn't. Even if he did there was a chance he might have taken it to Tarlton."

From the narrow gate passage into the open square before St. George's Chapel, they went. St. George's was a long gothic building that made its supplication skyward in tall lines. Its tall windowed cavities of stained glass gazed down piously at them. It was a building of most serious religion. It was also the tomb of Henry VIII and Jane Seymour.

George took Miao by the arm and made for the entrance. The guards at the entrance stopped them. "I'm sorry; you and the Lady will have to remain outside while the ceremony is in progress."

George nodded and wandered off with Miao and was soon surrounded by Kit, Will, Richard, Ned and Luce. He knew it would be useless to argue.

"What's the problem?" asked Richard.

Miao was beginning to feel her dream bubbling up into reality. If they didn't get in soon, the Queen would die. She had to do something and soon.

"We need to get in," said Miao, "but we're late."

Will shrugged. "Why don't we try the same trick that we used at St. Paul's?"

"A diversion?" said Ned rubbing his hands together in delight.

"Yes, yes," said George anxiously. He had to do something soon, before Miao started to run for the small entrance into St. George's. He knew it when his charge was about to do something irrational. "Create a diversion and we will slip in along with Kit and his letter."

Will looked offended, "Diversions, diversions, all you ask for is diversion...well, that's a good thing because my life is just one long diversion. Let me just set up everyone."

George Bryan nodded. "And Richard and I can do our fight. You can use that as a cue."

It was set. George and Miao waited for Will to circulate through the players, explaining their plan. They noticed that Will and Ned were arguing again with Richard. At first he was shaking his head, and then when Luce and two of the girls converged on him he seemed to give up and nod. Then Ned separated himself from the group and began. He addressed the few guards as though they were a full house. His voice boomed about the square.

"Since you've been so kind to escort us here to wait until the end of the Maundy Ceremony, we thought we would give you a private taste of our entertainment. So, without ado, here is a section of Tamburlaine the Great, by our esteemed playwright, Christopher Marlowe.

Kit took a little bow. No one clapped.

"Richard Cuthbert," continued Ned, "the famous impresario, of no less, The Theatre itself, will assist me. We will perform a scene between gentle Zenocrate and Bajazeth."

"I hope it has some slaughter," chirped one of the guards with a grim face. "I do love a bit of slaughter. Don't you?"

The guard beside him nodded in agreement. "I do."

"You will not only have slaughter," promised Ned lavishly, "but you shall have the sweetness of love, an apple presented by Aphrodite herself."

One of the guards puckered up his face. "An apple in the spring? It's most likely to be a shriveled thing. What's Aphrodite's got to do with shriveled things?"

Another guard swatted him in the head, knocking his silver helmet down over his eyes. "Don't be rude. You can't have slaughter without love, the bitter without the sweet."

"Absolutely," Ned enthused, vindicating the guard who couldn't stop eyeing Luce and her girls. "Onwards," he shouted and with a swirl of his cape he began.

'Zenocrate, the loveliest maid alive,
Fairer than rocks of pearl and precious stone,
The only paragon of Tamburlaine;
Whose eyes are brighter than the lamps of heaven,
And speech more pleasant than sweet harmony;
That with thy looks canst clear the darken'd sky,
And calm the rage of thundering Jupiter;
Sit down by her, adorned with my crown,
As if thou wert the empress of the world.
Stir not, Zenocrate, until thou see me march victoriously with all my men,
Triumphing over him and these his kings,
Which I will bring as vassals to thy feet;
Till then, take thou my crown, vaunt of my worth,
And manage words with her, as we will arms.

Richard looked as though he had swallowed a lemon. Luce's girls had done their best to dress him up as a woman, they had even found him a dress to wear. But at best, he looked like some poor harridan that had been dragged through the streets. How he wished they had permitted Ed to come along. He cleared his voice forcing it up at least an octave, any higher and he wouldn't have been able to deliver the lines. He'd get even with Ned, somehow.

And may my love, the king of Persia,
Return with victory and free from wound!

Ned puffed up in his glory now and braked out his lines.

Now shalt thou feel the force of Turkish arms,
Which lately made all Europe quake for fear.
I have of Turks, Arabians, Moors and Jews,
Enough to cover all Bithynia:
Let thousands die; their slaughter'd carcasses..."

Richard threw off his woman's clothes and drew out his rapier into the en-garde position. No sooner had he done this than George Bryan had lunged at him and they began their choreographed sword fight designed by Silver.

"What's this?" complained one of the guards, trying to understand what was happening. "The lady is now fighting this other chap, that's not right is it?"

The man received another swat knocking his helmet over his eyes again.

"It's a montage," said the knowing guard. "Any fool can see that."

"Never liked the French," muttered the surly guard as he tried to straighten his helmet.

The other guards crossed their arms and watched the sword play. The fighting held them to such a degree that they didn't notice the three figures slipping into the entrance to St. George's Chapel.

Chapter Twenty One: Assassination

They found themselves out of the light of the day and into the dark of a vestibule. Miao, George and Kit took off their cloaks and let them fall to the stone floor. Their first idea was to blend in, but they were running out of time. The problem was, where exactly, were they on that line continuum?

As they forged on they soon came to the large open chapel that was crammed with people. Fortunately, the poor women were just being ushered into the chapel, so that the nobles and clergy parted before them, creating a path.

Miao took in a breath, she had forgotten to breathe. Before the crowd could close back in on the group of women, she felt George grip her by the arm, forcing her to follow. One priest, not so high as to be awarded a closer view, made to complain about the buffeting that George had given him, but when he saw Miao, her hair seeming to glow in the filtered light that was entering into the chapel, he turned to the man next to him and whispered something.

The singular, sibilant sound began and multiplied until a hiss rolled through the room like a cresting wave. It was easier to move through the crowd after that, which made Miao apprehensive at being in the open. Kit had disappeared into the crowd, lost in the swirl of fabric, of silks and taffeta, of big ruffs and tall hats.

Finally, they came into position of the ceremony itself, and that's when Miao, for the first time, saw the Queen. At their distance she couldn't see the details of the Queen's face, but around her swirled an aura of virtual colour. In that tempestuous whirlwind there were signs and symbols. There she saw roses, both red and white and a great crown; she also saw fire and waves and blood, a sea of blood. But the strongest impression she had was that of intellectual brilliance coupled with overwhelming familial sadness. And she saw death. It was like a specter rising up behind her, black and faceless. She had begun to wash the poor women's feet.

It was then that Miao also noticed other shadows about the room. Shadows to her were an augury of death, of change. Sometimes those with the shadows about them were destined to die soon, and sometimes they were the ones who would deal out death. There were so many. She had never been in a room with so many people with so many shadows. She did not remember, but it must have been like this at the Emperor's Court, and then she wondered. Her father seemed so sad most of the time. Did he see the things she saw? Did she get this curse, or blessing from him?

Then she saw Kit, or where his aura was, and there was something black and brooding behind him. She trembled with dread: so much death here today, at a time of life, of great service and sacrifice.

George had told her about the Maundy Ceremony, how it was to imitate what this great teacher Jesus Christ had done. For someone to wash another's feet was symbolic of the willingness to serve, that no matter how great one was, his purpose was to serve the people. The dark shadow that seemed to be following Kit was almost on him.

"George," Miao tugged on George's sleeve, getting him to bend to offer her his ear. "Kit, he's in the back. You have to go to him. He is in danger."

George tightened his lips on his face. He did that when he was presented with a difficult choice, when he was going to refuse her.

She reached up and placed a hand against his cheek. Not one for overtly touching anyone, it was a gesture of intimate pleading, and George recognized it. Miao also knew that George could be convinced to do almost anything, if the request was done in the right manner.

He grumbled. "Fine, but I'll be back." He glanced at the Queen who had just started to dry the first woman's feet. He turned and pushed through the crowd.

If the Ceremony hadn't been in progress, a few shouts of complaint would have filled the chapel, but most feared the Queen's displeasure on disturbing the reverence of the day.

She was a great performer, the Queen, moving with grace and incredible focus on the task at hand, even so she was aware of everything. She saw, albeit out of the corner of her eye, the young lady and rough gentleman who reminded her of the Captain of her Guard. They were cut from the same cloth. She had indeed invited them to Court, insisting on it even to the discouragement of Lord Burghley. Lord Burghley and Sir Francis were like two dogs occasionally fighting to see who would most please her. This was by design, and by yoking them to her chariot, she found she could steer them. She was not displeased with this appearance; Sir Water had told her to expect something like this. Indeed, she was most entertained. She dried off the feet of the girl she had been ministering to and handed her a silken purse with some Maundy money in it. Such beautifully white hair and her complexion was one which would evoke a great admiration in her Glories. She moved onto the next woman, but she continued to watch...everything.

George searched for Kit, but the writer was nowhere. Then he heard scuffling and muffled sounds of someone struggling down one of the exits. As he rushed down the hall, he found something dark stooped over the unconscious form of Kit. The dark form fled and George noticed the glint of steel in the man's hand. Out of some side passage, Richard Tarlton converged on the prone playwright. Not a big man, Tarlton still managed to give the impression of size. The presence of so many clerics had driven him away from the Queen to lurk in the passages until the Ceremony was over.

"That's Kit," he said with a slight slur to his voice, "what's he doing here?" Tarlton squinted at George. "I know you, don't I? George, George Silver, what are you doing here?"

216

"Getting permission for me and my Lady to attend the Maundy Ceremony," said George wryly. He wanted to chase after whoever had clubbed Kit, but he also felt the overwhelming urge to get back inside.

"Well, you have it, there," said Tarlton with his slightly googly eyes. There was something about his face that was incredibly malleable, able to take on whatever shape he wanted. George noticed he was carrying a rapier.

"You sober enough to use that?"

"Am I sober enough not to use it, of course I am. You want me to chase down yon perpetrator, don't you?"

"If you don't mind, somebody is about to try to kill the Queen."

Tarlton's face twisted into a cold, immobile mask, the façade of the drunken fool gone. "No one stops the fountain of Bacchus! I'll get the blighter, you save the Queen."

When George returned to the ceremony everything was in tumult, women were screaming and men shouting in fear and confusion. George groaned, leave the girl alone for a moment and look what happens.

Miao Juzheng began to grow tense. After she had sent George to check on Kit, the Queen's progression down the line was beginning to worry her. She began to doubt herself. Was the woman in her dreams exactly in the centre? She thought so, but it was hard to tell because she had been seeing everything through the eyes of the woman. Her mouth went dry, her palms clammy and she began to chew on her lip. From her perspective she was just behind and off to the side of the women. She could see only glimpses of the Queen through there. Then something, on one of the women caught her eye: red hair. Then she recognized that out of all the women who were being administered only one of them had red hair. The

217

Queen had just begun to bathe her feet. And then she saw the aura.

Miao took a step forward and pushed past the Lady in front of her, who perturbed, began to scowl at such a presumptuous action...and then she stopped. Miao was moving forward too slowly. The Queen was going to finish before she could reach her.

The Queen's Guards had noticed her and began to move to intercept her. She had only moments before the Queen would be dead. Everything slowed down, the sounds, the movement of the people in the press. Miao had no idea what she was going to do once she reached the woman and the Queen. If she reached them, suddenly the Guards, in their royal livery, began pushing through the Lords and Ladies roughly out of the way, which was met a cry of outrageous offense.

Everything seemed to slow. The Queen handed the towel she had just used to dry feet to the bishop and was reaching for the purse of Maundy money. There was a slight, happy tilt to the Queen's lips, even though they were still closed. She was enjoying this, truly enjoying this, thought Miao.

The red haired woman was pulling something out of a secret fold in her skirt. In moments Miao knew that a dagger would be thrust into the chest of the Queen. The tumult that Miao was creating caused the smile on the face of the Queen to melt away, replaced with the sudden curiosity and fear as her eyes rested on Miao.

Three steps and the Guards would be on her, three steps and she would be on the woman with red hair, but what then? What was she going to do? The woman had a dagger, and all she had was her hands – and her quick mind.

Rapiers were even more a fashion accessory than a weapon. The hilt, the length often matched the outfit the man wore, and for that, Miao was grateful.

218

Unsheathing a rapier was at the best of times an awkward thing. There was no 'drawing the sword,' it was more a wrist flick forward while the other hand pulled the sheath back so the rapier could be cleared. It was more like throwing the rapier forward hilt first, and this worked to her advantage.

Miao, as she shoved past a Lord, grabbed, with her left hand the ornate basket hilt of his rapier and threw it. As it flew forward she caught it with her right hand.

High pitch screams of women were now reverberating through the chapel at the barred steel. Strange, thought Miao, the Queen's face was not a mask of fear or horror. She was supremely resigned in a peaceful way. It was as though she had been expecting this or something like this to happen and was prepared for it. She was prepared to meet death.

The horror, the true horror of the moment, for Miao, was that everyone thought that she was trying to kill the Queen. George had prepared her for this. After every practice they would talk about killing, how terrible it was and how it took a toll on the human mind. He was very sensitive about this, which was odd for such a gruff, old soldier.

'The reason I train men to kill, is that they will be able to do so, without thought, because if they think, they will invariably hesitate, and if they hesitate they die."

"But what happens to the ones who live through the battle?" she had asked.

He had looked at her, his face as though it had been turned into stone. "No one lives after a battle. Everyone dies, in a way. It's the price of taking life."

Miao had time to turn the rapier about, to use the point on the back of the woman who was now intent on plunging her dagger into the heart of the Queen. To kill or not to kill, that was indeed the question. She drove forward as the dagger surged upwards and hit the young woman in the back of the head with the hilt of the rapier. Even though Miao was a slight woman, her momentum took her right into the back of the woman, and both of them fell onto the Queen.

George was bellowing with abandon now, striking left and right with his fists, knocking down whoever was in his way. It didn't matter if they were Lord or Lady they went down. He used every dirty, unarmed fighting skill he had learned or taught, but when he got to the place where he saw Miao go down it was too late. The three women were in a tangle of skirts and arms. He noticed there was blood on the floor's tiles. He reached for Miao at the same time his benefactor, Sir Water reached for the Queen.

There was a snarl on Sir Water's face, but when he recognized George, he held up a hand to stop the half dozen men behind his friend.

"Silver, speak, quick and well," snapped Sir Water.

"One of the poor women...the dagger."

Sir Water noticed the dagger on the floor at the fingertips of the now insensate woman. The Queen was being helped back up to her feet by several of her Glories that had rushed to her aid. Miao had not been so lucky; she had hit her head on the floor, spinning off the back of the much bigger red haired woman and was now unconscious.

The Queen stood there in startled paralysis, unable to speak. Her Glories and Guards converging to usher her away.

Both Miao and the would-be assassin lay unconscious on the floor.

"Take her into custody," said Sir Water about the red haired woman. As the Guards bent over and George scooped up Miao, another cry went up at the far end of the Chapel. George twisted about, Miao in his arms. Richard Tarlton staggered into the Chapel, his sword arm, clutching his rapier, dragging and dripping blood. His face was pale as he staggered forward.

"My Lord," said Tarlton grimacing smartly. "I apologize for disturbing the Ceremony, but there is a villain more so than I in the castle and I thought to remedy the situation."

Sir Water took Miao from George's arms. Tarlton staggered and George caught him. The wine fumes were strong on the man's breath as George stabilized him by propping him up on the cold tiles. He whispered in his ear, "George, he pretends to be right handed, but is equally good with both."

"Go," snapped Sir Water to George, and George went knowing exactly what he had to do.

Chapter Twenty Two: Duel to the Death

When George burst out onto the street in front of St. George's Chapel, he knew he had lost Della Massa. A jubilant roar went up from those who were waiting in front, taking him as a symbol of the cessation of the Maundy Ceremony. A larger group which now included some of the Castle staff had formed. A confused silence settled on them when nobody followed George out of the Chapel.

"Did you see a man coming out?" he yelled.

"No, you're the first to come out since going in. What's wrong? What happened?" yelled back Richard.

"There has been an attempt on the Queen's life."

A great concerned rumble went through the crowd. Everyone knew the trouble which could occur in a succession with no apparent heir. For her entire reign Elizabeth had kept her country from the religious wars which were threatening to engulf the continent. Would this be the tipping point where all England would burn?

He caught hold of one of the guard's arm. "Is there a way out of the Chapel, other than the front entrance?"

The guard shook his head. "You could go up."

After getting instructions to the location of the maintenance stairway that led to the roof, George dashed back into the building, found the little alcove that hid the stairs and began climbing them. On the roof there was a narrow cap ridge running the length of the building. It was a relatively flat roof with little grade. Along the roof's edge were the beasts rampant: seventy six statues, heraldic devices carved at the founding of the Chapel. And at the far end, he found Berto Della Massa, his back turned to him. It was as though he was admiring the scenery. From the roof they could see far into the green countryside threaded by the ribbon of water that marked the Thames.

"I'm glad it's you," said Della Massa turning to face him, sword in one hand, pistol in his other. He looked down at his small arm ordinance as though seeing it for the first time. "Oh, this? I was supposed to use this one on the Queen, if the woman failed." He gave a wan, twisted smile and tossed it off the roof. It fell silently off into the air. He gave a couple slashes with his sword. "Suddenly, I do not have the heart for regicide. Your Queen is no fool. You could do much worse."

"Could have," said George tersely. Most Kings and Queens cared little for the people they were supposed to serve. Generally the people could tell when a monarch cared about them, and when they did not. "We could have ended up with Phillip."

"Still might, poor England," said Della Massa.

Instead of wearing his rapier today George had strapped on his two handed long sword. It was a sword that bore a resemblance to its distant medieval cousin, but it was a lot lighter and had some flexibility to it. Still it needed two hands instead of the rapier's one. He drew the blade.

Della Massa's face brightened appreciatively. "Ah, good; the Fool had a rapier, not a good choice."

"You seem to be the fool," snapped George as he moved cautiously forward. He knew with the roof having such a low grade, that the fight could move in any direction. It wouldn't be very long, or protracted, before one, or both of them would be bleeding out their life on the roof, or on the ground below. He suspected that was why the man had come here. There was no way out. This would be their last stand before death.

Della Massa was regarding one of the statues. He approached it and placed an admiring hand on its pedestal. "The griffon, perseverance: the symbol of perseverance. Let me ask you a question, as one soldier to another."

The wind had suddenly picked up and a fine mist of rain began to fall. This would make their footing treacherous. George began to move down the grade and forward, his sword held high and ready.

"It doesn't matter, does it," said Della Massa cutting at the wind, "because in a moment we will both be dead." He chanced a look down at the square. The crowd had noticed them and were pointing. "It seems we have an audience."

Cries came from below. The Queen's body guard and the braver Lords in attendance had flooded out onto the street below and joined those already there. They pointed at them, at the two men balancing on the edge of the roof silhouetted against the sky.

"Seems so," said George grimly. All his instincts told him this was to be the fight of his life. Every soldier mused about his own death, when it would come and how and what would be the manner of it. Death would dance with them up here, for one, or for both and he knew it.

"That Witch of yours, can she tell the future?" he asked his sword still held in a casual, almost lazy grip.

George thought that the man must be either a fool or suicidal. He was within striking distance, so George made the first pass. The point of his sword made for Della Massa's eye, but it flickered into air. George pulled back just in time for the counter, parrying the blade that would've slashed open his thigh. George took a couple steps back.

"Now that you've sounded out my reflexes, the questions; don't you think it would be comforting, going to our graves knowing?"

"Knowing what?" snapped George. He had no appetite for conversation, not now.

"Know how your beloved, stench filled country will be invaded." Della Massa suddenly lunged forward, his blue blade making for George's own eye. He slipped to the side and slashed at Della Massa's leg. It seemed only appropriate to return like for like. Except this time his balance was a bit off and he could feel his feet slipping on the damp slate. He held his breath, his toes digging into the souls of his boots in an attempt to regain balance. Della Massa was insisting on them fighting next to the rail and the edge of the roof.

A sudden bolt from a crossbow caromed of the upright bear to the side of Della Massa. The deflection almost hit George.

"No crossbows," bellowed George down to the men below. "No arrows!"

Della Massa gave him a respectful nod and saluted him with his sword.

"So, how is my cesspool of a country going to be invaded?" asked George taking the time to make sure his footing was sure.

"The death of your Queen was supposed to be the signal. With her death, Catholics would rise up and take Dover. The armada, after all, needs a place to land."

George grunted. He thought 'good luck with that'. One of the things that Phillip and the rest of them hadn't realized that Protestant or Catholic they were all English, and they all, with few exceptions, hated Phillip. "Sorry, my Lady disappointed Phillip."

Della Massa shrugged. "So, she stopped the killing, too bad. I don't think she disappointed The King of Spain though."

"What are you talking about?"

"It was Sixtus that wanted your Queen dead today."

"Sixtus, the Pope?"

"Yes. Phillip wanted to humiliate your Queen, and then perhaps execute her, but he does not want her dead, not yet anyway; after all, it is a family affair with him."

Their swords darted at each other simultaneously, barely missing each other's chest. George now knew they were equally matched, that in reality, they would most likely kill each other as so usually happened with twinned combatants. He felt the damp sweat beginning to roll down his back and collecting in its hollow.

"Tell me then, if you know so much," said George through his clenched teeth as he continued to study the man. Tarlton was right; the man could use both hands with equal alacrity. He could tell this by the way he alternated his lead foot.

"Anything," he said with a shockingly sincere expression on his face.

"The red hair girls that have been showing up all over London, you are the killer."

"If you know, why do you ask?"

Della Massa shifted his sword from his right hand to his left (as Tarlton warned) and lunged. George had been waiting for the trick. Two things saved him; the fact that he knew before hand, and the double handed long sword he used. He caught Della Massa's blade on its length and turned it away. Instead of countering, which was expected, he assumed a defensive stance again, and waited.

A shadow of doubt passed over Della Massa's face. A rapier was no match for his sword of Damascus steel, but this two handed monstrosity was more than a match. His free hand inched toward the spot where he kept his dagger. If he could get passed the length of his opponent's sword, the dagger would end both their lives, end all of the misery.

"It was you," said George.

Della Massa nodded, tasting the cool of the mist that had now turned into rain. It ran down his face and into the corners of his mouth. He was strangely parched. "Ask your Witch, or maybe your precious bald Queen."

George knew what the man was doing and he let him come. The talking was to distract him so that he could get in close. It was harder to kill a talking man, because the talking reminded one of humanity. Fortunately, George held no such prejudices.

Della Massa moved quickly like a striking serpent, and managed to get inside the Englishman's long sword and pulled out his dagger. It should have been a quick thrust, but instead of the severing of flesh, he felt the steel like grip of the other man's hand around his wrist. The dagger halted inches from George's chest. How was this feasible? The man, who had the silver of age in his beard, could not possibly be holding onto his long sword with one hand, but he was.

George used all his strength to hold on, to both his sword, and the dagger arm of his opponent. Then he did the only thing a real Englishman would do, he brought up his knee into Della Massa's groin. Unfortunately, he just missed the man's stones, which would have debilitated him. As it was, Della Massa dropped the dagger, twisted away and back.

"You have no honour," spat Della Massa in pain.

"You have no balls," quipped back George. "The Lady you serve, the one close to the Queen, who is she?"

Della Massa's sword came in low, this time at George's feet and he had to leap. He brought down his long sword intending to cleave the man's head, but Della Massa slipped aside. It was all George could do to bring around his blade to create a bar of steel through which his opponent could not get through.

Della Massa smiled. "She is a Lady of Great renown, whose name shall remain – nameless."

"Thought so," said George. Up until now he had been fighting a reserved style, hoping that the man would divulge something useful. Even so, Della Massa had brought him close to the edge. He began to think that maybe he should let someone below skewer the man with a dozen bolts. Yet he hesitated. Even though he had made jest of the Chivalric Order of The Garter, he did, deep down in his heart desire to be made a knight. But without a great, incomparable deed that was impossible. A Knight of The Garter had lineage. He wasn't even sure who his parents were. Yet, here, on top of St. George's Chapel, the ancient home of the Order of The Garter, he could feel the possibilities. "That sword, I've seen that sword before."

The cold intensity of the cornered man seemed to lessen somewhat, replaced with curiosity. "My sword?"

"At the Battle of The Three Kings, I noticed a Turk with a blue sword." George had been waiting to use this trump card. An enemy that was off guard was an enemy you could defeat. He had never been to the battle, but Miao had read this above Della Massa's head: a blue sword held in the hand of a Turk and the sliced throat of King Sebastian.

"You were at the Battle of The Three Kings?" he asked in disbelief.

George shrugged. "I was in a lot of battles. I'm surprised you didn't tell Don Antonio what really happened with your precious Sebastian."

Della Massa spit. "Don Antonio is a fool and will always be a fool." He shrugged. "Sebastian would have died anyway."

"That's what I always say about the men I kill. Some of my best friends are fools." George had hesitated just too long. He could hear Miao berating him for talking too much. "Why don't you give up and you can turn yourself in."

Della Massa laughed at the absurdity of the suggestion. The only thing he had to gain here was the measure of a wonderful swordsman and a quick death. If he did as Silver suggested he would be tortured and then drawn and quartered. Not a pleasant death that: to be hung until unconscious, cut down, and while still alive have your belly slit open and your entrails paraded before your eyes. A good executioner would make sure you were still alive while they hacked off your limbs. Della Massa attacked.

George felt the abandon of the man as their swords crossed. A man who had given up on life was either easy to defeat or impossible because he no longer feared death, but had embraced it. He suspected the latter with Della Massa. They were so evenly matched that their swords could've crossed until their strength failed. Neither had the advantage over the other, and Della Massa knew it. That was why once he was inside George's sword he dropped his fabled, blue blade to grapple with him.

George dropped his own sword that spun and clattered on the slate tiles. He caught a fist on the side of his head and reeled, not feeling much because of the intensity of the fight. His own fist caught Della Massa on the chin. Then they turned, pressed up against the railing that separated them from the fall to the paving stones below.

The world was twisted from beneath George's feet as he felt Della Massa pulling him over the railing. The man had thrown his entire weight out into the air and was purposely dragging George with him. George reached out, desperate to latch onto anything as he flipped over the railing. His arm jerked painfully as it caught on one of the plinths that supported one of the many stone beasts. His hold slipped, but then held fast giving an agonizing jerk; he was still holding onto Della Massa, who was now swinging free. Below the up turned faces of the Court watched the events unfold. George felt their tightly grasped hands slip. The mist had now turned into a constant rain and was seeping in between their fingers, slowly loosening their grip.

"I can't hold on..." grated out George. "Try to grab my arm with your free hand."

There was no panic, or terror on Della Massa's face, just a cold acceptance. He ignored George's instructions and released his grip. He was saved so why should he fear death?

He relaxed his grip and his fingers slipped through George's and he was gone. There came a shout from below, and then the sound of men above, sliding over the slates, and then he was being pulled up and supported by the arms of several castle guards. It was then that he saw it. It had not fallen off the roof when Della Massa abandoned all hope. George bent down and picked up the blue sword of Damascus' steel.

Chapter Twenty Three: In The Privy Chamber

Out of the darkness she climbed, up into the light, and the slow focus of a world of colour. There were candles blazing about her. She always liked the light, but only if it wasn't too overwhelming. She could smell the sweet scent of burning bee's wax, and there was the scent of perfume. She wasn't in London, because the prevalent odour of sewage wasn't in the air. Then she remembered her mad dash at the woman about to stab the Queen and her hitting her and her own fall.

Her head hurt, but the warm, wet cloth that was being applied to it soothed. She blinked and opened her eyes focusing on the face of the woman who held her head in her lap. The woman's face was thin and pale, her hair wrapped in a tight fitting cover. Miao realized suddenly she was staring up into the eyes of the Queen herself. She jerked, trying to sit up and her head pounded. There was a twittering sound of concern off to the side and the Queen scowled.

"If you cannot endure the sick and injured, then leave us."

A voice took in air as though preparing to complain, but the Queen shut her down.

"Now..."

It was a voice that brooked no disobedience. There was the sound of skirts whisking out of the room and then silence, blessed silence. Water ran as the Queen dipped the cloth and wrung it. It felt good on her forehead.

"There, finally, alone at last. Do you know it almost takes an act of God to get some privacy?"

The Queen's voice was an earthy contralto. Miao had never thought about what the voice of the Queen should sound like, but this fit. It was a voice of supreme control. She tried to sit up again but was pushed back down.

"There will be time later for you to bow and scrape before me. Right now, let me do this for you."

"Your Highness..." started Miao. "The woman with the dagger..."

"Oh, that," she said with aplomb. "Unfortunately, she died."

"She died?" and Miao struggled to rise.

Queen Elizabeth sighed in pretend exasperation. "Well, if you no longer intend on playing the patient and insist on a dialog you best be up."

Miao's head spun as she was assisted in sitting up, but after a few moments her world began to settle.

"That is a nasty bump you have, but fortunately, not fatal. The woman, who tried to kill me, was killed herself."

"I didn't..." stuttered Miao.

"Oh, no, you didn't kill her. One of my overzealous courtiers, I'm afraid – the barbarian. That's all men can think about, their swords and where to place them."

Miao tentatively touched the bump on her head. "How convenient."

There was a flash in the Queen's eyes. "Exactly so. I thought about having him banished, but I think it would be better if I have that particular courtier watched. It is too bad about my Cat and your Silver."

Miao felt herself confused. Cat? Her Silver? Then she tensed up realizing whom she was talking about. "Are they all right?"

The Queen looked amused. "It suits us well to have someone else, other than Lord Burghley to question me, and that stupid Fool, getting himself stabbed. They are all right. Comedy can be so inconvenient. You know, he was against me inviting you to court."

"He was? The Fool?"

"Oh, no, for him, the more the merrier. It was Lord Burghley who was against you. He has some peculiar notions about religion. I had to send my dear friend Doctor Dee abroad because of him. You see, unfortunately he sees witches and sorcerers behind every chamber pot."

"And you don't?"

The Queen chuckled and tapped her on the end of her nose. "Indeed, you are very darling. Isn't there a strange belief, in the East, where if you save a person's life, you are then required to care for them the rest of your life...or their life? I suppose that only applies to whomever lives the longest."

Miao was fortunately familiar with that particular Buddhist belief. Old Lao had taught her about as many faiths as he could. He said, a person's belief was important; right or wrong often did not matter. She nodded distinctly feeling that this extremely intelligent Queen was weaving a net of filial service about her. "Yes, I am familiar."

The Queen clapped her hands together and a woman stuck her head back into the room. "Oh, shoo, not you, we are just expressing our delight.

"Now to the events that nearly killed my Fool, knocked my Cat insensible, nearly killed your Silver and has upset my own Sir Water, horribly." She paused and took a deep, bracing breath. "I cannot remember having such an entertaining Maundy Ceremony in such a long time. It was so exciting it put me into temporary paralysis," she said wryly.

Miao felt the shadows around the Queen's colourful aura dissipate slightly, but only slightly to lurk in the corners of the room, waiting to be summoned back.

"Your Highness," began Miao, "there is someone close to you that may be a traitor." She had wanted to tell her about the woman who was one of her Glories, but something restrained her.

The Queen suppressed the smile that came to her lips, but the force was too strong and her lips parted, revealing some of her missing teeth. "I keep many traitors about me. They are easier to watch that way." Then she considered her with a cold, sober gaze. Her eyes seemed to have frost in them. "The question is, can I trust you?"

"If you did not, I would not be here. I have no reason to betray you."

"Have you not," said the Queen contemplatively, "no, I believe you do not. I have decided: you, like Doctor Dee, are beyond reproach."

"May I ask a question?"

"You may."

"George, George Silver. He is all right?"

The Queen told her of the fight that most of the Lords and Ladies had witnessed along the roof's edge of St. George's Chapel, and the fall of Berto Della Massa. "I do think," finished the Queen, "that Silver's guardian saint is indeed his namesake. Do you think Don Antonio had anything to do with this mess?"

"No, I don't believe so."

"Nevertheless, nevertheless, I will inquire of him. I shall submit this matter to Francis; he will know the proper channels of the mind to plumb." The Queen readjusted herself. "My Cat told me that you can delve the future, is this true?"

Miao's throat went dry. "Sometimes I see paths, directions. The future is determined by our present actions."

The Queen gave a pleasant chuckle. "You even sound like Doctor Dee, how fortuitous. Will my land burn, crushed beneath the boots of the Spanish?"

Miao shook her head. "No."

"Tell me," she said heatedly, "what message comes this way."

Miao felt her breath grow thick and heavy. She realized that this was the moment where she proved her worth to the Queen. She had saved the Queen's life, but there were men and women who had saved her life multiple times. In the moment of terror, in the moment before knowing she needed assurance.

"I need to feel your face," said Miao.

The Queen leaned in and Miao touched her. She had not told Black Luce the entire truth. She did 'see' things through touch, personal things and for some reason she had not wanted to share that with the woman. Immediately images shot through her mind. "I see you sitting in a dark indigo dress with great cream coloured sleeves. A lace ruff is flared around your head. The dress, along with your hair is festooned with pearls and red and blue bows. Behind you, partially covered, are two pictures. They are either pictures or they are windows with curtains I don't know which. In one of the windows is a vast fleet, sails full of wind, and they are sailing away, and in the other window there are – tempestuous waves and wrecked ships. The fleet is destroyed. Your Queen's right hand is resting on the world while her left hand is holding handle a scepter.

Just then there was a noisy tumult of voices outside the Queen's privy chamber which was met with the shrill complaint of her ladies in waiting, like hens at the approach of a fox. Over all rose a deep sonorous voice commanding order. A woman stuck her head back into the room and when she saw the disapproval on the Queen's face she fell to her knees.

"Your Highness, the Captain of your Guard seeks an audience."

She waved the woman away. "Since when does my Captain need to seek an audience you silly woman? Be gone with you and fetch him presently." The Queen turned her regal gaze on Miao, who was feeling much better. The worst of it was gone, although she did still feel a bit faint.

The Queen rose and sighed, "But she is right. As you can see, I am in no state to receive anyone. Would you be so kind, as to help me dress, one Queen to another, so that we may continue our private discourse."

Miao didn't know if she could be of any help, but to the Queen's satisfaction, she rose to her feet and after a moment of dizziness nodded.

"Good, now, my hair."

Miao saw several wigs sitting on wooden head forms. She moved hesitantly to them.

"The one on the right, that's it, the one that looks like I've just woken from bed."

As Miao touched the wig the images of the dead women shot through her head. The value in telling the Queen now that some of the hair may possibly have come from heads of murdered women faded. Unless she had the killer, it would upset without purpose, so she decided to say nothing. She fitted the hair on the Queen's head, and immediately she looked younger.

"The cloak, over there."

Miao fetched the cloak and wrapped it around the Queen's shoulders. Just then one of her ladies stuck a head back into the room, there was resentment and hurt in those eyes at seeing the Queen with her hair and seated. The Queen patted the seat beside her. "Sit. We must not be anxious to receive men."

Sir Walter Raleigh, resplendent in his silver armour, strode into the room. Immediately his eyes dashed from the Queen to Miao in quick assessment. He went to his knee and bowed his head.

"My Queen..."

"Queens," corrected Elizabeth, "I'm sure you are quite aware of the blood that flows in Lady Juzheng's veins, considering you have been protecting and providing for her this past year. I wish to know the reason for your duplicitous secrecy."

Miao noticed Sir Water go a little stiff, but then he smiled. He was a rogue and Miao suddenly understood the Queen's attraction to him. He was cut from the same cloth as George. "Forgive me; I was waiting to introduce her to Court..."

"Had you waited any longer, I would be dead," admonished the Queen. "Now, what is this urgent news that you bear us?"

His face glowed exultantly. "Drake has burned the Spanish fleet at Cadiz."

Elizabeth rose to her feet. She rubbed her hands together and her chest heaved, but controlled her passion. "This is good, but it will not stop Phillip. At best, it has bought us some time until our victory."

"Victory?" asked Sir Water confusedly.

"Yes, Lady Juzheng has promised us victory."

Sir Water gave Miao a worried glance and then gave a stiff nod.

It should have comforted Miao, so why did she just feel that the Queen had just ordered her execution and Sir Water was about to perform it?

Chapter Twenty Four: Cast Party

The Unicorn at Bishopsgate was as good as any other tavern in London, perhaps better because they were able to get a cut on ale price from Ned's elder brother, Jack. Jack was not an easy man to forget. He was larger than his brother and sported a great black beard. He would stare at you with his one good eye, while the other was as blank as the wall.

They were all there in the drinking cram of the place; George Bryan, Agustine Phillipe, Will Kemp, Richard Burbage, Thomas Pope, Edward Allyen and Ed along for the ride. George Silver, Miao Juzheng and Kit Marlowe sat in a threesome, the two men sitting protectively on either side of Miao. They had retired there, after another successful showing of 'Tamburlaine the Great.' Money was flowing freely into The Theatre's coffers which added to the already jovial nature of the house. Even so Richard was keeping a good count on what would be owed tonight.

"Dear brother," shouted Ned, "we'll need some food to sop up this offering to Dionysus!"

Jack glared down at him with his one good eye. He was wearing a once-white apron, now smeared with many layers of the brownish-yellow of grease and blood. He crossed his hairy arms creating a great wall of a man. "No gelt, no food," snapped Jack.

Ned laughed. "Will, you've been teaching Jack some Lowlands. Not to worry, dear brother, we have money," Ned searched around hopefully his eyes falling to appeal on Richard.

"Don't look at me," said Richard, "Cuthbert keeps the purse. If you've spent your pay, don't blame me."

George flipped a bag of coin up to Jack, who caught it and held it up to his ear as though the coins had a voice and could tell him how much was there. He gave a terse nod, turned and bulled his way across the room.

"Thank you," said Ned graciously.

"The Queen's coin," explained George.

Will leaned in across the table with a grin more like of a wolf than a man. "So, tell us about her," said Will. "What's she really like?"

Miao found the place hot and stuffy and because she didn't drink she was beginning to find it intolerable. Besides, she didn't feel like talking about Elizabeth. She just shrugged. She was about to ask George if they could leave when the mob noise of the men and women that filled the Inn came abruptly to a stop.

Standing in the open door of the Inn was Sir Walter Raleigh.

Ned leaned in. "Now that's a beard. It juts into the room like the prow of a Turkish galley."

"Couldn't ask for a better entrance," quipped Will.

Ned gazed at Kit hopefully. After the success of Tamburlaine he had been feeding Kit with endless lines for his next work. "I've got more where that comes from."

"No doubt," groaned Richard under his breath. If his father hadn't a will of steel, Ned would have a series of one man shows, which would be the death of everyone, including Ned; some courtier would probably skewer him.

Even dressing down, Raleigh stood resplendent above the Unicorn's patrons. He was wearing a black velvet doublet and hose. His sleeves were studded with pearls. For someone less confident, stepping into a place dressed like that might have caused some reason for hesitation, but his station carried him. Raleigh spotted his target and strode through the press which parted before him like the red sea before Moses.

"Nice outfit," muttered Will into his cup.

George and Miao tried not to grin.

Raleigh stood over them and the sounds of the Inn resumed its deafening timbre. He waited expectantly.

There was no seat at the table, so Tom gave Ed a boot. "Since you're the youngest...you have been elected to provide a seat for our unofficial patron Lord."

Raleigh held up his hand. Most Lords had taken to the effete habit of wearing gloves with lace dangling from the cuffs. Raleigh eschewed such, preferring to exhibit his calloused, large hands. He wanted everyone to know that first of all he was a man of Devon and that meant a working man of the sea.

"No, don't rise; I'll make space for myself." He swung about and placed one of those large hands on the back of the chair of the man seated at the next table. "You don't mind if I take your chair, do you?"

The man, knowing exactly who was talking, tried not to spit out his ale. "No, no, take the chair." He stood up hastily. "Take my wife if you want." Everyone laughed providing the man a way of saving face.

Raleigh swung around and seated himself side-saddle, the way men with rapiers at their side were forced to sit. "I hope you don't mind..."

238

"Any friend of the Queen is a friend of ours," proclaimed Ned who stood bolt upright, raised his cup and bellowed, "To the Queen."

Not everyone was besotted with the Queen, but with the Captain of her personal Guard in attendance, everyone stood and shouted and drank.

After the toast, Raleigh leaned in conspiratorially, a very grim expression on his face. "I hope all of you realize how close you came to being hung, drawn and quartered."

Will rubbed his neck and took a long pull on his cup. "Indeed, I did feel a final jig coming on." He clapped George on the shoulder. "But our Sword Master here and Lady Juzheng saved the day! So, we live to jig another day."

"Unfortunately," muttered Richard under his breath.

"Yes, that's why I'm here. Ned, does your brother have a room where we can meet privately? I need to talk to George and Lady Juzheng, alone."

Ned gave an enthusiastic head wag. "Oh, yes, yes. It's in the back. We call it the 'Traitor's Nook,' you would be surprised how full it is. Come on, I'll take you there. It might be occupied."

As it turned out there was no one in the 'Traitor's Nook,' and Ned left them to themselves.

As Raleigh sat down he seemed to relax, all the show went out of him as he gave a long sigh, his face carrying the sudden weight of many worries. "It wasn't a jape when I said about some wanting to draw and quarter the lot of you."

"I know," said George.

"It was a risk we had to take," said Miao trying to assuage her benefactor. "It turned out all right didn't it?"

Raleigh ran his hand through his hair. "Yes, but it was a close thing." He leaned in. "There still is this matter of *the woman*."

"We believe her to be one of the Queen's ladies in waiting," said George.

Raleigh grimaced. "She's very possessive of her Glories. Did you know what Walsingham had to go through to gather enough evidence to condemn Mary Stuart? Even then, the Queen hesitated, for months, to sign her death warrant." He paused. "You were alone with the Queen," he said to Miao. "That doesn't happen very often, to anyone."

"That's good, right," said George.

"Could be, could also be very bad. She is much like her father. His closest companions were often the ones who lost their lives."

"She is not her father," said Miao. She had heard about Henry VIII, and his mercurial fits and his unyielding justice. She had felt this pain in Elizabeth but had not spoken of it.

"Maybe so, maybe so, but I would advise much caution at Court. You are most likely to create much envy and malice."

Miao felt a cold breeze and shivered. It wasn't a physical breeze, but that of long suppressed emotion.

"What's the matter?" asked George.

She said, "Nothing:" A one word statement which gave the opposite feeling to the two other men in the room.

"You know," said Raleigh his voice rather dry, "if you don't want..."

Miao smiled. "Does anyone refuse the confidence of the Queen?"

"Well, no."

"Then I am fine." But she wasn't, because it was at Court, albeit a different Court, that her own family had been murdered.

ENDE

Other Books by M.E.Eadie:

Rivertown Cycle:
Book 1: Colin and the Rise of The House of Horwood
Book 2: Colin and The Little Black Box
Book 3: Colin and The Revenant
Book 4: Colin and The Courts of Faerie

A Fantasy:
A Thousand Kisses Deep

Hard copies available through Amazon

Ebooks through Smashwords, Barnes & Noble, Kobo and Apple's Ibooks.

To find out what I'm currently working on –

My blog: http://adambookhouse.blogspot.com/